FAMOUS
MISS FEVERSHAM

"Fanny," Neville said sternly, " do you realize what a confounded farce you have forced me to play during these last few hours? Consider. I have dressed up in a ridiculous masquerade as a highwayman, called a man out, received an injury, and delivered an even worse one."

Fanny bit her lip, trying not to cry. "I know I have been very selfish, Julian—"

Neville continued as if he had not heard her. "In short, I have played the fool. You have caused me to do things I would never have dreamed of doing for any other woman, Fanny."

"I am so sorry, Julian. How can I ever . . . " She looked down, desperate to end the scene.

A tender smile stole across his face, and he lifted her chin. "Well, I am not sorry, little vixen," he said softly. "Sometimes a man must be willing to play the fool to find out how much of a fool he has been."

Other **Regency Romances**
from Avon Books

THE BLACK DUKE'S PRIZE *by Suzanne Enoch*
DEAR DECEIVER *by Elizabeth Lynch*
THE FICTITIOUS MARQUIS *by Alina Adams*
AN IRRESISTIBLE PURSUIT *by Rebecca Robbins*
MY LORD LION *by Rebecca Ward*

Coming Soon

A DELECTABLE DILEMMA *by Cathleen Clare*

Famous Miss Feversham

CHRISTIE KENNARD

AVON BOOKS ◆ NEW YORK

FAMOUS MISS FEVERSHAM is an original publication of Avon Books. This work has never before appeared in book form. This work is a novel. Any similarity to actual persons or events is purely coincidental.

AVON BOOKS
A division of
The Hearst Corporation
1350 Avenue of the Americas
New York, New York 10019

Copyright © 1995 by Christie Kennard
Published by arrangement with the author
Library of Congress Catalog Card Number: 95-94150
ISBN: 0-380-78135-2

First Avon Books Printing: September 1995

AVON TRADEMARK REG. U.S. PAT. OFF. AND IN OTHER COUNTRIES, MARCA REGISTRADA, HECHO EN U.S.A.

Printed in the U.S.A.

RA   10   9   8   7   6   5   4   3   2   1

*For John,
steadfast and true,
who made Miss Feversham possible*

1

At the very center of Gentleman Jackson's Rooms in Bond Street, two half-clad men ducked and swayed within the roped-off ring, each seeking a momentary lapse in the other's defense. With their bare fists held close to their faces, their muscled shoulders hunched, the sparrers bore a marked resemblance to each other in height and weight. Their athletic bodies gleamed with a light film of sweat. Both wore buckskin trousers laced at the calf, and low-cut leather shoes that allowed them to move with a predatory grace. But all resemblance ended there.

With an air of quiet concentration, the fighter with sandy brown hair and a military moustache fended off his opponent's blows. His sparring partner, wet black curls plastered against his pale skin, fought back with a ferocious tenacity, his stare unflinching.

A third, more lightly built fellow sat astride a chair at the periphery of the ring, occasionally flinging back a thatch of dark-blond hair from his eyes. Other fashionable young gentlemen lounged against armchairs or billiard tables, mesmerized by the sight of Gentleman Jackson in action. One fellow glanced alternately at the sparring partners and his large gold pocket-watch.

1

"Let it fly, Neville, you can chancery him now if you look sharp," cried the young man at ringside.

The black-haired fighter erupted into action. He jabbed an upper cut at his opponent, who ducked swiftly out of reach, his expression impassive.

"What a rum one!" cried the ringside enthusiast. "Try again, Neville!"

At that moment Jackson moved in, crouching low, landing two punches to his opponent's mid-section.

The black-haired fighter grunted as the wind was knocked out of him. But rather than collapsing, he closed in, rounding with a parry and punch that found its way to Jackson's jaw.

"Round!" cried the fellow with the pocket watch.

Jackson dropped his fists and rubbed his jaw. His opponent lowered his hands to his side, his chest heaving as he gasped for breath.

"A tremendous blow, Neville," cried his companion, as the room broke into an excited hubbub.

The dark-haired fighter ran a bruised hand across his forehead, attempting to wipe away the sweat that streamed down his face. He smiled weakly at his fellow members of the Pugilistic Club, then winked at his ringside companion, who was already untying his cravat in readiness for the next match.

"Excellent fight, my lord." Jackson pumped Neville's hand enthusiastically. "Can't say I remember any student of mine ever ticking me after the third lesson."

"Thank you, Mr. Jackson," Neville said, clapping his hand on the other's shoulder. "Coming from you, that is indeed a compliment."

"Ready for another go, Neville?" The companion, now unbuttoning his shirt, squeezed between the ropes and began dancing about the ring, practicing feints. "I've never seen you in such top form. Try me now?"

"Perhaps on Friday, Kit," Neville replied. "A stroll in St. James will do more to revive me just now."

"I'd not recommend it today, Mr. Feversham." Gentleman Jackson lay a restraining hand on Kit's shoulder. They both watched as the dark-haired nobleman walked away, vigorously toweling the sweat from his hair. "He's in a devil of a temper and might draw your claret accidentally. He nearly did mine." Jackson nodded goodbye to his latest convert to the sweet science and summoned another student to the ring.

As the tonnish young men stepped into Old Bond Street half an hour later, there was no trace of the passionate pugilist in either. Julian Carrothers, ninth Earl of Neville, pulled on his buff-colored gloves with a cool air and dusted an infinitesimal speck of lint from his dark-blue frock coat.

"I say, Kit," he said, glancing approvingly at his companion's ensemble, "that color suits you. Best not to let Petersham see you in it, though. He's mad for that shade of brown and will have you matched to his horses and carriage before you know it."

"That would suit me, as long as he let me handle the ribbons. A finer set of cattle I've never laid eyes on," his friend, Christopher Feversham, replied.

As the two sauntered along in the crisp autumn air, they acknowledged greetings from passers-by and the occupants of fashionable carriages that wheeled smartly past them.

"It wouldn't be too much of an imposition, would it, Kit, if we stopped at Grantham House? I'd like to have Jenkins set my cravat to rights before we dine at Brooks's."

"No trouble at all," came the affable reply. "But tell me, Neville, what got into you back there at Jackson's? I've never seen you in such a taking. You were practically breathing fire."

"I have found that the ring is the only antidote for the tiresome creature who continues to plague me," Neville said.

"Lady Stanbury again?"

"As usual, Kit, your perspicacity astonishes me." Neville's bantering tone turned cold. "It isn't enough that she calls on me at midnight unannounced; now she has begun to cause scenes."

"Brought on by that young heiress in Hertfordshire?"

"I was hoping that tale hadn't already made the rounds," Neville muttered. "Yes, Lady Lyte had kindly invited me to view their Palladian temple—which I must say exceeded my expectations."

"And what of the Lady Honoria?" asked his companion.

"She, also, exceeded my expectations," Neville replied. "Statuesque, as wise as Minerva, and with skin like alabaster. Amiable, as far as I could tell, until the Stanbury creature arrived."

"Uninvited, surely!"

"She wrangled an invitation on some pretext or other, but once she had Lady Lyte's ear, the sun set rapidly on my hopes of claiming the handsome Honoria."

"What were her methods?" Kit asked as they rounded the corner into Piccadilly.

"The usual stratagems—blemishing my character through innuendoes and false pieties. As if Lady Stanbury is any model of virtue. Bah!" he let out a despairing laugh. "It was obvious that Lady Lyte questioned Lady Stanbury's motives, but she was not about to wed her precious daughter to some Medmenham Abbey monk." Neville grimaced and stopped to dab at his brow with his monogrammed handkerchief—a dandified gesture that briefly masked his expression of intense distaste.

"What galls me is the increasing effrontery of her conduct. Take heed, my dear fellow, it is worse to be a lover than a husband. In fact, the idea of being a husband is beginning to appeal to me. Not so much is expected of husbands, once the nuptials are past."

"I must say, you are bearing up manfully after losing Lady Honoria," Kit observed.

"Wonderfully well. Poor girl was almost as baffled by my attentions as I was. Much too virtuous for me." Neville tucked his handkerchief into his sleeve with elaborate attentiveness. "You were right, Kit. You tried to warn me against beginning anything with Lady Stanbury. Now I must find a way to end it."

"She *is* very beautiful." Kit began.

"Beauty such as hers often conceals the worst deficiencies of character," Neville retorted flatly.

They had just crossed the street when Kit seized Neville's arm. "I've hit upon it, Neville! I've got the perfect solution for you!"

"Eh?"

"To your predicament," his companion said. "Come stay with me at Henley for a month or so." In response to Neville's blank stare, he continued. "You remember, my family's estate in Wiltshire. We could rusticate together." Kit laughed delightedly, while his friend openly blanched.

"You mean, stay in the *country* . . . for a month?"

"Yes, the country. It is most entertaining, I assure you," said Kit. "Weren't you just rusticating in Hertfordshire?"

"That was different." Neville sniffed audibly. "My purpose was to view Lord Lyte's Palladian folly, not to camp beneath it. Tell me, Kit, what does one do in the country for a month?"

"Oh, any number of things. There's prime fox hunting this time of year, shooting, country dances, fairs, races, all manner of fêtes. And if you're feeling especially repentant, you could go on pilgrimage to Salisbury Cathedral," Kit teased. "Then there are my sisters. I've praised them to you any number of times."

"Quite so," Neville replied absently. "Arabella and . . . the other one."

"Fanny!"

"Ah, yes. The one you taught how to shoot."

"And a crack shot she is, Neville. You should see

her. At a full gallop she can hit a bull's eye with a Mortimer revolver.''

"Astonishing. I may have to employ her as my second in a duel,'' said Neville dryly. He narrowed his eyes to ascertain the markings on the carriage that was pulling up to No. 54, Picadilly Square.

"And the very best thing about the country,'' continued Kit, ''is that it's not the town.''

"Well, of course it's not the town,'' said Neville haughtily.

"What I mean is, you can go there and be forgotten. Whereas, here in London, everyone is always talking about what everyone else is doing. Perfect set of rattle-traps, if you ask me.''

"Hmmm.'' Neville was staring fixedly at the steel-blue carriage just ahead. A door bearing a familiar coat of arms swung open, and a liveried servant descended carrying a vellum packet.

"Lady Stanbury's carriage?'' Kit asked, shading his eyes for a better look at the crest.

"The same,'' Neville replied grimly. "Obviously sending her servant with an apology for the 'unfortunate occurrences' at Lord Lyte's.''

"While refusing to admit her hand in the matter,'' Kit added.

"You have it, my boy.'' With a decisive air Neville turned to Kit. "How soon can you be ready to leave for Wiltshire?''

"This very evening, if you like.''

"Then send word to your family, Kit. I apologize for the short notice, but the idea of Wiltshire suddenly appeals to me. Be ready by seven if you can.''

"Yes, of course.'' Kit turned to go. "You'll see. You'll like my family, Neville. You might even turn into a proper country squire!''

"I've no doubt of it.'' Neville waved farewell to his friend, then slowly resumed his stroll toward No. 54. A whole month in Wiltshire—and with people he'd never even met. Neville twirled his walking stick and tried to remember if he'd ever been able to tolerate anyone's company for even a fortnight.

He shrugged his shoulders philosophically as he watched the steel-blue carriage round the corner. "At least it is farther from London than Hertfordshire," he sighed.

2

With great stealth, Fanny Feversham pulled the strand of green embroidery thread toward her, all the while keeping her eye on the tortoiseshell cat that was wiggling into a crouch and digging its claws into the carpet.

"Come, Silky, your thread is getting away," she coaxed softly. As the green strand inched between two white kid slippers, the cat's whiskers twitched in excitement. "That's right, puss, go after it," she urged.

"Fanny, whatever are you doing crawling about behind my chair?" Arabella called haughtily. "You know how displeased Mama will be if you haven't finished your needlework." She proudly held up the square of white lawn she had embroidered with poppies. "You see, my handkerchief is nearly done."

"Perfection, Arabella, as always." Fanny tugged hard at the strand, causing the cat to pounce on her sister's stockinged feet.

Her satisfaction at the loud yelps quickly evaporated as she looked up to see her mother standing in the doorway.

Even in her striped morning coat, Dorothea Feversham exuded a commanding air. Matthews, the ladies' maid, stood behind her mistress, nearly obscured by an armload of frothy gowns. Like a general surveying a battlefield, Dorothea Feversham quickly appraised the scene before her.

"Idle pranks, girls, when we have so much to do?" she inquired. She entered the room with a determined air, Matthews close on her heels.

"Mama, Fanny made Silky scratch me," Arabella whimpered, rubbing her stockinged instep.

"My poor Bella," Mrs. Feversham said soothingly. "That cat is almost as provoking as your sister." Her expression softened at the sight of her dark-haired daughter daintily seated on a Sheraton chair, nursing her injured foot. "Fanny, come here at once."

Her elder daughter dutifully emerged from behind the chair, cuddling a purring ball of tortoiseshell fur.

"Put that nasty thing down. I won't have any of your bamming today, especially with that witless cat. Now, girls, attend. Matthews has brought the new gowns we ordered from Mrs. Pinkney. I should like you to try them on, then Mrs. Pinkney will come for the final fittings."

She pointed to the sofa, where Matthews obediently deposited her burden and retreated. The two sisters crowded about the billowing pile, uttering cries of ecstatic delight. Mrs. Feversham watched contentedly as her daughters held up their new sprigged muslins and chintzes, finding each one more elegant than the last.

"Oh, Mama, this walking dress is truly enchanting," Fanny said, holding out the Pomona green skirt of an India muslin. "I shall look as if I stepped down from one of Mr. Wedgewood's vases."

Her mother's brow clouded as she recognized a familiar dress printed with bluebells at the bottom of the heap. "Fanny, this was your gown, was it not? It appears the sleeve has been mended."

"Why, yes, Mama," Fanny replied meekly. "I sent it out because it had a great gash in it."

"I can see that, my girl. Whatever were you doing?"

"Only riding Vulcan, Mama," Fanny said meekly.

"In a gown instead of a habit! You're nineteen years old, my girl. You can't just leap onto a horse in your best clothes. Really, Fanny, you simply must not go on behaving in such a harum-scarum manner!" Mrs. Feversham fixed her daughter with her most severe look. "One would suspect you do not want a Season, Fanny."

"All young ladies want a Season, Mama," Arabella said urgently.

"Why, of course, child. And so you shall have one. As to you, Fanny, I must make it clear that I will have no malingering like last year. Do you hear me?"

"But, Mama, even Dr. Smirke said it was the worst case of ague he had ever seen," her daughter replied, affecting mild surprise.

"An ague brought upon by ingesting large amounts of horse tonic and a great deal of stage acting," snorted her mother. "Besides, Dr. Smirke is completely near-sighted—he could have been diagnosing Silky and been none the wiser. No, this year you will come out with Arabella, and that is an end to it." Mrs. Feversham shook her head despairingly. "I must say, I pity the London beau who chooses such a hoyden. If only you were more like your sweet sister."

While Arabella gazed devotedly at her mother, Fanny buried her face in Silky's fur. "Sweet! Laced with enough false sentiment to sicken the likes of us, puss-cat."

Mrs. Feversham fixed her daughters with a stern gaze. "Let me remind you, girls, we have but a few months until the Season begins. We must prepare ourselves. After you have finished your embroidery, you may try on your new gowns. Matthews will assist when you are ready."

Satisfied at the sight of both girls taking up their embroidery hoops, Mrs. Feversham turned toward the door. "Try to keep your stitches small and neat, Fanny, like Bella's, not those elephantine ones you favor. I leave you girls with the thought that young ladies are never more quiet and well-bred than when doing their needlework." With that, she firmly closed the door behind her.

From beneath her lashes Fanny stole a look at her younger sister. Why, the little gudgeon was actually sewing away. Arabella bent over the frame, chestnut curls carefully arranged about her oval face—the very picture of modest feminine beauty, to judge by the engravings in *La Belle Assemblée*. Fanny judged her own looks to be less pleasing than Arabella's. The dark eyebrows that arched over her luminous blue eyes gave her face an expression of eager perceptiveness, which contrasted unfavorably with Arabella's perpetual docility.

Feeling Fanny's gaze, Arabella lifted her head and a fearful look clouded her soft brown eyes. "Pray, Fanny, don't start. I know you're up to something when you stare at me like that."

"I don't know what you could possibly mean, Bella," Fanny replied innocently. "If I stare, it is to study my virtuous sister and become more like her."

"Stop it, Fan," Bella said warningly.

Fanny threw aside her embroidery in exasperation. "It's positively tiresome, Bella, the way you have to be so good all the time. You looked a perfect goose when Mama began canonizing you. You must show more backbone, you know, and not lap it up so."

Arabella reddened with embarrassment. "If I am good, it is because I am not clever like you, Fanny."

"And if I were so clever I'd know how to avoid this ridiculous come-out," her sister replied hotly. She began sorting through the new dresses with a distracted air. "It is all so silly, don't you think, Bella?"

"Fan, you can't mean you don't want a Season in London," her sister said incredulously. "Just think of the balls and routs we shall attend."

"Think of the stiff-necked coxcombs ogling us from the corner of every drawing room," Fanny replied with distaste. "I would rather be sold off at the Bradford Fair.

That's what the Marriage Mart is, you know, Bella, a glorified cattle auction.''

"Why, Fan, I don't think of it that way at all.'' Arabella went to her sister's side and took her hand. "You're putting yourself in a fret for nothing, my dear.''

"You forget, Bella, the purpose. It is to find husbands with at least ten thousand a year.''

"And what is wrong with a wealthy husband who adores you and gives you presents?'' her sister countered earnestly.

"Everything—if that same husband turns outs to be a rake who shuts you in an airless London house to breed a tribe of pasty-faced whelps, while he runs up gambling debts.''

"Oh, Fan, you know Papa would never sanction such a match,'' Arabella whispered.

"But they never seem like such a match at first. Take, as an example, that horrid thing Cousin Alethia married.''

"Lord Lansden? What of him?''

"A man twice her age, fat, bald and little red eyes like a maddened boar.'' Fanny shuddered irrepressibly.

"But we all know Alethia married Lord Lansden for his fortune.'' Arabella patted her sister's hand consolingly. "I know what has happened to you, Fan. Lord Neville has ruined you for marriage. He has stolen your heart.''

Fanny looked up at her sister quickly.

"I mean as Lord Rothermere,'' Arabella added, examining a delicate *jonquille* batiste.

Her sister sighed pensively. "I suppose you're right, Bella. A man created on paper has caused me more heartache than any man of flesh and blood ever will.''

"We shall see how true that is after our Season is over,'' Arabella said, holding the dress against her. "Speaking of Lord Rothermere, do you think he would find this color attractive?'' she asked archly.

Fanny considered for a moment. "It is one of his favorites," she decided. Then she bit back a smile at how adroitly Arabella had manipulated her mood. Her hero, Lord Rothermere, was the one thing she cared passionately about.

It had all begun as an innocent diversion. She had modeled him on what she imagined the present Lord Neville to be, the London beau who figured so prominently in Kit's letters and the pages of *The Morning Chronicle*. According to the reports, the gallant Julian Carrothers, ninth Earl of Neville, was constantly embroiled in intrigues with ladies of London's fashionable *ton*. The latest rumor was that he had decamped to Hertfordshire to court an heiress.

The Feversham girls had practically memorized his misadventures. As soon as their father was finished with the paper, they pounced upon it for news of London life and the wayward lord. He had once entered Brooks's accompanied by an exquisitely dressed monkey. The creature wore a cravat tied by Brummell himself. Neville pretended to play a hand with the hairy beast, contending it would have as much luck at whist as he. After that escapade he had been barred from Brooks's for a month.

Aside from the *Chronicle*, Fanny occasionally received carefully edited accounts of Neville's indiscretions from Kit, who was rated one of Neville's greatest friends. Although Neville was somewhat older than Kit, they shared a love of mills, riding, gaming and dancing. Neville had sponsored Kit for membership at Brooks's, and Kit had introduced Neville to the Four-in-Hand Club.

As Fanny's novel progressed, the real life dandy and the fictional character had merged, making Lord Rothermere the perfect embodiment of the gothic hero.

"Actually, Bella, Melinda is just about to meet the wicked lord," Fanny said with a mysterious air. She moved to her mahogany writing desk in the corner. From the furthest depths of the desk drawer she retrieved a portfolio bound in dark-green morocco leather, from which manuscript pages protruded. Her sister promptly sank onto the sofa as Fanny arranged the pages.

"Now, Bella, do you recall where we left off?"

"How could I forget!" Arabella's eyes widened in excitement. "Melinda Earnshaw, although warned against it by her headmistress, has taken the position as governess in Lord Rothermere's household. She began her journey despite her misgivings about her employer's dissipated reputation."

"Quite so." Fanny smoothed out a page of manuscript. "Here we are. We find our heroine en route to Castle Locarno in the Italian Alps." Fanny began reading in a hushed, dramatic tone:

> Melinda drew back from the coach window with an involuntary shudder. From its windswept position high atop the distant tor, Castle Locarno presented a forbidding aspect with its craggy battlements etched against the tumultuous sky.

The young authoress paused and regarded the paragraph critically, pleased with her effort so far. The thrilling combination of gloom and romance she had experienced upon reading the gothic novels of Mrs. Radcliffe was no less present in her own work.

> Melinda drew her cloak about her. Even more chilling than the forbidding appearance of Castle Locarno, was the thought of her inevitable meeting with Lord Rothermere.

A *frisson* of delicious dread, much as Melinda must have felt, passed through Fanny.

> "The Wicked Lord" some had called him, since his banishment from England ten long years ago.

She glanced up to find Arabella leaning forward, impatient for Rothermere's entrance.

"Go on, Fan," she urged. "What does he look like? Is he grim and horribly disfigured?"

Fanny had spent hours designing her hero's appearance. His face was as familiar to her as Bella's. Lord Rothermere was tall and agile, with tousled black curls. His countenance was pale as death, etched with the painful memories of his many transgressions. She returned to the page before her.

The coach bowled into a cobblestone courtyard which was eerily lit by blazing torches. In the doorway stood Lord Rothermere, his ebony curls windswept by the impending storm. He strode over to the coach and opened the door, bowing gracefully.

"My dear Miss Earnshaw, I am pleased to welcome you to Castle Locarno," he said. His voice, although well-bred, sounded cold and harsh to Melinda's ear. A cruel smile played about his mouth. But as he helped her alight, his touch was strangely reassuring.

Arabella sat back, murmuring, "Oh, how very gothic!"

With a heavy sigh, Fanny continued:

Standing in the shadow of the doorway was Rothermere's child, a delicate creature with long black ringlets and questioning eyes.

At this point, they were rudely transported back to Henley Hall by the strange and barbaric sound of their mother having hysterics. Fanny hastily thrust the portfolio aside, and the two sisters raced downstairs to find Wilkins standing just outside the drawing room.

"All I did, Miss Fanny, was bring her a letter from

young Mr. Feversham,'' he said, nervously turning a tray.

The girls dashed into the lemon-colored drawing room, where a fire burned brightly in the grate and the morning sun streamed through lace curtains. Usually a cheerful place, it now held a tragic scene worthy of Mrs. Siddons.

Mrs. Feversham had collapsed onto the divan, her morning coat twisted in disarray. One hand clasped a letter and the other was at her throat. She appeared to be gasping for air.

Arabella swooped to her mother's side and patted her hand, making soothing noises while Fanny handed her mother the hartshorn.

''Mama, what is it?'' Fanny asked anxiously.

''Good heavens, whatever will become of us! Oh, my poor girls, what shall we do?''

''Has Kit gambled away all our money?'' Fanny cried. She drew closer, trying to make out the handwriting on the letter her mother brandished.

''He's bringing someone here . . . in a few days, if you can imagine! They are coming in a carriage from London.'' Mrs. Feversham, her imminent collapse momentarily forgotten, managed an indignant stare. ''A *nobleman's* carriage, I must add. We are to have a titled guest in less than a week. Oh, my dears, we are ruined!''

''What nobleman, Mama?'' Fanny exchanged mystified looks with Arabella. Kit was always dashing off on some new adventure, but so far Henley had remained outside his periphery.

''He will be accompanied by that man . . . that fellow with the monkey . . . you know,'' Mrs. Feversham spluttered.

''You mean Lord Nev—'' Fanny began.

''Yes, that's it, Julian Carrothers.''

''Lord Neville . . . coming here!'' Fanny gasped. There were exclamations from the entire household—from Wilkins and the maidservants gathered in the door-

way, to Arabella, who clasped Fanny's hand in astonishment.

"This is your doing, Fan," she whispered. "You've
conjured him here with Lord Rothermere."

Fanny was overcome—first, with curiosity, then a
heart-pounding excitement she could barely contain. She
stared blindly at Arabella. Lord Neville, here at Henley
Hall? It was unthinkable!

"But, Mama, how very thrilling," Fanny finally
blurted. "Think what charming stories he'll tell us of
London society."

"*Charming!* Really, Fanny, I can scarce believe my
ears. Think what charming stories he shall tell London
society of his month at Henley Hall, where all is topsy-
turvy and the Feversham girls set clawing cats on one
another!" Mrs. Feversham waved her lace-trimmed
handkerchief and dabbed at her eyes. "Oh, where is my
husband? Someone fetch him instantly!"

"Please, Mama," Arabella said soothingly, "we
promise to be well behaved, don't we, Fan?"

"Opportunity knocks but once in a lifetime and it has
found me unprepared," their mother wailed. "Whatever
shall I do?"

"Mrs. F., what is it, my dearest?"

Mr. Feversham, summoned from his business with the
estate manager, appeared at his wife's side. He was accompanied by Brutus, the ancient retriever, who leaned
sympathetically against Mrs. Feversham.

"Oh, Mr. F., a disaster brought upon us by our provoking son! He is arriving in a few days time with a
titled guest. They are stopping at Devizes to watch a
mill, then they shall be here—for nearly a month," she
finished in sepulchral tones.

"Well then, Mrs. F., we shall do our best to make
Kit's friend feel at home," her husband replied calmly.
"Take him riding, take him shooting. Invite people to
meet him. Have a big dinner. You know what to do."

"Why, Mr. F., whomever could we invite to supper?

"I know, Mama," Arabella prompted helpfully. "We could have Mr. Burleigh and his son, Clive."

Fanny spluttered at the mention of the name. "Clive Burleigh! Oh, no, Mama, not him. Not that popinjay!"

"Fanny, how dare you call that refined young man a popinjay! When was the last time you saw him?"

"At the Bradford Fair two years ago, Mama, when he wore those horrid trousers and pretended to speak with an Italian accent."

"I think Mr. Burleigh a very feeling sort of young person," Mrs. Feversham replied severely, "quite unlike the other ruffians who inhabit this countryside. Besides, he has just returned from Italy, so he should provide Lord Neville with very stimulating conversation."

"I think Mr. Clive Burleigh quite admirable altogether," Arabella ventured.

Fanny waited to catch her sister's eye, then smirked mockingly at her.

"Oh, Fanny, you are a beast!" Arabella burst into tears and fled from the room.

"Really, Fanny, that's outside of enough," her mother commanded. "Take this awful dog away from me. Why must he always lick my hand? And you can stop spying over my shoulder to read Kit's letter—you may have it."

Fanny seized the letter and called to Brutus. She made her escape through the front door to the surrounding parkland, letting out loud whoops punctuated with leaps in the air.

Panting, she fell upon a mossy turf where she was joined by the hoarsely yelping retriever. The pink band that held back her curls had come loose and, like one of Romney's young bacchantes, her golden hair streamed about her shoulders. Oblivious to the grass stains on her gown and her torn stockings, she scanned Kit's letter eagerly.

"My great friend, Lord N . . . seeking the healing balm of nature . . . his charm and erudition . . . a month's rustication.''

Fanny crushed the letter to her breast in an effort to quiet her pounding heart. So, it was true. She was to spend a whole month in Lord Neville's company. The hero of her book and she—beneath the same roof!

"Aren't we a lucky pair, Brutus?" She entwined her arms about the dog's neck while he whined and licked her face excitedly. "But you must promise to help me. We shall have to be very, very good. I know it won't be easy for you, my dear, but we must try." She kissed the dog on his forehead, causing him to bark gleefully.

3

The next few days passed in a flurry of preparations for Henley's distinguished visitor. The servants, from Wilkins to the stableboys, were kept in a constant state of activity. Horses had to be reshod, carriages polished, and the hedges clipped. Pacing among the terrace gardens, Mrs. Feversham nervously counted the blooms on the chrysanthemums, praying they would keep their blazing golds and clarets for a few more weeks.

Fanny gazed down the gravel drive and tried to envision what Neville's impression of Henley Hall would be. As Mr. Feversham was fond of observing, the approach was as fine a sight as the Georgian manor itself. Nestled against a slight hill, Henley commanded a fine view of the surrounding gardens, grassy terraces, parkland and woods. Rows of majestic oaks lined the serpentine drive that led to the pedimented doorway.

As to accommodations, a debate quickly ensued as to which bedroom was best suited to their guest's requirements. Mrs. Feversham finally decided on the room next to Kit's, but she continued to torment her family with questions. Were the bed hangings too dreary? What of the room's situation? It overlooked the entrance. Did they think the morning sun would disturb Lord Neville if he were to wake, er, indisposed?

In her spare moments, which were few, Mrs. Feversham drilled her daughters on table manners and correct forms of address. When Fanny muttered it was as if Good Queen Bess herself were coming, her mother fixed her with a gimlet eye and intoned, "Mark you, Fanny, you shall have reason to be glad of this." Invitations to the neighboring families, the Monktons, the vicarage and Burleigh House, flew out with great dispatch.

Just when Fanny began to think their honored guest had chosen to forego nature's healing balm, Kit's whoop announced their arrival. She ran to the window, and saw two young men swathed in greatcoats driving an elegant curricle drawn by a pair of well-matched bays. Kit jumped down off the box. The driver, Fanny realized with a lump in her throat, was Lord Neville. He calmly handed the reins to the stableboy and alighted, following in Kit's wake.

Fanny and Arabella scrambled to take their places in the hall, while the others streamed out the front door.

"Kit, my dear boy!" Mrs. Feversham trotted as fast as her legs would carry her toward her son. Wilkins directed the footmen to gather up portmanteaux, bags and parcels.

There were many kisses and embraces, then Kit introduced his friend.

Mr. Feversham, with a hearty handshake, welcomed his guest and congratulated him on his conveyance. "Well, well, never saw the likes. Quite splendid horses you have there. We are honored indeed, my lord."

Above the hubbub Fanny could hear Kit's excited voice. "Pater, you should have seen Neville handle the ribbons. We had a remarkable race to Trowbridge, for who should we meet at the mill but Tom Moore. He challenged us to a dash from Devizes to his house in Trowbridge, and of course we couldn't refuse him. Must say, he was a devil with the four-in-hand, but nothing like Neville, here." Still talking, Kit burst through the door, then fell upon Fanny and twirled her in the air.

"Fan, you're the quiet one! Waiting so politely by the door—not much like the Fanny I knew. Still practicing with the pistol like I showed you?" He set her down and hugged Arabella. "And, Bella, aren't you a picture!" Kit put an arm around each girl. "Neville, come meet these fine lasses!"

For the first time, Fanny actually dared to take a closer look at the Earl of Neville. The chiseled planes of his face lent him an aristocratic, yet sensitive, appearance. As he removed his hat, Fanny gasped. His hair was exactly the color of Lord Rothermere's—black as night— and brushed forward in the windswept manner. He was tall and slender, wearing spattered boots whose overturned white tops elegantly set off the many-caped greatcoat which he gracefully shrugged off. Fanny watched him adjust his cravat, mesmerized by the elaborate Waterfall style. She caught herself staring, but not before Neville did. He met her glance and smiled slightly.

"Well, girls, what do you say?" prompted Mrs. Feversham.

First Arabella, then Fanny, dropped a small curtsy and murmured a greeting.

He took each hand as it was proffered. "You must be Miss Arabella. You are even lovelier than Kit said you were. And you must be Miss Fanny. What stories I've heard of you! I'm glad to see you are a connoisseur of cravats."

Fanny allowed her hand to lie in his, while she gazed up into his eyes despite her embarrassment. They were unlike any she had seen before, she thought, certainly very different from Lord Rothermere's hardened glance. Their caressing warmth could melt any heart. She glanced around dreamily, to see Arabella blushing furiously nearby. To think she was actually meeting the Wicked Lord, himself . . .

"Brutus!" her mother shrieked, as a shaggy thunderbolt streaked through the front door. Barking madly, the dog thrust itself between Fanny and their guest. Before anyone could restrain him the retriever leaped up, licking Neville's face and covering his snowy cravat and linen waistcoat with muddy paw prints.

"Oh, my heavens, oh no, oh, Mr. F., do something! Oh, I shall faint!" Mrs. Feversham's face turned an apoplectic shade as her hands fluttered helplessly.

Kit threw himself upon Brutus. "Down, boy, down, I say," he commanded, his voice convulsed with laughter.

"Filthy beast," Neville muttered flatly, dabbing at his waistcoat with a monogrammed handkerchief.

"I should have warned you about country hospitality," Kit said. "Sorry, old man. You're not used to dogs greeting you with mucky paws in St. James Square, are you?"

"Terribly sorry, very nice weskit," ventured Mr. Feversham.

"I beg you," Neville replied, sniffing slightly, "do not be distressed on my account."

"Oh, my lord, I hope that wasn't your favorite waistcoat," Mrs. Feversham said anxiously, swabbing ineffectually at the muddied linen.

"No, ma'am, I have several favorites," he said distantly. "This was simply my most recent one."

"Now it has a sufficiently antiquated appearance," Kit returned cheerfully.

As the group moved awkwardly toward the drawing room, Fanny exchanged a look with Arabella, who bit her lip anxiously. Far from taking Brutus's onslaught with good grace, Neville had retreated into a haughty silence. The knot in Fanny's stomach tightened. The prospect of a month-long visit began to loom before her like a dreaded Latin translation.

As they settled in chairs and sofas, the men stood politely until the women had been seated. Then Mr. Feversham began in conversational tones, "So, my lord, Kit informs us you are a newcomer to Wiltshire."

"Yes, to my discredit," Neville began pleasantly. "For it is enchanting countryside and full of interesting novelties—the ruins at Stonehenge, the White Horse at Westbury."

"Some say it was carved there by Alfred the Great himself after defeating the Danes," Fanny interjected, surprising herself with this long-buried scrap of erudition.

"You don't say?" Neville turned to regard her, an eyebrow half-raised behind his quizzing glass.

"Well, Fan, tell us what battle it was," Mrs. Feversham urged.

"Ethandune, I believe."

"You see, already I have learned much about the charms of Wiltshire," Neville responded, sitting back in his chair. The quizzing glass that hung about his neck by a black silk ribbon plopped against his sleeve.

Fanny blanched to recall how Melinda and Lord Rothermere had been swept away by an undeniable passion from the very beginning. Neville, it appeared, would soon be swept into sleep by the unremitting boredom of this first meeting.

As silence threatened to engulf them once more, Mr. Feversham embarked on another sortie. "And what of the mill at Devizes, Kit? Was it worth leaving London for?"

"I should say. Perfectly ripping," Kit responded with gusto. "Ned Turner was deemed to have the advantage. Superior tonnage and all. But Jack Randall quickly showed he was a man of talent, eh, Neville?"

"I would call him a man of genius," his friend replied. "He's been dubbed The Nonpareil. Beating Turner wasn't an easy task, but Randall has tremendous spirit. The fight lasted thirty-four rounds."

During this last exchange, Silky had leapt quietly into Fanny's lap. The presence of the warm, purring creature comforted her, enabling her to study Neville at leisure. His aquiline nose and pale skin lent him a poetic air, decidedly at odds with the drawling sophistication of the town dandy. Where was the real Neville in these contradictions? Lost in her ruminations, she barely noticed the cat's departure. Silky took up a position below the arm of Neville's chair, raptly gazing at the quizzing glass that dangled just out of reach.

"Dash it, nearly forgot in all the excitement," said Kit, jumping up and disappearing into the hallway. He quickly returned, his arms filled with parcels, and handed each family member a gift.

A tiara set with cameos of agate and onyx evoked a delighted cry from Mrs. Feversham. She immediately placed it on her head and solicited everyone's opinion of its effect.

Mr. Feversham received a beautifully chased silver snuffbox which he weighed in his hand appreciatively, pronouncing it a "monstrous fine piece."

Arabella and Fanny lost no time tearing into their gifts. Sighing with pleasure, Arabella wrapped herself in a fawn-colored Kashmir shawl.

"Just look at these!" Fanny gasped as she pulled on a pair of lavender kid gloves. "They're perfect, Kit." She ran over to her brother and began tickling him. "Exactly what I'll need for driving a gig with a pair of high steppers in Hyde Park!"

"Oh no, my girl, no gigs for you yet," countered Mrs. Feversham severely. "And quit pestering your brother. Really, Kit, you mustn't encourage her so."

"Someone call off this sister of mine!" Kit yelped, fighting off Fanny's attack. Between fits of laughter, he choked out, "What say, Neville, isn't she a perfect gammoner?"

"I dare say she is," said Neville blandly, holding up his glass the better to see Fanny, now emitting shrieks at her brother's counterattack.

"Stop it, this instant, you two," Mrs. Feversham commanded, her tiara glinting in a threatening manner. "You have forgotten our guest."

Immediately chastened, Fanny took her place next to Kit on the sofa. With arms outstretched, she proffered her gloves for Brutus's approval.

Gammoner, to be sure, Neville thought. Kit had told him all about his sisters—Arabella, the family beauty, and Fanny, the hoyden, who had taken as naturally to pistol shooting as a highwayman, and who had concocted a *maladie imaginaire* to avoid last year's Season. But there was one thing Kit had forgotten to tell him— that the elder sister was a diamond of the first water.

Neville appraised her looks with a connoisseur's detachment. She was a golden girl with the enchanting eyes and brows of a Greek nymph. Her unabashed manner announced as clearly as any words that she was utterly free from the affectations of recognized beauties like Lady Stanbury. But beneath her looks she was still a green girl, and a rather backward one at that, judging by her antics.

He stifled a yawn and looked about the drawing room with its air of unassuming comfort, against which several pieces of superb furniture stood out like eighteenth century courtiers. Plunged amid the Fevershams, he was beset by an unusual mix of feelings. Although he had the warmest regard for Kit, he had frankly winced at the prospect of enduring the sisters, no doubt a pair of smirking country maids. Thus far, the Feversham girls were neither an inspiration nor a torment. They appeared to be gently bred—at least the dark-haired one. A cynical smile played about his lips at the sight of Mrs. Feversham prattling away to Arabella while her husband surreptitiously fed lumps of sugar to the retriever at his side.

What fun Sally Jersey would have with that sight! Yet, despite their gaucheries, he could see that the family was close-knit and kind. Being among them reawakened a reassuring feeling, one he hadn't experienced since his boarding school days. Returning to his family in Derbyshire during the holidays then had been his only chance to shed the protective armor of artifice, and to bask in the warmth of family affection.

His gaze lingered on the honey-haired creature petting the dog. He was about to rouse himself to make some gallant remark, when she raised her head, meeting his glance.

"Do you have pets, Lord Neville?" she asked.

"Pets? You mean animals? Good heavens, no!" The directness of her question momentarily stunned him.

"That is too bad," she said in a disappointed tone.

Recovering his suavity, Neville replied, "My valet, you see, would never hear of it."

Seeing his sister's questioning look, Kit intervened. "Too many dog hairs, Fan. Jenkins is very strict about his master's clothes."

Fanny gave Neville a pitying look that he found most annoying. "I take it, Miss Feversham, you would prefer it if I lived with a menagerie," he asked mockingly.

Stung by his tone, Fanny was about to make a caustic reply when she noticed Silky make a leap for the quizzing glass on the black ribbon. Narrowly missing its target, the cat dug its claws into Neville's hand.

"Good Lord!" he expostulated, shaking off the cat and nursing his hand. "What a vicious little monster! What other rabid creatures are you going to unleash on me, Kit?"

"Fanny, do something about that vile cat at once," Mrs. Feversham commanded.

The small bundle of fur jumped into Neville's lap, circled briefly and collapsed. "What's this?" he asked distastefully, pointing to Silky. "It's behaving in a most familiar and common fashion."

Fanny, who had approached with some trepidation, blushed angrily. "Cats are anything but common," she said severely. She leaned toward him to gather up her animal. "You should be honored, for they are very particular about whose laps they sit in."

Neville's disdain was held in check by her stern tone. He looked up into her bright blue eyes, which assessed him with unusual clarity. Protectively, she nuzzled her cat.

"Fanny, how dare you speak to Lord Neville in such a manner," Mrs. Feversham remonstrated.

"It's all right," he responded blandly, "your daughter is merely initiating me into the mysteries of felines. Very well, give the creature back, then." He held out his arms. Fanny hesitantly handed him Silky, who promptly curled into a ball on his lap, blinking lazily. "It seems I am to feel honored for some time," he muttered, as the cat yawned and went to sleep.

He watched as Fanny took her seat across from him. What an odd little creature, he thought. She certainly didn't lack fire when it came to defending her beast. He observed his scratched hand with profound annoyance and tried to remember the last time anyone had told him their true feelings at the risk of insulting him.

Suddenly, Kit began to chuckle. "Would give anything for your Bond Street tailor to see you now, Neville. Muddy boots, ruined waistcoat, wounded paw, alternately bammed by my sister and her cat. Looks like you've lived here all your life."

"Don't think I would have lasted this long, old chap," Neville replied dryly, watching Fanny take a sip of tea. "One of 'em would have been the death of me by now."

4

6 6 A nd now your opinion, Fan," said Arabella breathlessly. She tucked back a strand of hair that had escaped from the small cluster of roses behind her ear. "Are you not surprised to find Lord Neville so agreeable?"

"How do you mean, Bella?" Fanny replied vaguely.

"To be so forgiving of the indignities he suffered."

"I s'pose," Fanny answered distantly, twisting from her vantage point behind Arabella to gain a look at herself in the pier glass. "Although I'm sure Silky meant no harm."

"Well, Fan, you must confess you were less than agreeable," said Arabella smugly. "I tremble to think what the poor man must think of us!"

"I assure you, Bella, he hardly thinks of us at all," Fanny replied dryly. She recalled the distracted way he had gazed about him, taking in her family as if they were sticks of furniture, worthy of no more than a cursory glance.

Her last reply was lost on Arabella who regarded herself critically, smoothing her hair and her gown. Of the two sisters' dresses, Bella's was by far the finer. A layer of pale pink tulle over an underdress of white silk set off her ivory skin and brown eyes to perfection.

"What I meant to say, Fan," Arabella observed, as she pulled on her white kid gloves, "was that after Lord Rothermere, I rather expected Lord Neville to be more . . . wicked." She moved away from the mirror, giving Fanny her turn before it. "You don't think we could have misjudged him, do you? Perhaps the *Chronicle* showed him in a false light. He seems not the least bit wicked to me."

Fanny caught the tone of disappointment in Arabella's last observation. "Well," she said judiciously, "perhaps he's only a bit tired at the moment. I imagine he could be wicked if he wanted to," she added helpfully.

While Bella ruminated, Fanny spun delightedly before the mirror, lost in clouds of filmy muslin. The dress was her favorite, even though it had been cut down from one of Mama's and was hopelessly out of style—the rage for classical clothes being long past. The dress was elegantly simple, consisting of yards of white gauze and pale blue silk ribbons that criss-crossed and tied under the bosom *à la greque*. A single gold fillet kept the thick curls from cascading down her slim neck.

"Fan, you still haven't answered my question," Arabella continued petulantly. "What do you think Lord Neville is really like? With us he is very polite, but think of all those poor heiresses he pursued and lost interest in. What possesses him to act in such a manner?"

"Can't say for sure, Bella. Maybe because he doesn't have a family to go back to as Kit has. Even the gayest of London beaus must get blue-devilled at times." Then Fanny remembered the way he had grimaced at Silky. "Frankly, I think him rather a bore."

"Fanny!"

Just then Mrs. Feversham appeared dressed for dinner, as gaily decorated as Nelson's flagship. A spray of coquelicot feathers drifted lazily above her head, while her yellow-green satin gown, trimmed with poppy-colored ribbon, completed the ensemble.

"Dear girls, how lovely you look!" she said, squeezing her fan in delight. "Pretty as anything painted by Lawrence! Come now, Lord Neville awaits us. Our guests are due to arrive at any moment. Fanny, mind those silk stockings."

As the sisters made their way into the drawing room, the men standing by the fireplace turned expectantly. Mr. Feversham crossed the room and kissed each daughter affectionately. Kit made a low whistling sound and muttered, "Well, I'll be a blind monkey."

Neville, Fanny marked, was by far the most elegantly dressed person in the room. He was attired in a pair of black pantaloons buttoned tightly over highly polished pumps. His coat was of a midnight blue superfine, cut to reveal a clean white waistcoat with gold buttons. A heavy gold chain, which supported two fobs and a finely crafted watch, appeared just below his waistcoat. His cravat, Fanny noted appreciatively, had again been tied in a devastatingly ornate manner.

"What style, eh, Fan?" remarked Kit, following her gaze. "I've tried to master the Oriental for months with no luck."

"All depends on one's valet, old man. Jenkins is both my manservant and mentor. The torture of tying my own cravats will be over when he arrives next week." Neville smiled with satisfaction as he took up a position next to Fanny.

"My apologies about your hand, my lord," said Fanny glumly.

"It's of no consequence." Neville examined his wound and sighed. "No doubt it's to be expected. The countryside positively teems with unseen dangers." When there was no response to this quip, Neville continued. "Tell me, Miss Feversham, do you sing?"

"Oh, no, my lord."

"Do you play?"

"A bit. I play the piano a little. Usually I accompany

Arabella when she sings. You'll no doubt have the pleasure of hearing her tonight.''

Fanny traced the outline of an acanthus leaf in the carpet with her slipper—her desultory air an attempt to suppress the excitement she felt in Neville's presence.

''I recollect Kit saying that you're a versifier, are you not, Miss Feversham? A scribbler of some sort?''

She gave a start. ''Yes,'' she answered tentatively.

''And what do you write—verses, plays, novels?'' he pursued relentlessly.

''This and that,'' she answered vaguely. ''Mostly novels.''

''I suppose, then, they're gothic novels in the style of Mrs. Radcliffe, are they not? Those seem to be the rage.''

''Yes, quite,'' Fanny said, ''although I'm sure they're deemed passé now.''

''Well, how very splendid of you,'' Neville answered, ignoring her last remark. ''And who, might I ask, has been your inspiration for a gothic hero?''

Fanny glanced about the room, desperate for a way out of this trap. She answered with the name of the first person she saw.

''Wilkins, my lord.''

''Wilkins?'' Neville exclaimed, turning to catch a glimpse of the aged butler, now shuffling into the drawing room. ''What an interesting chap he must be. I dare say, Miss Feversham, I never would have presumed Wilkins to be particularly heroic, but then—''

Fanny's precarious situation was momentarily relieved by the entrance of the Monktons and the vicar, Mr. Sutcliff. Mrs. Monkton was swathed in a heavily fringed shawl, and on her head she wore a Turkish turban—her appearance, Fanny thought, startlingly theatrical. She swept into the room, and upon meeting Lord Neville, curtsied deeply as if to a member of the royal family.

Mr. Monkton, looking very florid in a cravat that

pushed his jowls into his cheekbones, sketched a bow with many flourishes which was quickly terminated by the creaking of his stays.

"Your lordship, such a great honor." Mrs. Monkton was practically prostrate with awe.

Fanny knew that in five minutes' time Mrs. Monkton would have monopolized Neville, rattling off the names of her titled acquaintances from London and Bath. She resolutely made her way to the vicar's side.

"Tally ho, my girl," he called out in the friendliest of tones. "How is the fox hunt progressing?" He quaffed a glass of punch and nodded toward Mrs. Monkton, chatting vigorously with Neville. "I fear our quarry is chased by hungry hounds."

"Just so, Mr. Sutcliff," Fanny agreed, "her blood is up."

They were diverted by the sound of Mrs. Feversham shrilly greeting new guests. Standing in the doorway was old Mr. Burleigh, one hand on a cane, the other holding a brass trumpet to his ear. He was accompanied by his son, whose appearance caused the vicar to splutter and say, "Eh? What's this?" in a thoroughly aggrieved manner.

Although, Fanny wagered, Neville and Clive had doubtlessly both spent equal care in their dress, Neville's understated taste put everyone at ease, while Clive's costume drew baffled stares. First of all, his hair was all wrong. Although the mousey brown locks were combed forward, tightly curled and pomaded *à la Titus*, they lacked the deceptive casualness of Neville's windswept cut.

Next, the points on his collar were so high they grazed his ears, giving his already sharp features a weasel-like cast. And his cravat, it appeared, was straight out of the *commedia dell' arte*, its broad green and white stripes tied in an absurdly large bow. Added to all this was an embroidered waistcoat beneath a maroon frockcoat, and nankeen trousers tucked into highly polished and tasselled boots.

"Ah, Clive, what a sight you are!" Mrs. Feversham began uncertainly. "Please meet my distinguished guest, Lord Neville. Mr. James Burleigh and his son, Clive Burleigh."

Clive had just embarked on a series of outrageous compliments to Neville when Mrs. Feversham summoned her daughters to join them.

"Ah, here is Miss Arabella Feversham, a rare English rose—a type of beauty my travels have taught me to appreciate," Clive said with great feeling. "And Miss Fanny Feversham. Something more wild, uncultivated, springing directly from nature's hand . . . "

"A weed, perhaps?" Fanny offered sweetly.

"No, not a weed," Clive replied tersely. "The two of you together put me very much in mind of, let me see . . . which two goddesses?" Clive held up a triangular-shaped quizzing glass. "Tell me, Lord Neville, do they not remind you of Venus and Flora, goddesses of love and spring?"

Neville appeared at Clive's elbow and regarded the sisters with equal solemnity through his own quizzing glass. "I should think something earlier," he said. "Greek, perhaps."

"Greek, indeed!" Clive dropped his quizzing glass and turned an appreciative countenance on Neville.

Fanny could no longer abide their airs. "How challenging life must be for men of taste," she said lightly, "to be always examining persons as if they are objects in your collections of virtu. Why, I feel myself crumbling away into the dust of antiquity as I stand here. Greek dust, perhaps. Come, gentlemen, I see that it's time for our dinner."

She imperiously led the way to the dining room, which had just been opened by Wilkins. Neville fell into step beside her, offering her his arm.

Once out of earshot, he murmured, "I fear you have

given young Mr. Burleigh quite a fright with your lecture. Perhaps the Medusa's head would suit you better than Flora's blossoms, Miss Feversham. The poor fellow is still licking his wounds, as I am mine.'' He indicated his scratched hand with great solemnity.

''Thank heaven he has Arabella to offer him solace,'' Fanny observed. Her calm demeanor barely disguised her delight in Neville's teasing manner.

He bent close as he seated her at the table. ''Just look at him now. See how willingly Miss Arabella listens, how pliantly she leans upon his arm. And look at me,'' he gesticulated dramatically, taking the seat on Fanny's right. ''Bruised and rebuffed, scratched and scorned. A poor dandy adrift in the country.''

''If I might speak plainly, my lord, it seems you are no stranger to country life,'' Fanny retorted. ''I recall a recent report of you leaving another adrift—in Hertford-shire, I believe.''

''There is more to that story, Miss Feversham,'' he answered in low tones. ''Mind, you still have not solved my dilemma as to how a man of fashion may find solace in the wilds of Wiltshire.''

''I believe, my lord,'' said Fanny demurely, unfolding her napkin, ''that men of fashion rarely find solace for long, whether in or out of the country.''

''And just what do you mean by that, Miss Feversham?'' he asked, visibly piqued.

''That fashion is a thing of whimsy,'' Fanny replied, her heart beating rapidly. She felt carried away by a torrent of words, unable to weigh their consequences. ''It is forever changing. Solace rejects change. It is something that comes from within.''

''Then, you are saying that to be solaced, I must change. Cruel Miss Feversham. You show me no mercy.'' He lifted an eyebrow and regarded Fanny more keenly.

Without realizing it, she had touched on the very

thing that had been plaguing him lately. He had been feeling as dissatisfied with himself as a snake that needs to shed its skin. No matter how much diversion he sought, the badly needed change seemed to elude him.

Snatches of dinner conversation reached Fanny while she reviewed her exchange with Neville. Replying to his sallies, no matter how clumsily, had been exhilarating. She tried not to smile at the way he had called her cruel. Suddenly, she felt very grown up.

She stole a glance at Neville, seated next to her. In the candlelight, his dark eyes shone against his pale skin. He appeared to be attending to what Arabella was saying—more the result of good manners, Fanny reasoned, than of interest. Her sister was usually hopeless at conversation.

Across the table, Mrs. Monkton was battering away at Clive about the Italian contessa she had met at Brighton last year. Mr. Monkton and Papa discussed which horses they would show at the Bradford Fair, while Kit repeated their conversation twice to old Mr. Burleigh— once to him and once to his ear trumpet. As the gooseberry fool was being served, Mr. Sutcliff engaged Neville in a lively discussion about the possibility of reform while Castlereagh served as Foreign Secretary.

Clive had been regarding his own reflection in the bowl of a spoon, but now he looked up with a discontented expression. "Why must we always concern ourselves with politics," he said, "when there are greater matters before us?"

"Greater matters?" drawled Neville.

"Why, yes, would you not consider art a very great matter, my lord? I believe that improving sensibility is one of the most important tasks before us. Our age is one of unparalleled cultivation and taste. Why, the very treasures of the Continent lie at our feet."

"If you are speaking, Mr. Burleigh, of the recent looting of France for objects to be sold in London's auction houses, then I beg to disagree with you.'' Neville's sharp retort was followed by a pall of stunned silence.

Mrs. Feversham looked anxiously about the table for a rescuer. Finding none, she began bravely. ''We are all most anxious to become more refined. Perhaps Mr. Burleigh would like to tell us of his travels.''

A heavy sigh escaped Fanny, which earned her a quick look from Neville.

''As I'm sure Lord Neville will agree,'' Clive began pompously, ''the Grand Tour only increases one's appreciation for the perfection of the past.'' Gathering courage from his hostess's civil smile, he continued. ''No sooner was the Treaty of Paris signed, than I set sail for Naples. Italy—how can I describe it? I only truly understood the theory of the picturesque as set forth by our Mr. Knight when I viewed the plane trees upon the Tuscan hills. Each scene under those sunny Mediterranean skies was a picture by the divine Rosa. I must confess,'' he smirked, ''that the sight inspired me to apply my humble talents to canvas.''

''How very charming,'' exclaimed Arabella. ''You must show us your pictures, Mr. Burleigh.''

''Nothing would please me more, dear Miss Arabella.'' Clive replied unctuously. ''I invite everyone here to visit Burleigh Abbey. I think you will find it greatly changed.''

''How do you mean?'' asked Mrs. Feversham uneasily.

''Why, ma'am, my travels throughout the Continent put me in the mood medieval, and upon arriving back on English soil I immediately set to work to renovate our home in a gothic manner. I now prefer to call it Burleigh Abbey for it resembles one of Horace Walpole's follies.''

''Folly! There you've hit the nail on the head, my lad,'' chuckled Mr. Burleigh. ''Clive has reduced our home to rubble.''

"What, that lovely Palladian estate!" Mrs. Monkton exclaimed.

"Father, as I have explained to you countless times before, the improvements to Burleigh Abbey are a supreme example of Mr. Knight's picturesque style. As you can see," Clive favored Neville with a world-weary gaze, "the style is not widely understood here in the provinces."

"On the contrary, my dear Burleigh," Neville answered pleasantly, "I find that it is in the country where the picturesque can be most readily apprehended—in its most natural state." He glanced in Fanny's direction. "Those who dwell in the country claim to find great solace there."

"I daresay, Neville, perhaps you are confusing the picturesque with the sublime. It is with the palette of the sublime that nature paints her strongest colors. The picturesque, I believe, depends upon man's cultivation to achieve its effect."

"Now we are embarking upon a debate of Taste," Mrs. Monkton observed smugly.

"I put it to you, Neville," Clive began, warming to his subject, "do you not agree with Edmund Burke that it is the sublime which induces awe, terror and inspiration? The sublime is found in a torrent's rushing cascades, in craggy Alpine scenery, in those sights and sounds whose immensity reduces us to trembling reverence."

"As one might find in one of Mr. Wordsworth's poems?" asked the vicar.

"Exactly, my good man," said Clive. "There you have hit upon the sublime, *point-device*. Now, assuming the picturesque can be equated with Mr. Burke's definition of the beautiful, we have a different canvas entirely."

"I think I'm going to like the beautiful better than the sublime," Mrs. Monkton whispered to Mr. Feversham.

"The beautiful, you will recall," Clive continued, "is

that which is small, pretty, pleasing, smooth in texture, not alarming in any way. Now, I ask you, Neville, which is the object of more sublimity? Say, a dog which has been defending his master from murderers and, mortally wounded, dies by his side, or—"

"A dog has been wounded?" interjected Mr. Burleigh waving his ear trumpet in Clive's direction. "Not old Brutus, I hope!"

"No, Father," Clive said impatiently, "we are speaking of an imaginary dog, not a real dog."

"Give me a real dog every time," muttered Mr. Burleigh into his wine. "Can't see what Clive wants with all these imaginary dogs."

"Or, say, a tiger springing on an unsuspecting sheep from the covert of a thicket," Clive continued.

"What are a tiger and a sheep doing in the same thicket, Burleigh?" asked Mr. Feversham crossly. "Don't recall ever seeing any tigers springing on sheep around here."

"Let me see," Kit said, working it out slowly, "the dog displays loyalty to his master, but the tiger is a splendid beast."

"But isn't the tiger taking unfair advantage?" asked Mrs. Monkton. "After all, he was hiding, wasn't he? I've never liked it much when people spring on me from thickets."

This remark earned her a curious look from Mr. Monkton, while Clive shrugged, indicating that any further discussion was hopeless. Neville coughed gently behind his hand, fighting for composure.

"Then here is an easier question. I put it to you, Neville, of the Feversham girls here before you, which do you find the more beautiful?"

Fanny shot Clive a nasty glance, for she knew Arabella's looks were rated far superior to hers. The insufferable little prig was having his revenge upon her at last.

"Oh, that's an easy puzzler, Burleigh," Neville answered lazily. "One I don't even need my quizzing glass to answer." He turned to Arabella, who was gazing at him with rapt devotion. "I find Miss Arabella the more picturesque because she is as pretty as any of the pictures painted by Salvatore Rosa. Only I much prefer Arabella's eyes to any landscape."

A general sigh went round the table at the gallantry of this remark. Then Neville turned to Fanny. "And I find Miss Feversham, my dear Burleigh, the more sublime."

"Why is that, Neville?"

"Because," came the answer, "she is an unrestrained force of nature."

To the sound of general merriment, Fanny met Neville's glance. It was cool and detached—the look of a connoisseur who was appraising an odd little ornament.

In a single second, all her confidence vanished. She longed for the brittle wit that would counter his jest with an easy rejoinder, but could find none.

Fanny adjusted the music before her and moved her chair closer to the pianoforte. Arabella leafed through the pages of her favorite song, "The Sojourner," which Fanny found extremely insipid. Neville's presence would no doubt encourage the little goose to new heights of saccharine warbling.

Fanny watched as guests drifted into chairs and sofas. From a vantage point at the back of the room, Neville lounged easily against the mantelpiece. When all were settled, Mrs. Feversham rapped her fan against her palm for silence and Mr. Burleigh raised his ear trumpet expectantly.

Fanny nodded to her sister and they began. It was immediately apparent that Arabella's nervousness had made her a little breathless. Fanny accelerated the tempo slightly to keep Arabella from lingering on the high notes, and was irritated that all the legato had unaccountably vanished from her own playing. Relief swept over her as they galloped into the final chords.

"Brava, brava!" Clive clapped enthusiastically, executing a willowy bow to the singer. "Very much in the Italian style! *Carissima*, Arabella, what phrasing!"

"Thank you," Bella murmured, gazing at the applauding Neville.

"Perhaps, my dear Miss Feversham, you would allow me to join my humble talents with yours in a *concertante*." Without waiting for a reply Clive began to approach the pianoforte, much to Fanny's dismay.

"We'd be honored, Mr. Burleigh," Arabella chirped. "I had no idea you sang."

"Sing! When I was in Naples I studied with the great master, Scribelli," Clive said reverently.

"Whose belly?" shouted old Mr. Burleigh, adjusting his ear trumpet.

"Please, Father," Clive said with great self-restraint, "we were not speaking of anything corporeal. Let me see . . ." His white, elongated hands sifted through the stack of music. "Shall we try the Mozart?"

Arabella stared at the score of *Don Giovanni* with a look of pure panic, but Clive was determined. The three of them plunged into the playful duet of "La Ci Darem La Mano," with Arabella panting through the soprano part.

Clive and Signor Scribelli, Fanny noted dourly as she dutifully played, must have concentrated heavily on Mozart, for he pranced and mugged his way through the aria with a practiced ease. Clive's outpourings reached a crescendo in the last measure, when he added extra vibrato to an already earsplitting tenor. Glancing up, Fanny saw Brutus slinking out of the room and envied him.

A round of furious applause greeted the final crashing arpeggio. Fanny looked up in time to see Neville's expression change from cynical amusement to feigned appreciation.

A flush of shame crept up her neck, as she imagined

the scene from Neville's perspective. How ridiculous her family and friends must seem to him, with their provincial pretensions and eagerness to win his favor. He mocks us for being country simpletons, she thought, furiously gathering up her music. For lacking *tonnish* ways.

"What, no encores, Fan?" Kit appeared, grinning broadly. "Wasn't Clive a corker, singing through that striped cravat?"

At that point Neville joined them, handing Fanny a cup of tea. "For the valiant Fanny," he said smoothly, "your musical exertions have fatigued you."

"It is not my musical exertions that have made me tired, Lord Neville," said Fanny, flashing him an angry glance as she seized the cup, "but barely disguised hypocrisy."

"Good Gad, Neville, do you think Clive tried to pinch her?" Kit gasped as Fanny moved away.

"No, my dear Kit," Neville said lightly, "I do not think she was referring to Mr. Burleigh."

Kit shrugged, his attention now riveted on Mr. Monkton reciting "The Old Churchyard." Neville watched as Fanny took a seat next to her sister. He would grant that she was young. But she definitely was not a green girl.

As the sisters prepared for bed that evening, Fanny steeled herself against Arabella's inevitable comments on Neville's charm.

With a languid motion, Arabella brushed her lustrous brown hair until it hung sleekly down her back. "Did you notice, Fan," Arabella asked dreamily, "how Lord Neville praised my looks at dinner?"

"Yes, I did," Fanny retorted brusquely. She turned to the portfolio that lay before her on her desk.

"Really, Fan, sometimes I cannot fathom you. Here is the actual Lord Neville in our very midst, and all you can think about is your precious Lord Rothermere. I, for one, am very glad he's here. I think he might be forming a real attachment to us," she added.

"Bella, he's only being polite out of fondness for Kit," Fanny replied coldly. "And now, if you'll pardon me, I must tend to my precious Lord Rothermere."

After pouting for a few minutes, Arabella climbed into bed and quickly fell asleep. By the light of a single candle Fanny worked well into the night, unaware of the hours that ticked away. In the scene that unfolded before her, Melinda was teaching her little charge how to form her letters. They had just been interrupted by Lord Rothermere's unexpected visit.

"See what Miss Earnshaw has taught me, Papa," said Augusta proudly indicating her exercise book. "Isn't she clever?"

A sardonic smile played about Lord Rothermere's mouth. He slowly took full measure of the governess's simple brown stuff gown, so different from the brocades and silks of his Italian contessas.

"Yes, Augusta," he said coldly, "at lessons I'll warrant she is sublimely clever. But I find your picturesque beauty just as charming." He softly kissed the top of his daughter's head. "Beware of becoming merely clever, my little mouse." With a mocking smile he held Melinda's glance, then turned quickly and was gone.

5

Rising early the next morning, Fanny quietly slipped on her white muslin dress and kid walking boots. She tied the ribbons of a chip straw bonnet and drew a paisley shawl about her shoulders. Moving with great stealth, she managed to slide through the door without awakening Arabella. She tiptoed down the hallway to the back stairs, which led to the kitchen. The warm aroma of toasting bread told her that Cook was well along with breakfast.

An instant later, she was picking her way through the kitchen garden. She climbed the low stone wall into the orchard, where apples hung in ripe clusters from drooping branches, and helped herself to a glowing russet, which she dropped into her pocket. It was only as she entered the park that she dared to take a deep breath of the crisp October air.

Once free of the confines of Henley Hall and Neville's disturbing presence, she felt she could examine matters in a clearer, more objective light.

She had been so eager to meet Julian Carrothers. To her disappointment, though, he had proved more of the dandy than the haughty hero. He hadn't much liked Brutus's making a nasty mess of his waistcoat, but then,

what man of fashion would? And he had positively recoiled from Silky. Beneath the fine manners, Fanny wagered, he felt a certain repugnance toward all the
Fevershams, with the exception of Kit, of course.

She had hoped to glimpse some of the Wicked Lord
in him, but his nature seemed more fashionable than
fiery. She had seen no hint of the man of action in him.
Once he returned to the *ton*, she suspected, he would
recount the horrors of country life to the amusement of
London's best supper tables.

Ruminating on Neville's character, she climbed the
stile which separated the estate from the vicarage. After
taking her seat on the rough stone step she absentmind-
edly polished the apple against her muslin skirt. Pushing
her bonnet back so that it hung from her neck by a blue
ribbon, she gazed at the broad expanse of sky, dotted
with a few white puffs of clouds. As she took a deep
bite, she sighed with pleasure at its tangy sweetness.
Who could not love the country? Fanny thought, gazing
at a yellow and black butterfly that had perched on her
sleeve. As it departed, its flight led her gaze into the
middle distance, filled with the hedgerows and low stone
walls that divided the neighboring farms and estates into
neat patches of green.

She was well aware of how country farmers were always portrayed in print as crude Johnny Raws. To be
sure, she and Kit had laughed themselves senseless over
the pair of bumpkins in *The Countryman's Guide to
London*. But the truth was that, unlike London, the country was filled with endless variety and beauty. The
thought of London stifled her.

The *ton* evoked the image of a great mill wheel turned
by the onrushing waters of gossip. What better fodder
for idle chatter than the green girls who made their de-
buts there each spring, hoping to marry well? The *ton*
lived only for fashion, for conversation and scandal. Her
own cousin, Alethia Mainwaring, now Lady Lansden,
had come back from London full of prattle and waving

her fan in the most ridiculous manner after only a few months' stay.

As for her own come-out, the Marriage Mart loomed before her like the guillotine. What if she were surrounded by young men who thought her as gauche as Neville did? What if she were forced to marry one of them and spend her entire life surrounded by clattering carriages, snooping visitors and disapproving in-laws? The very thought of such an existence made her ill.

Just beyond the stone wall, she could see a thin wisp of smoke curling up from the vicarage. She sprang up from the stile, hoping that Mr. Sutcliff was in the mood for a visit.

Thomas Sutcliff wiped his brow with a polka-dotted handkerchief and rested upon his spade. Although the morning was cool, the exertion of digging turnips had overheated him. When he saw Fanny appear at the gate, his face lit up with welcome. Her refreshing company was a welcome respite from gardening.

"Heigh ho, Fanny," he cried. "What brings you out so early?"

"Walking seemed prescribed, sir, after last night's supper." The smell of freshly turned earth mingled deliciously with the crisp morning air, stimulating her senses. "Your turnips are looking well."

"They're a robust lot. Not much to look at, but honest and nourishing," he said, holding one up admiringly.

"Not like Londoners," Fanny muttered.

"What's that?" he asked, somewhat baffled. "I don't believe I've ever heard townfolk and turnips compared before."

"I've decided I will not be going to London—or the Marriage Mart," Fanny blurted out.

The sight of the girl biting her lip and twisting her bonnet ribbons told the vicar all he needed to know. He tossed the vegetable into a nearby basket, saying, "Let's have some breakfast, my girl."

They followed a mossy path to the red brick cottage. Fanny had always regarded the vicarage as an extension of Henley, and therefore as home. Mr. Sutcliff had taught the Feversham girls their Latin, history, mathematics and composition. More importantly, he never condescended to them, so Fanny had always thought of him as a wise, somewhat eccentric uncle. His Christian teaching was the hearth fire round which Henley warmed itself.

"I can only give you bread and jam today," he said as his housekeeper bustled about his small, whitewashed parlor, laying the table for breakfast.

Fanny took a sip from her cup and began resolutely, "You see, it's like this, sir. I've been thinking about marriage. That is, the philosophy of marriage."

"I see," he said evenly.

"I know that as a vicar, you regard marriage as a holy sacrament, but I wondered, sir, if someone such as myself might be permitted to, ah, avoid the matrimonial state altogether."

"What's this, Fanny? Not marry? You are barely out of the schoolroom, dear girl." He took a long sip of tea. "Something's put you in a fright about this marriage business."

"There, you've said it perfectly," Fanny replied, setting down her cup firmly. "Marriage business. I don't want to be ogled and bartered for and sold like a prize sheep! Bella and I were always taught that one day we would be married and happiness would follow, but I find less and less about it that is admirable." She pulled at the fringe to her shawl. "It's simply a way to show off one's wealth—to drive about in a carriage bearing a coat of arms in exchange for . . . well, you understand."

She sprang up and began pacing the floor. "To think of a girl Alethia's age marrying that scaly monster puts me in a taking every time."

"Fanny, my dear, calm yourself. I've never seen you in such a tangle." The vicar poured her another cup.

"To begin with, not every girl is expected to marry. It's a matter of opportunity and inclination." He stirred his tea slowly. "Now, Fanny, I believe you have several ideas that have run headlong into one another. First, you have confused your imminent come-out with the less imminent possibility of marriage. By that I mean," he added, "that because your Season is next spring, you think you must decide how you stand on the question of marriage once and for all. As to your suitability to marriage, I have always found your company extremely amiable. I think you would make some young gentleman a splendid wife."

"Indeed," she replied warily, sensing that the vicar's ultimate intent, like a well-trained sheepdog, was to guide her intentions into more domestic environs.

"I know how you love country life, my girl, particularly life at Henley. But have you ever considered what kind of match you would make were you simply to rusticate, without any town bronze?" He took the poker and made a few desultory stabs at the fire. "Tell me which country lad of acceptable family you might wed."

"Well, let me see." Fanny smoothed out a wrinkle in the tablecloth. "There are the Winthrop twins. I beat Brandon once in a steeplechase. And Edward is a fine lad at a mill. Why, Kit told me he went four rounds with Ned Scroggins."

"Fanny, fighting and racing do not make a match. Most of the lads hereabouts are a rough and tumble lot, with the exception of Mr. Clive Burleigh, who puts on airs before clothes in the morning."

"Preposterous!" exclaimed Fanny. "I'd never consent to such a marriage. I'd run away first."

"And how would you keep yourself if you ran away?" the vicar asked calmly.

"I should become a governess . . . in the Italian Alps perhaps," Fanny ventured desperately.

"Mmmmm. Your Latin is not good enough. I can testify to that. Take my word for it, Fanny, your best chances of a making decent match are in London." He refilled his pipe. "Kit seems to like town life exceedingly well."

"He's a man. It's different for Kit. He can racket about the town or country all he wants."

"And Lord Neville seems most amiable. Thought you and he got on rather well last night."

"Not really," said Fanny, looking away. "I think he finds us rather preposterous."

The vicar smiled, as if he suddenly understood a matter which troubled him. "Fanny, London ways are different from country ways. Townfolk are cool as cucumbers, then one day they're your best friend. Kit will shake some of the fluff out of your guest. Then we'll see what Lord Neville's made of."

The slanting rays of sunlight, which had illuminated the blue and white porcelain on the table, suddenly vanished. The vicar peered out the window at the gathering clouds, looming low and grey.

"Storm's coming. I'd send you home on my mare, but Finch has her today. You'll have to make a dash for it." He handed the basket of turnips to Fanny. "Take these to your cook, please, with my compliments. I daresay they'll end up in one of her delicious stews."

Fanny tied her bonnet, stood on tip toe and kissed him on the cheek. "Thank you for hearing me out," she murmured. "I feel less plagued by this silly business."

He stood at the door, watching as she latched the gate behind her. "God bless you, Fanny," he called as a fat raindrop plopped heavily at his feet. "Keep your nerve! To the chase! London's your best chance, don't forget!"

Fanny had not travelled far from the vicar's gate when a near rumble announced she was in for a drenching. She glanced up at the churning clouds. Feeling the heavy raindrops begin to pelt her bonnet, she shuddered with pleasure at how this scene of gothic gloom would have suited Lord Rothermere.

She had just reached the verge of Henley Hall's park when a jagged finger of lightning cracked the sky, illuminating the entire landscape in a dazzling, sulphurous brilliance.

From the east, sheets of rain advanced toward her. Nearby, treetops began to sway in the wind. It must be the wind, Fanny thought, that sounded so much like a horse's hoofbeats.

Following the sound, she saw galloping through the gathering darkness a huge black stallion whose rider clung to his neck. At first she thought it an untamed vision from her imagination, until she realized the horseman was making straight toward her. She stood stock-still, able at last to make out the rider.

"Neville," she gasped. Her earlier misgivings about him were swept away by the dashing sight. Never before, she thought, had horse and master been so perfectly matched. The stallion was a deep-chested, strong-legged brute bred for speed. His noble head and flashing eyes evinced a fiery spirit held in check by his rider's splendid horsemanship.

Neville was hatless and his black curls were swept back by the wind. He reined in just short of where she stood.

"Miss Feversham!" he cried. "I thought it was you!" He dismounted, throwing his reins across the beast's neck. "Come, we haven't much time. You're not soaked yet. That's good. We've only just outrun the storm."

Fanny met his burning glance, and felt her resistance to him weaken at his unmistakable concern. She shivered beneath the paisley shawl, her hands still clasped tightly about the basket of turnips. Like an admonishment, his supercilious stares of the previous day came back to warn her.

"No. My thanks, but I cannot ride with you," she answered.

"I would never have guessed the redoubtable Miss Feversham to be puddinghearted," he teased. "You're

not willing to go neck-or-nothing with me on Tammuz?'' As if seeking the horse's agreement, he firmly
patted its flank.

"He's a fine one, all right," Fanny admitted grudgingly.

A deafening thunderclap brought a drenching gust of
rain.

"See here, Miss Feversham, no more idle chatter.
We'll have to make a run for it." Neville briskly began
removing his coat. "Kit tells me you're a fine
horsewoman. Just keep your seat as best you can. Hang
on to his mane."

Fanny blinked the rain from her eyes. She wondered
how she was to keep her seat when there was no side-
saddle. It would take nerve, no doubt about it.

"We have contraband as well?" he asked, noticing
the turnips for the first time. "A gift from some rustic
admirer?" he teased. Seeing her expression stiffen, he
added quickly, "Then wrap your shawl around the
wretched things so they don't spill. Here, take my coat."

"But you'll be soaked," she protested.

"We both will, dear girl, but unless we fly I'll wager
that gown will soon be your winding sheet."

Fanny looked down to see the damp muslin clinging
to her legs. As Neville slid his coat about her shoulders,
she was grateful for its lingering warmth. It smelled deliciously of musk and leather.

"Up we go. Not a second to lose." He grasped her
by the waist and effortlessly lifted her onto the saddle.

"Steady, now," he commanded the horse, handing
Fanny the basket and reaching for the reins. In an instant
he was seated behind her, his body pressed against hers
so that she could feel his heartbeat through the thin fabric of his shirt. He reached his arms through hers and
adjusted the reins over the basket, muttering, "Confounded turnips."

Tammuz circled nervously, adjusting to the additional
rider. "If you lose your balance, lean forward," Neville

instructed. "I'm holding you, Fanny, and won't let you fall."

A sudden streak of lightening blazed before them. Tammuz reared, his ears flattened against his head, his front hooves cleaving the air while Neville swore, working the reins and digging his heels into the horse's flanks. Tammuz whinnied and snorted, his nostrils steaming, and then sprinted away.

With Neville's strong arms about her, Fanny felt no fear for her safety. Kicking up clods of earth, Tammuz thundered across the open parkland. She leaned forward, grasping the horse's black mane. A hedge rose up before them and Fanny instinctively knew that Neville would take the jump.

"Steady on," he cried, pressing his weight against her. "Ready . . . *now!*" Together, they leaned against the horse's foam-flecked neck. Tammuz sailed over the tangled hawthorn branches, landing neatly on the opposite side. She felt Neville's breath on her neck as he murmured, "Good show, my girl."

She could just make out the roof of Henley Hall's stable through the trees. As they drew nearer, she could see a small knot of people gathered at the stable door, peering anxiously in their direction. Kit was at the forefront, along with the groom.

Neville slowed Tammuz to a walk. As they entered the stable, the groom came forward to take the reins, and Neville sprang to the ground. Fanny handed the turnips to a stableboy and prepared to slide off the horse.

"May I offer some assistance?" Neville held up his arms to lift her. A wet sleeve fell back and Fanny saw the white S-shaped scar that snaked up his arm. Feeling his hands about her waist, she leaned down, bracing herself against him. For the briefest of moments he held her close. The next second she was on the ground.

"Well done, Fanny. You are a fine rider," he said, his eyes warmly appreciative. "Kit has been your instructor, I take it."

Ignoring his praise, she asked, "How did you come by such a scar?"

"You mean this?" He laughed shortly, buttoning his sleeve. "It's nothing. I received it in a duel of honor. That was when I thought duels could decide such matters." He produced a lace-trimmed handkerchief and wiped some mud from her cheek. "I'll wager that once you're scrubbed and in a proper habit, you'll far surpass those pale beauties in Hyde Park."

Unsure if it was a compliment to skill or looks, Fanny blushed with confusion. She was rescued by Kit who rushed in and patted Tammuz admiringly.

"By Gad, what a ride, eh, Neville? Rare bang-up horse you've got. I saw you take that jump." Turning to his sister, he demanded, "And, Fan, how did you manage to stay aboard? Did Neville secure you with a ship's anchor? And what the deuce are these? Turnips? I say, Fan, you look a bit sticky. What's that—Neville's coat? So, we've ruined the poor chap's wardrobe and he's barely been here a day. I don't envy you having to explain this damage to Jenkins." Kit directed this last remark to Neville while distributing coats, shawls, turnips and general good cheer. "Neville, I ask you—what should we do with this filthy little creature? Give her a bath or turn her out?"

"She deserves a trophy," Neville said, casually inspecting a curry comb. "She took that jump better than my jockey at Epsom."

Kit took Fanny by the arm and led her through the gate to the kitchen garden. "Never known the fellow to be so full of compliments. Must've been knocked on the noggin by a tree branch."

Fanny barely heard her brother. Despite her wet, bedraggled clothes, she glowed with intense excitement. "He called me Fanny," she thought. "No more polite Miss Feversham." She remembered the way he had held her against him, and decided she had never liked anything half so much.

6

As news of Henley's distinguished guest travelled quickly throughout the county, invitations to dances, fêtes and dinners began pouring in, especially from local squires with unmarried daughters.

No sooner had Wilkins brought in the day's correspondence, then Mrs. Feversham set aside her morning cocoa and eagerly fell upon the stack of letters.

"Oh, Lord, no!" she exclaimed suddenly. "Fanny, Arabella, attend. Another invitation from Mrs. Monkton. This one is for Friday next. I simply can't face that drawing room of hers with those dreadful Egyptian chairs. What does she call them?"

"*Á la* Napoleon, Mama," Fanny answered.

"Well, she can send them back to that upstart Corsican for all I care," Mrs. Feversham sniffed contemptuously.

"By Gemini," said Fanny, scanning a carefully written note, "The Winthrops are having their harvest home the same evening as the Monktons' dinner." She handed the invitation to her mother. "You must agree, Mama, the timing is fortuitous. It's almost lucky that they had to postpone it for so long."

"Hmmm." Mrs. Feversham scanned it with a critical

eye. "Except tenant farmers as well as guests, are invited to the harvest home."

"Exactly, Mama," said Fanny enthusiastically.

"It might dreadfully offend Lord Neville's sensibilities," her mother said dubiously. "I remember last year, all that stamping and clapping. And what about those awful Winthrop twins? Those boys utterly lack any refinement."

Any further criticisms of the Winthrop twins were curtailed by Kit throwing open the drawing room doors. Back from their morning ride, he and Neville strode into the room. Fanny could not help but mark the change in Neville's appearance. Gone was the pale dandy of a only a week ago. Dressed in a pair of buckskins and elegant riding boots by Hoby, he now seemed the ideal country squire, his powerful shoulders emphasized by the close fit of his snuff-colored riding coat.

"Morning, Mater," said Kit, bending down and bestowing a kiss. "Bang-up ride we had—all the way to Devizes and back. What have we here, a stack of petitions from the local gentry? No doubt begging for our guest's presence. Why, look here, Neville," he deftly plucked the Winthrops' note from his mother's fingers. "Seems we're bidden to a rustic dance in a neighboring lodge. What say you to a little fiddle music?"

"Famous!" exclaimed his friend. "Haven't been to a proper harvest dance in years. Country dancing in Mayfair is like watching Kemble rather than Kean do Richard III. Elegant, but lacking a certain verve."

Before Mrs. Feversham could remonstrate, the sound of carriage wheels on the gravel drive drew everyone's attention. Fanny ran to the window in time to see a magnificent coach and four drawing up to Henley's entrance. A liveried footman unlatched the door emblazoned with a coat of arms, and an exceedingly slim young man, dressed in a dark frockcoat and trousers, alighted. He held a beaver hat in one hand while he surveyed Henley's exterior disapprovingly.

As the footman deposited three bulging portmanteaux at his feet, the visitor's glance fell upon Fanny's face and his disapprobation intensified.

"There's a rather sour looking young man outside. He has arrived in a very handsome black and green carriage belonging to a nobleman," Fanny reported. "He seems to find the sight of me extremely disagreeable."

"That must be Jenkins, my valet," Neville drawled. "I sent for him several days ago and asked him to bring my carriage. I find tying my own cravats to be most exhausting." He flashed Mrs. Feversham a smile. "He will make me presentable for the country dance, I assure you."

"Good heavens, Lord Neville, cutting a dash is the last of your worries," Mrs. Feversham retorted. With a greatly satisfied air, she began rearranging the tea cups.

"Let's intercept Jenkins before he finds the back stairs," Neville said to Kit. Fanny joined them, overcome with curiosity about Neville's fashionable valet. As Jenkins caught sight of his master, he stopped stock-still, stupefied by the change in Neville's appearance.

"My lord, if you'll pardon me." He dusted a particle of lint from his master's sleeve. "I have never seen your lordship looking so . . . robust," he observed.

"Not much in the way of dissipation here at Henley, Jenkins," Neville said coolly. "No gambling and hardly any hock. Of course, Miss Feversham here tried to kill me one day by leaping onto my horse when she was dripping wet."

"Indeed," said the valet flatly. He searched Fanny's ensemble for some sign of taste and could find none. His glance drifted down to her feet where, to his amazement, a tortoiseshell cat was tugging at the back of one of her scuffed slippers. The valet squeaked and involuntarily took a step backward.

"Do not take fright at Silky, my good man," Neville said, scooping up the cat. "This animal is one of the finest felines you're likely to meet. Here, Silky, put out

a paw.'' Neville proffered one of the cat's white-stock-
inged feet as Jenkins shrank back in horror.

"Cat hairs, my lord," he pleaded.

"Oh, you'll grow used to them."

The valet began his grim ascent to upper regions as
one called to the scaffold. Neville winked conspiratori-
ally at Fanny.

As their carriage rounded the final curve leading to
the Winthrops' house, Fanny's pulse raced with excitement. The long windows of the hall glowed with light.
She pressed her face against the carriage window and
counted the conveyances.

The carriage rumbled to a stop beneath the portico.
Mr. Feversham stepped down and handed the ladies out
as Kit and Neville rode up and dismounted, handing
their reins to the waiting groom.

Shivering with both cold and anticipation, Fanny
smoothed her gown of pale ivory sarsenet. She straightened her moss green spencer and rebuttoned one of the
frogs, reckoning her appearance to be quite dashing. She
plunged her hands into the rabbit fur muff, grateful for
its warmth.

She stole a glance at Neville who wore a magnificent
dark blue cloak over a black coat, doeskin breeches and
an embroidered waistcoat. Jenkins, Fanny wagered, must
be very pleased with his efforts.

At that moment Kit gave Arabella his arm, while Neville offered Fanny his. "Come, everyone, let us prepare to sacrifice our guest to the county gentry. You
were wise to choose Fanny, Neville, as she's looking
very menacing and military tonight. Remember, you
must dance with every young lady the Winthrops have
summoned, no matter how little you favor 'em. Standing up twice with the same one is likely to produce the
banns.''

As they entered the hall, Fanny thought the lodge had
never looked more festive. Chairs had been placed

against the walls, and sheaves of corn filled the corners.

"It seems we are making our mark upon the old lionesses," Neville murmured, returning the dowagers' nods of approval.

"Then I have you to thank, my lord. For when I am unaccompanied by nobility they maul me without mercy." Fanny smiled dazzlingly at Mrs. Winthrop, who was advancing on them with great determination.

"Very well then, we shall make a pact," Neville vowed solemnly. "I have granted you safe conduct into Wiltshire society, and you must rescue me from country hospitality. No doubt I shall be made to quaff our host's most wretched homemade wine."

Before Fanny could reply, they were descended upon by a throng of fluttering matrons, their daughters in tow. Heading the contingent was the determined Mrs. Sedley and her plump, pink-cheeked daughter, Serena.

While Kit supervised the numerous introductions to Neville, Fanny and Arabella found seats near the windows. Fanny especially liked the harvest dance because it brought all classes of folk together, tenant farmers as well as gentry. The young laborers, some dressed in simple trousers and ill-fitting fustian jackets, were in high spirits, drinking glasses of punch, talking loudly, and ogling the partners they hoped to claim for the first reel. The girls, when not seated primly next to their mothers, congregated in knots and produced deafening giggles and high-pitched squeals. By leaning sideways Fanny could see into the gallery where the musicians were taking their places, arranging their instruments and making a stir.

"Isn't that Clive Burleigh over there?" Bella asked tentatively, gazing at the opposite side of the room.

"Why, yes, I believe it is," said Fanny, recoiling somewhat at the sight of Clive in a burgundy velvet frockcoat. He held his quizzing glass listlessly and occasionally turned it in the direction of the chattering mob that surrounded Neville.

"It seems we have been discovered," Arabella observed. Mrs. Feversham was headed toward them, as the Winthrop twins approached from the other direction. Old Mr. Burleigh, his ear trumpet grasped firmly, began trotting unsteadily toward them from the vicinity of the punch bowl. The Winthrops were the first to arrive.

"Quite a stir, eh, what?" ventured Brandon, always a bit uncomfortable out of the saddle.

"Ah, the Feversham gels," Mr. Burleigh called out with a delighted cackle. Fanny steered him into a chair beside her, where he collapsed gratefully. The twins leaned toward the girls in constrained, polite postures, both fidgeting with their tight collars and cravats.

All attempts at conversation were drowned by the sound of fiddles being tuned and the tin whistle emitting some ominous squeaks. The musicians finally sustained a note which they agreed to be a true one, then swung into "Sellenger's Reel."

Fanny began tapping her foot in time to the music as the Winthrops asked Mrs. Feversham's permission for her daughters to dance. The sisters hastened to join the line of girls that was forming, facing a line of young men. After clasping Arabella's hand on her right and Serena Sedley's on her left, Fanny looked for Neville among the dancers but did not see him. She quickly scanned the room for a sign of him.

No longer bedeviled by females, Neville had joined Clive and Mr. Winthrop at the punch bowl, where they were all taking small sips of a dark purple liquid. Clive, looking horribly bored, examined the couples on the dance floor who were spinning back to their places.

Caught up in the complicated patterns of the reel, Fanny and Brandon had arrived at the end of the line. The couple at the opposite end clasped hands, making a bridge with their arms. The fiddles embellished the mischievous refrain as Fanny and Brandon slid sideways between the two lines and ducked beneath the bridge. They emerged clapping in time to the music, at which point Brandon bowed to Fanny and she curtseyed in reply. It was now their turn to be the bridge, and she beamed good-naturedly in Neville's direction. To her surprise, he was watching her with a keenness that brought a hot flush into her cheeks.

When the reel was over, Fanny and Arabella returned to their seats. Mrs. Feversham had just handed her daughters their fans when Neville appeared, carrying two glasses of punch.

"The Feversham girls dance divinely," he said suavely. Arabella smiled sweetly while Fanny remained silent. She could not tell if there was sincerity behind his compliment or derision at their raucous imitations of the *ton*'s refined country dances.

"Remember, you promised not to abandon me to country hospitality," Neville said to her in a low tone. "Thus far, I have been made to drink three glasses of Winthrop's mulberry wine, I have endured a lecture from Burleigh comparing the dignity of medieval dancing to the immodesty of country dancing, and . . . what else? Oh," Neville looked away, a bored tone coming into his voice, "I have been forced to watch you disporting with that young bantling, leaving me easy prey to every rattle-trap mama in the county."

"What would you have me do, my lord?" Fanny asked innocently.

"Take me to the sanctuary of the dance floor. I have asked your mama and she has agreed to let me partner you in the 'Roughty Toughty.' Good heavens, what a name."

As Neville led her onto the floor, Fanny saw that it had been taken over by milkmaids and stable boys, red-cheeked from stamping and clapping. The more refined dancers, it appeared, had gone in to supper. The band swung into a rollicking version of the "Roughty Toughty" as couples swarmed into groups of four. Those who were not dancing began hooting and clapping in time to the music.

With their hands clasped behind their backs during the opening bars, Fanny and Neville faced each other. His expression was a curious mixture of detached amusement and intense regard. Their shoulders brushed one another's as they sketched a square. Then, as if dancing a Highland fling, Neville swung her by the waist, while she held one arm aloft in a graceful arc.

The music raced faster and faster as he spun her close against him. Her world compressed into a single moment of happiness that was intensified by the smell of sawdust on the floor, the merry rhythm of the music, and the feel of Neville holding her so close that her feet barely touched the ground. The fiddles played even more furiously, urged on by the whistles and cries of the dancers.

When it was over the foursomes separated, each dancer bowing first to the other couple and then to his partner. Enthusiastic applause greeted the musicians. Feeling hot and strangely excited, Fanny searched in vain for her fan. Neville offered her a fine cambric handkerchief which she gratefully accepted, immediately pressing it against her face and throat.

For the first time she heard him laugh spontaneously. "You are quite a sight, Fanny. Such a change for me, I must admit. I should warn you that I am so well disposed to the world at this point I even find Mr. Winthrop's wine excellent."

"Then you must be foxed," Fanny observed wryly.

"No, Fanny, I am not foxed. I had merely forgotten how pleasurable things can be . . . until tonight. Now I am starting to remember." Neville smiled, taking in the way her eyes glistened, the flush that was now creeping up from her throat to her temples. "I shall be eagerly awaiting your Season, Fanny, to see how many hearts you break."

"I'll be lucky to survive it," Fanny murmured, looking down at the damp handkerchief. "I do not seem to be the sort of young person society has much use for."

"Society! What do you know of society?" Neville snorted dismissively. "Mark me, Fanny, you will bring new spirit to that dull, dissipated crowd that feeds on warm lemonade and stale cake."

Kit appeared at his elbow. "Good hock, this stuff of Winthrop's. Tried it yet, Neville? See here, you're not bamming my sister, are you?"

"I must warn you against that horrid mulberry wine, Kit," Fanny declared. "It's made your lips all purple." She hoped the diversion hid the agitation that Neville's attention had aroused in her. He ceremoniously escorted her back to her chair, bowed, and returned to Kit's side.

"Demned fine girl, that Fanny," said Kit. Neville was silent for a moment, watching her converse. "Wouldn't you agree, old man?"

"Agree? Lord, yes. One of the finest I've ever met. I'm not sure what to make of her, though."

Kit chuckled under his breath. "Now you sound like Mater. Here, have the last of Winthrop's hock."

It was close to 3:00 a.m. by the time the Fevershams set off for Henley Hall in their carriage.

"Here, Fan, bundle yourself in this fur rug or you'll catch your death," said Mrs. Feversham in a sleepy voice. Fanny snuggled against her mother and plunged her hands deep into her fur muff. The clear night air was icy, but she had never felt more warm and protected.

As they tumbled along the narrow country road, Fanny reviewed the evening's events, all of which seemed to center around Neville and his absurd compliments and attentions. No wonder he had such a reputation for charm. She thought of how his eyes caressed her as he offered her his handkerchief. She had to keep telling herself such things meant nothing to him. If she mistook his playfulness, then she was no different from all the other girls whose hearts he had set pounding tonight.

Arabella stirred, then stared out the window. "Look,

Fan.'' She pointed to the flat plain etched in moonlight where two riders stood out in sharp relief, black shadows skimming across the silvery ground.

"Why, it's Kit and Neville!" Fanny exclaimed. Neville was in the lead, his black cloak billowing, with Kit on Vulcan some thirty paces behind. Both were riding neck-or-nothing, probably with a bet on the race's outcome.

"A very gothic sight, is it not, Fan?" asked Arabella, sighing.

As much as Fanny made a show of disparaging her sister's sentimentality, she was bound to agree. She recalled what it had felt like to ride Tammuz at full gallop, with Neville holding her so tightly it nearly crushed the breath from her lungs.

She gradually realized she was clutching an object in her fist. Removing her hand from her muff, she discovered the cambric handkerchief with Neville's monogram plainly visible. Holding the faintly scented fabric against her cheek, she whispered, "Rothermere."

7

Fanny had the next morning to herself. Rising late, she was filled with a languid contentment whose source she could not trace. Then she remembered last night's dance with Neville. His touch, how he had held her, the way he had looked at her—it all came rushing back. She dressed quickly, wondering if she had already missed him before his morning ride.

Once she had descended the stairs, shyness seized hold of her again. What if his manner was cold and supercilious? She didn't know if her composure would hold. The door to the morning room stood open, and through it she could see Arabella, Kit and Neville seated round a card-table with Papa. They were evidently engaged in a convivial game of whist, judging by the levity that prevailed. Fanny was especially vexed by the disgusting way in which Arabella, like a love-sick spaniel, gazed at Neville.

"Good morning, Miss Fanny, keeping a close watch, are we?"

Fanny jumped at the sound of Wilkins's voice so near. He had appeared silently and was now peering over her shoulder at the company within.

"Missed much, have I, Wilkins?" Fanny whispered.

"Nasty weather has prevented Mr. Christopher and Lord Neville from their customary ride," he whispered back. "They arranged a game of cards instead." As an afterthought he added, "Mrs. Feversham has invited Lord Neville to accompany the family to church next Sunday."

"And he accepted?" asked Fanny, incredulous.

"Yes, miss. Said he would go as long as the communion wine was good." Wilkins continued his perambulation down the hallway.

"Gemini!" Fanny murmured. Neville was proving more of an enigma each day. Kit had told her how his friend scoffed at all religious practice as mere superstition. It seemed his gallantry in accompanying the Fevershams everywhere was outrunning his convictions.

The sound of Neville's low laugh, as he chided Arabella for misplaying a card, strengthened Fanny's resolve to avoid the card party. It was well underway without her. She turned toward the stairs. Perhaps an hour or two with Lord Rothermere would help her sort out her feelings.

As she reached the landing, her speculations were cut short by Neville's valet stepping out of his master's room. Carrying an armload of cast-off cravats and waistcoats, along with a clothes brush and a scented packet of soap, Jenkins nodded at her briefly, then continued on his way.

As she made her way along the corridor, she hesitated for a moment, then turned back. Neville's bedroom door stood slightly ajar. To trespass on a gentleman's privacy was unthinkable, but the temptation was strong. She weighed the possibilities of being discovered. Jenkins's mission appeared to be a long and arduous one, washing yards of fine linen. It was pleasurable to imagine him in the scullery, up to his elbows in soapsuds under Cook's scrutiny.

Timorously, she pushed the door open further. She slipped inside, then shut it softly, exhaling slowly. The bedroom was a testament to gentlemanly good taste. With little rearranging of existing furniture, the suite now seemed much more simple, functional and ordered.

Fanny inched her way past the heavily carved, canopied bed, filled with a guilty excitement that made her uneasy. She crept over to the dressing table and examined its collection of brushes, combs, razor and scissors, all gleaming silver and laid out with great precision.

Placed at the edge of the table was a jeweled oval snuffbox with a scene from Greek mythology on its porcelain lid. An open bowl of potpourri gave off a scent of attar of roses. Next to it stood a bottle embossed with Neville's monogram. Fanny reached out a hesitant hand and unstoppered it. At once the intoxicating scent of musk filled the room, bringing back the feel of Neville's coat about her shoulders that day in the rain.

She wished she was one of those gypsy women who, by simply holding an object, could perfectly describe its owner. Outwardly, Neville was very different from the dark, romantic hero she had imagined. At times she had found him insufferably priggish, cold and distant. Yet, there were moments when he could be charming and intimate. Had she been wrong to cast him as Rothermere?

She gently rubbed the smooth glass against her cheek. There was a subtle link between Neville and Rothermere. She had seen flashes of a deeper, wilder side to his nature. Riding Tammuz before the storm, holding her close at the harvest dance, his eyes dark with emotion. But if Neville had a more passionate side to his nature, London must seem like a cage at times. Why wasn't he more dissatisfied?

The sound of voices emerging from the morning room plunged her into sudden panic. Fanny hastily placed the bottle back on the table and tiptoed to the bedroom door. She opened it a crack, making sure the corridor was clear, then darted into her sitting room. With her heart pounding, she heard Neville and Kit climb the stairs, discussing their next day's ride.

When Sunday arrived they all set off for church merrily, with Kit whistling a tune and taking Fanny by the arm while Neville courteously escorted Mrs. Feversham. Arabella unfurled her parasol against the bright morning sun, as her father fell into step next to her. Fanny's chief pleasure in attending Sunday services was following the country lane that wound through fields of wild daisies and tall blue larkspur, finally zigzagging up the small hill on which the crumbling twelfth-century church stood.

Various families crowded around the porch, waiting, it seemed, for a glimpse of the Fevershams' titled visitor. Fanny seated herself next to Arabella, and Neville took his place at her left. As the congregation settled in, she relaxed against the pew and opened her prayerbook. She had always loved this church—the mellow scent of waxed wooden pews, the uneven flagstones that paved the floor and, especially the leaded glass windows depicting biblical scenes. An air of tranquility seemed to emanate from the rafters which had sheltered seven centuries of worshippers.

After an introductory hymn, Mr. Sutcliff entered the pulpit. "I take for the text of today's sermon," he began, "Romans Six, verse twenty. 'For when ye were the servants of sin, ye were free from righteousness. What fruit had ye then in those things whereof ye are now ashamed? For the end of those things *is* death.' "

Fanny felt Neville's shoulders shift against her, and she stole a glance at him from beneath her lashes. His head was lifted nobly, his chiseled nose and strong, rounded chin adding distinction to his profile. But in his demeanor she thought she detected a vague melancholy.

Neville found this enforced reflection on human frailty not wholly welcome. For the last few years he had successfully resisted taking stock of his life, plunging instead into restless travel and a series of amatory adventures, some flagrantly dangerous, others merely amusing. What had he been trying so desperately to escape?

The scar burned along his arm beneath the fine linen of his shirt as if he had received it yesterday, rather than almost a decade ago. The duel had marked him forever. He had fought that day with no regard for his own life— only for the woman he loved. Camilla's exquisite face rose before him, her eyes begging him to fight for her.

Camilla had loved him with a desperate courage. He had given her hope, and she had given him everything to live for. But in the end she had gone back to her husband because he had threatened to take her children from her. No shred of her reputation would be left, he had assured her. She and her lover would have to run away, he had sneered, never to marry, to live on the Continent in disrepute. Society would never condone their love. He would see to that. So she had returned to the brute, the scoundrel who had beaten her, tormented her. She had died less than six months later in childbirth—denied not only Neville's love, but his child as well.

It had twisted him, made him bitter. His first love and, he vowed, his last. From then on, he dallied in only the most superficial romances, pursuing a life of pleasure with a vengeance. And when the black moods seized him, there were exotic worlds to explore—worlds which hadn't had the life squeezed out of them by blackguards hiding behind drawing room manners.

But Neville found that the life of ease came with certain iron-bound constraints. It had become increasingly difficult to do, if not what was right, then what was simply decent. If he did not alter his course soon he would end up a softened jade like his own prince. A man had a right, surely, to a life of purpose, if not of passion. In a strange way the vicar's words mirrored the direction his own thoughts had been taking at Henley.

" 'For the good that I would do, I do not, but the evil which I would not do, that I do.' "

Neville glanced at Fanny, so demure in her little bonnet and the lavender gloves she always wore. An uncharacteristic tenderness stole over him. The days at Henley had assumed their own gentle rhythms. The simple routines, morning rides with Kit, the interminable games of whist and the foolish but innocent conversations over supper had revived in him some connection with his youth at Wycherly Grange. Although dull by London standards, the Fevershams, with all their family prattle and country airings, had been good for him.

His eyes followed the Feversham girls as they accompanied their mother to the communion rail. Outwardly both were so compliant, yet one such a hoyden. He recalled dancing the "Roughty Toughty" with Fanny, her pliant body clasped to him. He had never expected to find such a rarity here, buried in the country. He envisioned her at the London assemblies, dazzling the reigning bucks and beauties. She should have little trouble making a good match. But her husband would have to be someone who could direct her vibrant spirit without breaking it. Neville sighed, thinking that whoever he was, he would be a lucky fellow.

As soon as the vicar pronounced the benediction, the congregation filed out of their pews and exchanged greetings. At the entrance, Clive and Mr. Burleigh awaited the Fevershams and Neville.

"Lovely flowers on the altar, don't you think, Mrs. Feversham? The rich, dark colors of autumn so remind me of Rembrandt's later palette," Clive observed. "My compliments to the Miss Fevershams this Sunday morn," he continued, bowing toward both girls.

As they walked outside he gazed rapturously at the church walls, sagging into the soft earth. "A fine example of twelfth century romanesque," he commented to Neville, "although the windows, I fear, are somewhat later.'' He snapped his fingers. ''A splendid idea has just occurred to me. If you would like to see some truly gothic architecture, why not come to Burleigh Abbey for an afternoon ramble? I'll even give you supper,'' he added magnanimously.

''Oh, Clive,'' Mrs. Feversham replied, ''we would find it most . . . edifying, I'm sure.'' Pleased with the invitation, she studiously avoided Fanny's disapproving scowl.

''Done!'' said Neville.

''A ramble, eh?'' said Kit, rubbing his hands together. ''Sounds capital.''

''Tuesday next, then. Would that suit you?''

''But that's All Hallow's Eve,'' said Arabella hesitantly.

''I shall lock away all the phantoms before your arrival,'' Clive reassured her gallantly. ''Well, Father, what do you say?'' he asked, turning to the ear trumpet. ''We're to have guests at Burleigh Abbey.''

''Pests?'' Mr. Burleigh returned in querulous tones. ''Only remedy I know is to poison 'em.''

The Sunday afternoon had warmed significantly, and the Fevershams were enjoying it al fresco. Chairs and tables had been moved to the back terrace, which commanded an excellent view of the flower and topiary gardens. Stretching off to the right was a long, level greensward used as a riding turf. Kit and Neville were busily occupied there, taking their horses through their gaits.

''Mama, how could you have accepted Mr. Burleigh's invitation?'' Fanny said accusingly. She swept aside the skirt of her riding habit and plopped down in a chair next to her mother. Settling her drawing board against her knee, she squinted into the distance and made a few quick outlines with her pencil.

''I couldn't have possibly refused, Fanny. Besides, I'm sure Clive will entertain us in a great deal of style.

I won't hear another word from you against him."

"But, Mama, think what a dead bore it will be. Lord Neville will simply hate it." Fanny reached over to pat the head of Brutus who, panting from the heat, had sunk down next to her.

"Lord Neville thinks Clive extremely amiable," her mother countered. "Besides, we have little enough in the way of grand architecture here. I'm sure he'll find Clive's efforts of considerable interest."

"So it's settled, we are going to Burleigh Abbey?" asked Arabella, putting down her embroidery hoop.

"Slow as treacle, thick as cream," her sister taunted.

"Fanny, stop it this instant. I won't have you baiting your sister that way. If anyone dislikes the outing it will be on account of your disagreeable manners."

As Arabella departed with a pout, Mrs. Feversham glared menacingly at her elder daughter. "Now see what you have done—you've driven Arabella away. I don't know what's gotten into you. And in heaven's name, stop making those gasping sounds. Why are you pulling on the collar of your habit?"

"Because I'm *hot*."

"Well, of course you are, in that habit. It's an impossible color anyway—robin's egg blue. Bright enough to scare the fox back into his hole. If you're going to sketch, why don't you change into something cooler?"

"I intend to ride, Mama." Fanny's gaze was locked on Neville and Kit racing up and down the turf.

"Stop petting that nasty dog. You'll get hairs all over your habit. Lord Neville doesn't want to race a girl, he wants to race Kit."

"I can outrun Kit on Vulcan," Fanny announced simply. She gazed at her drawing with immense satisfaction. It was an admirable likeness of Neville mounted on Tammuz, she thought. Brutus suddenly began barking at the horses streaking toward the lawn. Fanny glanced at the dog, and made a hasty annotation to her drawing as the two riders reined in sharply at the foot of the terrace.

"Care to ride, Fan?" called Kit. "I'll take Tammuz, you can have Vulcan."

"Done!" said Fanny eagerly, flinging down her drawing board. Before her mother could protest, she had run to Vulcan and held his reins as the groom changed the saddles.

"We'll race to the first copse of trees, Fan, then I'll see how your marksmanship has improved. I brought pistols for us," Kit said, brandishing a handsome pair of duelling pieces.

Neville stood on the steps, watching brother and sister ride away in a whirlwind of energy. As he approached Mrs. Feversham he mopped his brow with a handkerchief, then sank into the chair Fanny had just vacated.

"Splendid rider, Kit," he said, sighing. "I haven't had a run like that since . . . actually, since Fanny and I raced against the storm." He grinned widely at the memory.

"Lord Neville, you look as if you could use a restorative," said Mrs. Feversham, offering him a glass of lemonade. She nodded as he thanked her and quaffed the cold drink.

"I really must apologize for my children's harum-scarum behavior, my lord," she sighed. "I feel that you've been tossed about on a rough sea since your arrival here."

"Nonsense, Mrs. Feversham," he replied. "Their manners are simply the result of high spirits. I must confess, they've been a stimulant to my own."

"I concede that, in Kit's case, a certain wildness is acceptable. But, Lord Neville, Fanny has me greatly worried."

"Why so?"

At that moment shots rang out from the opposite end of the park, succeeded by wild whoops.

"As you have no doubt noticed, my two daughters are as unlike as night and day. Their come-out is this spring. I have no concerns on Arabella's account. She is all a parent could wish for in a daughter—sweet, obedient, and, I believe," she looked down modestly, "possessing a certain charm."

"Quite so," came the languid reply.

"My lord, you are a man of the town. I must beg your advice."

"Concerning?"

"Concerning Fanny!" Mrs. Feversham exclaimed, her patience at an end. "No doubt you have marked her headstrong behavior. Why, she's as giddy as a top! I am simply at a loss as to what to do. Her prospects for the Marriage Mart are, I fear, very poor. Oh, Lord Neville, my brains are in a dreadful tangle over this matter." Mrs. Feversham dabbed at her eyes with a handkerchief while her guest took her other hand between his own.

"My dear Mrs. Feversham," he said gently. "I must tell you that I judge both your daughters' prospects in London to be excellent." He waited while she had dried her eyes and regained her composure.

"Mr. Burleigh was quite right when he compared Arabella to an English rose. Her beauty is exquisite, her manners charming. And the *ton* has terms to describe young ladies of great beauty and spirit. The ones lucky enough to be born beauties, we call Incomparables. The spirited ones who have created their own beauty, we call Originals. And you must take my word, I find Fanny to be the rarest of Originals. I think you will find," he said slowly, "that she will command enormous attention in London. She has her own natural beauty, a vitality that lights her from within."

The look of relief that swept across Mrs. Feversham's face encouraged him to go on. "Perhaps she seems a bit outspoken at times, but we have a saying that to be eccentric is to be natural. Fanny is completely herself. Mark my words, dear Mrs. Feversham, your little wildflower will garner you as much praise as your highly cultivated rose."

"I know not what to say, Lord Neville. I am astonished by your assessment."

"I have rarely been wrong in such matters, dear lady."

"But, my lord, you can't mean that Fanny should be allowed to cavort through the drawing rooms of London as wildly as she does here. Surely, she must learn some restraint, acquire some polish."

"I wouldn't like her to lose her exuberance," he said thoughtfully, "but if you think she needs some town bronze, I have just the right person for you."

"Oh, really? Who?"

"Miss Beatrice Wigmore on Jermyn Street. Very respectable." He looked about for a piece of paper and Mrs. Feversham indicated Fanny's drawing tablet. He found a clean sheet and scribbled the name and address, handing it to her. "She'll teach the girls to waltz, all the latest on-dits, and she won't dampen Fanny's spirit."

"Oh, thank you, my lord!" Mrs. Feversham beamed ecstatically, clasping the paper to her bosom as if it were the *Book of Common Prayer*.

Neville sat back with a satisfied air and gave Fanny's drawing a cursory glance, then focused more closely on it.

It was a sketch of him astride Tammuz. He could tell that from the riding clothes and a certain nonchalance the artist had captured. But an unflattering addition had been made: the rider bore not his head, but Brutus's!

He scowled at the distant copse of trees where two marksmen, one clad in startling blue, emitted shouts of laughter.

8

It was with a certain misgiving that Fanny departed for Burleigh Abbey the following week. The thought of seeing Clive's pretensions translated to stone and mortar was a bit forbidding. Like her father who quietly napped in the corner, she feigned sleep in order to ignore her mother's excited chatter.

Over the last few days, Neville had treated her with a marked preference, inviting her on the morning rides with Kit and asking her to read aloud in the evenings. Although she knew his behavior was little more than brotherly affection, when translated to her imaginary world, it fueled Rothermere with passionate interest.

With an author's pride, Fanny contemplated the most recent turn of events at Castle Locarno. Unable to sleep one night, Melinda roamed the battlements, marveling at the midnight sky. Lord Rothermere joined her, closing his hand over hers as it rested against the rough-hewn stone. Wordlessly, he untied the ribbon that bound her dark curls. As they tumbled down her back he took her into his arms and covered her mouth with his in an urgent kiss. After a struggle, she yielded. There was no resisting him. His desire made him a savage tiger . . .

"Fanny, whatever is the matter?" Mrs. Feversham asked.

Her mother's question brought Fanny back to her cramped quarters in the carriage.

"You're wearing the oddest expression. You seem short of breath."

"I . . . I was just trying to imagine if Burleigh Abbey had battlements, Mama," she replied lamely.

"I never realized architecture could have such an effect," Mrs. Feversham observed dryly. "You shall have your answer soon. Here is the entrance now."

The carriage paused before gates bearing obscure heraldic devices and a motto in Latin. After a gnomelike gatekeeper had opened the gates, the carriage, followed by Neville and Kit on horseback, turned down the winding drive. Fanny noticed a ruined tower on a nearby hill, a folly evidently created by Clive, for it had never stood there before.

As the family sat forward in wonder, the carriage rounded the last curve of the drive. Through the tangled foliage Burleigh Abbey emerged, outlined in crocketed chimneys, fanciful turrets and running battlements.

"Remain calm, Fanny," Mrs. Feversham instructed. "Burleigh Abbey has battlements."

They gaped at what had once been an elegant seventeenth-century manor house, transformed into a gothic fantasy. As far as Fanny could tell, the abbey reflected no particular period in history. The library windows were capped by graceful trefoils, while arrow slits pierced the tower walls forming the entrance hall. A Tudor clock hung just above the massive oak door studded with nails, and as a final touch, a Jacobean weathervane surmounted the uneven roofline.

"If that don't beat the Dutch!" said Mr. Feversham, and for once no one took exception with him.

Fanny's eyes widened as a medieval monk stepped forth from the gloom of the entrance hall and bid them welcome, setting in motion a giant rosary that hung from his waist.

"Who is that papist Bedlamite?" Mrs. Feversham asked irritably.

"It must be Clive, Mama," Fanny answered, peering to see beneath the hood.

Mrs. Feversham narrowed her eyes suspiciously as the monk approached the carriage.

He removed his hood with a serene gesture, revealing that it was indeed their host. "Welcome to Burleigh Abbey, my friends," he intoned.

Neville and Kit dismounted from their horses and helped the ladies alight.

"Come," said Clive expansively. "I will show you some of my improvements to the abbey and then we shall wander for a bit."

As they entered the high-ceilinged hall hung with pennants and medieval standards, Kit fell into step beside Fanny.

"Haven't seen anything like this since the 'squerades at Vauxhall," he murmured.

"It seems Clive has combined the Grand Tour with too much Horace Walpole," Fanny whispered. Before she could make any further observation, Clive escorted them into the library, a room that stopped all conversation immediately.

Like everything else in the abbey, the fretted ceiling was of great height. Columns carved from the wall moldings supported intricate fan vaults, barely discernible in the gothic gloom. Overwhelmed, Arabella sank onto a crocketed couch. "It is . . . immense," she whimpered.

Although Fanny deplored her sister's show of overrefinement, she had to concur that their surroundings were somewhat alarming. Hundreds of mouldy, leatherbound volumes lined the shelves, reaching up into the vast darkness.

Their host seemed more pleased than disconcerted by

Arabella's reaction. "What delicacy of feeling you possess, Miss Arabella," he said approvingly, "to be so dismayed by my library. The gothic is a barbarous style, and I apologize for its terrifying aspects."

"Perhaps we should move to more congenial surroundings," Neville suggested quietly.

"Quite right," said Clive. "We shall adjourn to the sitting room. I haven't redesigned it yet, so I daresay we shall find Father there. It's the only room he will inhabit."

With his robe gathered about him, Clive led his guests down the hallway, his sandals slapping against the flagstones. They entered the sitting room to find Mr. Burleigh seated by a small fire. Although old-fashioned, the room was furnished in comfortable, modern elegance. Mr. Burleigh grasped his ear trumpet and began to rise.

"Pray, don't disturb yourself, Mr. Burleigh," said Mrs. Feversham, taking a nearby seat. "I don't know when I have been so pleased to see a simple chair by Robert Adam. Like coming across an old friend."

"Can't say I ever knew him," returned Mr. Burleigh.

Tea was brought in by a maid, and Mrs. Feversham poured. Gradually an air of normality returned, although Clive sniffed contemptuously at the sight of the Meissen tea service.

"Well, Clive, you've certainly left your mark on Burleigh Manor," Kit began bravely.

"It shall be my life's work," Clive said modestly. "And when I marry, it shall be to a very gothic sort of person." Noting his guests' blank stares, he continued, "By that, I mean that my wife shall shun modernity and share my labors here at the abbey."

Everyone stared fixedly at their tea, except for Arabella, whose gaze was riveted on a handsome landscape that hung above the fireplace.

"Ah, Miss Arabella," Clive said in a pleased tone, "I see that you have spied my little experiment with paint pots and brushes."

"You mean this is your work, Mr. Burleigh?" she asked wonderingly.

"Yes," he answered, strolling over to the painting. "Travelling northward to Rome one day I was struck by the desolate sweep of the Compagna . . . its undulating expanse recalled a vast inland sea. I immediately set up an easel, and my brushes have never flown faster. *Ecco*, you see the result."

To Fanny it appeared to be a competent work, well above the level of amateur, though not original in concept. The rustic scene, full of distant hills dotted with plane trees, was rendered in tones that resembled the varnished surfaces of much older paintings.

With the speculative air of a connoisseur, Neville joined Clive, regarding the work with calm approval. Unable any longer to resist soliciting a response, Clive said, "Neville, you have been uncommonly silent. What is your opinion?"

"I must warn you not to attach much worth to it," Neville said, "but your efforts have put me in mind of the view from the Capo di Monte—one of my favorites in all Italy."

The graceful compliment only whetted Clive's appetite for more. Like a greedy child, he continued, "And what of my improvements throughout the abbey?"

"Astonishing," came the reply as Neville turned away from the painting. "Your antiquarian vision is bold, indeed."

"*Grazie*," Clive returned humbly. He turned to Mrs. Feversham and said, "You will be pleased to know, Mrs. Feversham, some friends of yours will be joining us at supper."

"Indeed? Who?"

"The Monktons. Mrs. Monkton, especially, seems to have formed a lively interest in gothic architecture." Oblivious to Mrs. Feversham's pained expression, Clive continued, "Perhaps we should commence our ramble. I think you will be most pleased with my vertu. I have created a grotto using my most precious gems."

"Then let us away," Mr. Feversham prodded.

Clive led the party along a gravel path and onto a grassy promontory. Holding his robe in both hands, he clambered to the summit and stood with one knee bent, in the attitude of a conqueror. "You must come see the view," he called. "It is quite spectacular."

The others followed him as best they could, Mrs. Feversham toiling along the uneven ground, and Mr. Burleigh stopping halfway up, clinging breathlessly to the trunk of a tree.

Neville handed up the ladies, and Fanny clambered to the top to stand by his side. The crumbling tower capped the hill opposite them. In the valley between the two promontories, sunlight dappled the leaves of trees and played among the ripples of a sparkling stream.

"Very lovely, don't you agree?" Neville spoke softly, turning his gaze from the distant view to Fanny.

"Yes, indeed it is," she answered, strangely moved by the charming landscape.

"An Arcadian vision," Clive stated solemnly. From the folds of his robe he produced a small tinted glass in a carved ebony frame. He peered through it at the tower and sighed deeply, exceptionally pleased by the effects of his folly. "The sublime is enhanced by antiquity," he pronounced and handed the object to Mrs. Feversham.

"What do you call this?" she asked, turning it from side to side.

"It is a Claude glass," he answered. "It imbues landscapes with the appropriate tones, making them reminiscent of a painting by the divine Claude. It replaces nature's more vivid coloration with the palette of art. But come," he commanded. "Now I shall show you something truly picturesque."

After a quarter of an hour walking along another path, they reached the grotto. Fanny had to admit it was very prettily situated. Its outer shell resembled a small cave carved into the hill, with an oval entrance formed by large, jagged pieces of fieldstone. It overlooked a placid little pool spanned by a rustic footbridge.

"I dedicated this grotto to the Venerable Bede, who kept the lamp of learning alive through England's darkest medieval night," Clive announced. "The spirit lamp which I have placed on this pedestal burns in his memory. As you might imagine, it is wondrous at night."

Neville and Arabella were already examining the grotto's contents. As Fanny entered, she exclaimed, "Why, Mr. Burleigh, it is a jewel box!"

To her, it seemed that the grotto's perfection made up for all of Clive's preposterous improvements to Burleigh Abbey. The inside was a glittering shell, whose walls, even in the slanting light of the late afternoon, glowed with the refracted radiance of many gems, glasses and precious metals.

Everywhere she looked she discovered new treasures. Tiny seed pearls clustered around a chunk of lapis lazuli, outlined with diamond-like pieces of cut glass. Stamped gold fleur-de-lis, embedded with blood-red garnets, were strewn randomly throughout. Examining the walls closely, she found seashells scattered among malachite, amethysts and pieces of jasper. Spars of raw quartz protruded from the ceiling, adding to the feeling of an enchanted cave. Hugging the interior walls was a circular bench carved with rustic patterns. In the center of this bright little world stood the stone pedestal bearing the lamp.

"It is fine, Mr. Burleigh, very fine," said Neville, touching a large piece of coral near the entrance.

"I took the idea from Pope's grotto, of course," said Clive modestly.

"But your collection of vertu is really splendid," Neville added. "I have never seen anything to equal this quaint display."

"What say you, Miss Arabella?" asked Clive.

"Would you say it more picturesque or more sublime?"

"I cannot say, Mr. Burleigh," Arabella replied, slowly turning in astonishment. "It is fantastical."

"It must be magical in the evening," said Fanny, seating herself upon the bench. "You have created a place where the imagination can dwell."

Her heartfelt praise plunged Clive into confounded, but pleased, silence. Fanny gazed out at the silvery pond, a feeling of profound peace settling upon her. How perfect it had all been since Neville's arrival! She glanced about at her family and friends—Neville and Kit chatting amiably at the entrance to the grotto, Arabella and Mama examining the gems. If only she could preserve this moment forever.

Her meditation was interrupted by a strange sound emanating from the pathway.

"That cannot be the cawing of a gull, because we are too far from the sea," Mrs. Feversham said in puzzlement.

"Hieee, hellew, everyone," it continued.

"Isn't that Mrs. Monkton's voice?" said Kit, peering outside the grotto. "I say, you'd better see this."

The little party gathered at the entrance, and beheld a thoroughly astonishing sight. Like one of Scott's besieged heroines, Mrs. Monkton approached with little running steps, waving a white handkerchief. An undertunic of yellow silk was held in place with a heavily knotted girdle of gold rope with thick tassels. Her arms had been tightly laced into sleeves which appeared through slits of her eglantine velvet robe.

"Oh, dear, am I the only gothic one?" she queried in a chirping tone. Behind her panted Mr. Monkton, dressed in simple walking attire, his nankeen trousers showing signs of having been recently let out.

"My lady," said Clive, taking her hand with practiced grace, "welcome to the abbey. Your appearance adds human beauty to my efforts in stone and wood."

"Oh, do you like it?" Mrs. Monkton said coquet-

tishly. She held out her skirt. "I copied it from an il-
lustration of Eleanor of Aquitaine. I hope I was not too
enthusiastic a Francophile."

"I should say not," Mrs. Feversham reassured. "You
look every inch a queen." Turning to Fanny she muttered, "She has finally outdone herself."

Mr. Monkton heaved up alongside his wife. "Hullo,
Burleigh." He regarded his host phlegmatically. "Didn't
know you'd converted."

"Ah, no, Mr. Monkton. My robe only reflects my
mood medieval, not my spiritual persuasion, which, I
fear, remains unswervingly aesthetic." Clive took Mrs.
Monkton's arm and led the party up the path. "How
appropriate that you should dress as the Queen of Aquitaine, Mrs. Monkton, for tonight I am singing the
songs of the troubadours."

"On the pianoforte?" asked Mrs. Monkton. "Or is
that too modern?"

"Like the minstrels of old, I shall play the harp."

"So, our entertainments are to be gothic, too?" asked
Fanny in a low, mutinous voice.

"I'm surprised poor Mr. Monkton didn't arrive in
chain mail," Kit replied archly.

"Perhaps I shall order a suit of it from Weston upon
my return to London," Neville stated calmly. "It will
stand me in good stead when I enter my box at the
opera."

"Oh, Lord Neville, I hope you aren't planning on
leaving us soon?" Mrs. Feversham asked anxiously.

"Within a week, ma'am." Neville gave Mrs. Feversham his arm to steady her. "I assure you I am in no
hurry to depart, but certain business matters require my
attention."

Fanny caught her breath at his unexpected words.
Soon it all would be over! Within a week he would be
gone.

9

Supper in the rectory was a resplendent, though eccentric, affair, served in medieval style amid purple drapes and ebony chairs. Fanny looked down the long table at the variety of silver serving dishes set before them by an army of servants.

"I should like to propose a toast," Clive said, raising his goblet of rock crystal, "to my distinguished guests and neighbors who are always most welcome at Burleigh Abbey. And now, we shall feast like kings, for I have cooked you a wild boar."

Groaning under the weight, two servants carried in the boar on an enormous platter and placed it before Clive. Nonplussed, their host hovered over it, making vaguely threatening gestures with two large knives.

"Reminds me of a bullfight I once saw in Seville," muttered Mr. Burleigh.

Occasionally, during the disconcerting supper, Fanny's gaze met Neville's and they shared a smile. The guests were relieved when the dessert was finally over, and their brave efforts at transporting food to their mouths in overlarge spoons could cease.

Clive's idea of post-prandial entertainment was to serenade his guests with lays of the provençal troubadours.

Seating himself next to the fireplace on a Roman stool, he bent over the strings of a Celtic harp. In a slightly nasal tenor, he began to sing the story of Aucassin and Nicolete, two thirteenth-century French lovers.

The song had a decidedly soothing effect on the assembled company. Arabella gazed at Clive serenely, while the elder Fevershams and Monktons drew close to the fire.

Warming to his subject, Clive sang the next verse dramatically:

> *Of the pains the lover bore*
> *And the sorrows he outwore,*
> *For the goodness and the grace,*
> *Of his love, so fair of face.*

Fanny saw Neville stiffen at the words. A mask of sadness stole over his features. As Clive sang on of Nicolete's imprisonment, and Aucassin's fight to free her, Neville leaned further into the shadows.

Fanny looked away, not wanting to pry. He seemed to harbor a memory too painful to share. Instinctively, she wanted to console him, yet she had no idea how to do so. His wall of privacy was unassailable.

A gentle round of applause signalled the song's end. Mr. Monkton offered to recite "The Old Churchyard," which Clive rejected as lacking the proper gothic tone. Upon general agreement, the party set out for new quarters. The gentlemen chose to have their brandy and cigars in the library, while Clive, holding a blazing candelabra aloft, offered to give the ladies a tour of the portrait gallery.

Fanny hung back in the hall until the others were safely out of sight. As quietly as possible, she opened the front door and slipped through the narrow opening.

She was immediately thankful she had thought to

wrap her shawl about her, for the pathways and gardens were enveloped in a light fog. Despite the chill, her spirits began to soar as soon as she was free.

With no very clear idea of where she was going, she wanted to wander the grounds of this remarkable place and have time to think. She peered down the dark stretch of lawn. Behind the large clipped hedges of yew, she could barely make out a stone wall surmounted by gargoyles. She shivered slightly at their menacing images, and found her way to the path that led to the grotto. As she rounded the final curve, she stopped in awe.

With its colored gems and metals shimmering in the glow of the spirit lamp, the grotto was a twinkling cave of light and color, a haven of brightness in the surrounding gloom.

"Gemini!" she breathed, not knowing which cluster of treasures to inspect first. She lit a candle from the lamp's flame and held it up to the encrusted walls. The gems glowed with a deep radiance, revealing their full color in the candle's flame. Hundreds of raw amethysts winked from a sliced geode. Slabs of bright green malachite glinted between ancient Roman coins, polished to their original radiance.

After admiring her surroundings, Fanny blew out the candle and sat down on the bench. In the lamp's unsteady light, the walls seemed to shimmer with a life of their own. She folded her hands in her lap and breathed in the still night air. She felt safe and protected here. Gradually, her thoughts turned to Neville.

She tried to envision what her future with him would be. She was certain he would remain on friendly terms throughout her Season. Amiable, but a little distant. She shook her head at her own foolishness. Her feelings for him, misplaced as they were, were best left to novels, not life.

She closed her eyes and imagined the burning kiss Lord Rothermere had left on Melinda's lips. She blushed at the scene, thinking how it would be if Neville held

her so. She grew breathless at the idea of his strong
hands caressing her throat, stroking her loosened curls.
No, she reprimanded herself, such daydreams were fu-
tile.

With grim determination, she focused on the plot of
her novel. Devilish dealings in the occult and besotted
moments of passion were all very well, but what did
they add up to? She felt just as she did when Mama had
attempted to teach her embroidery. After much bungling,
she had ended up with a pile of tangled threads but no
sampler. Mama had called for the hartshorn and retreated.

What about an evil Italian count with supernatural
powers? His name? Count Orsini sounded suitably sin-
ister, she thought. He was under an ancient curse and
commanded a pack of ghostly white hounds. He could
be plotting to kidnap Rothermere's child, but to what
end?

Fanny had drifted far away to Castle Locarno and
didn't hear the footsteps coming along the path.

"At last I have found you." The familiar voice made
her start. "I have trapped the vixen in her lair!" Neville
laughed softly and entered the grotto, seating himself
next to her on the bench.

In the golden light she could have been a little fairy,
he thought. She looked startled to see him, and he was
careful to speak gently. "At the abbey they are worried
a Hallow's Eve ghost has abducted you. I remembered
how you loved the grotto. I thought I would find you
here."

"I am sorry to have given concern," Fanny stammered. "I merely wanted to sit here quietly for a few
moments. Perhaps we should return."

"No need yet. I apologize for intruding on you so
suddenly," he said. "This little grotto makes me hold
young Mr. Burleigh in higher regard. It is, indeed, a
thing of beauty." A teasing smile played about his

mouth. "Am I mistaken, or were you less cruel to him today than is your wont?"

"Perhaps it is the monk's robes that have caused Mr. Burleigh to spare us his usual compliments," Fanny replied. "If I am kind, it is out of thanks for the respite."

"What? I am amazed you haven't welcomed his attentions. I must confess, I think him quite a suitable match," he responded, polishing his quizzing glass.

Fanny looked up with horror. "For whom?"

"Why, you or Miss Arabella. Young Mr. Burleigh is obviously a man of taste and would make you a good husband. You could have sumptuous gowns from whatever period he was adopting. Think what history you would learn, Fanny! I think I shall recommend the idea to him," he said smugly.

"That's preposterous," Fanny spluttered. "Why, Mr. Burleigh and I merely vex one another. Besides, he well knows I would make his life a torment. We do not suit."

Neville laughed heartily to see her so outraged. "Forgive me, Fanny, I have teased you unmercifully. But now that we have broached the subject, what kind of man would be to your taste?"

"I could not say," she answered, drawing back slightly. "I haven't much experience in such matters."

"It is unfortunate I shall be leaving before I know your preferences," Neville replied.

"Yes," she stammered uneasily, "it will be soon, I suppose." She looked away to hide a tear.

"What is this?" he asked, brushing her cheek gently. "You weren't crying, were you, Fanny?"

"Oh, certainly not," she lied gallantly, trembling from his touch.

"You seemed preoccupied when I found you. What were you thinking, little sylph?" He leaned protectively toward her.

"Oh," she said, too startled by his use of a nickname to concoct an escape, "I was thinking about my book."

"Ah, the gothic novel you are writing. Is it so sad a tale, then?"

"Yes." She looked apprehensively into his calm eyes. "Yes and no."

"Does your hero suffer much? The one you have modeled upon Wilkins?" he queried.

"Yes, he has suffered in the past. Now it is my heroine's turn to suffer."

"She suffers, I suppose, out of love for him?" Neville asked, absent-mindedly straightening his cuff.

"Yes," she answered, unable to keep the emotion out of her voice, "she cannot help herself. But it turns out that she, the most helpless of creatures, is the one who saves him."

"Saves him, how?"

"When he falls in love," she answered softly. "When he sees that nothing in his past makes any difference to her. He sees that if he renounces her, he will renounce the best part of himself. And so he dares to love again."

"And he ceases to suffer," Neville finished. A silence fell between them.

With great care, Neville took Fanny's hand. "Fanny, there is so much I would like you to understand," he said in a low voice. "But there is no time just now to tell you all of it." He gazed into her deep blue eyes that shone beneath the dark lashes, then looked at the delicate hand he held, brushing her fingertips with his lips. To hold her, to kiss her now would bind her to him forever. How could he do that to her? She didn't truly know him.

"Sweet Fanny, could it be that your heroine has made a hero out of a man who has no heroic qualities?"

"What do you mean?" she asked.

"Perhaps he is not the man she imagines him to be. Perhaps he would only disappoint her." He drew her hand close to his heart.

"Do you mean he does not love her?" she whispered.

"No, my sweet. He loves her. More than she can imagine, but perhaps he fears disappointing her. He could not bear it if she came to look on him with anything less than love."

"Are you speaking of a woman you loved once?" she asked hesitantly.

"No, I am speaking of the present," he said tenderly. "You see, my dear, a very long time ago, I did love, passionately and completely. The story did not have a happy ending. Since then, I have permitted myself one ruling passion—vanity. It has been my mistress so long that if I were to trust my heart again, I might find that I lack one. Sharing my life with a person of sensibility could be a sentence of unending misery."

Even as he spoke these words, he fought his desire to embrace the beautiful young girl before him. She gazed back at him, her eyes fierce with the joy of first love, her moist lips slightly parted, begging to be kissed. He longed to crush her mouth to his now, to taste her sweetness.

Fanny felt Neville's touch upon her hair. His hand moved slowly along her neck, stroking her skin lightly, adoringly. With her eyes half-closed in a kind of lethargy, she felt her breathing quicken, aware only of a need to feel his lips on hers. In the glimmering light she could see his pale face grow taut, his eyes flickering with desire. With deliberate slowness, his fingers closed around the blue ribbon in her hair, untying it. Her curls cascaded to her shoulders as his hand explored their thick luxury, drawing her face closer to his.

His mouth hovered over hers, before claiming it in a kiss that took her breath away. Her arms crept around his neck as he pulled her close, forcing her against him in complete surrender.

She was overwhelmed by him—the softness of his lips, the lean muscularity of his chest, his powerful shoulders straining against the confining clothing. His kiss became more urgent, his tongue exploring her lips, then her mouth, demanding a response.

A flame ignited within her, sparking a deeper level of desire. Feverishly, she drew her hands through his hair, feeling its silky texture. Wanting more of him, she lightly stroked the face she had so long admired.

His lips moved from hers and began kissing her fingers fervently. "Fanny," he groaned, "I never knew . . . how very much I . . ."

"More, please," she said simply, her lips parted to receive his.

The spell was abruptly broken by the sound of Kit coming down the pathway, calling her name. Reluctantly, Fanny tore herself away from Neville, her heart pounding. He clutched her to him and would not let go.

"Fanny, forgive me for my foolishness," he whispered.

"Do not call it foolish," she implored.

They stared solemnly at each other, unwilling to relinquish the moment.

Neville released her and tenderly pushed back the disheveled curls from Fanny's face. With great gentleness, he traced her eyebrows, memorizing her features. "No words now, my little sylph. But I must tell you this, I do not kiss innocents lightly."

They could hear Arabella's voice joined to Kit's as they approached the grotto.

"I shall never forget this," he whispered. "Promise me you will remember it, too."

"Fanny! Oh, there you are . . . and . . ."

Fanny looked up to see Arabella and Kit peering

into the grotto from beneath a greatcoat they shared.

"So, Neville, I see you rescued Fanny from the ghost. You both look as if you've seen him!" Kit observed wryly.

"I see you came prepared for rain," Fanny said, trusting her voice at last.

"It *is* raining, you goose," Kit replied, offering Neville a cape.

"You mean you haven't heard it?" Arabella asked disbelievingly. She indicated the pond, where Fanny could see a hard rain breaking upon the surface.

"Mater says we must decamp immediately," Kit announced. "It's a matter of either taking our chances on the road, or spending the night in Clive's mouldy abbey."

"Then let's fly," Neville urged, pulling Fanny close and throwing the cape over them. They darted out of the grotto, scrambling up the rain-soaked path toward the lights of Burleigh Abbey.

Fanny bit back tears. Already the grotto was in the past. She had never dreamed she and Neville would share such passion. But in a few moments, they would resume their lives as if nothing had happened. Soon he would return to London—and forget.

But she would remember . . . always.

10

Riding back to Henley Hall in her family's carriage, Fanny relived the moment in the grotto, savoring every detail of Neville's embrace. A wave of longing swept over her as she remembered the feel of his mouth claiming hers. What she would give for him to kiss her like that again! Slowly the wave receded, leaving cold realization in its wake.

Everything had changed in that instant. How would she manage to conduct herself naturally while he remained at Henley? She thought of the numerous evenings he had joined the family at the fireside, chatting and playing cards, the morning rides, the afternoon walks. He had teased her unmercifully and laughed at her rejoinders. How, in heaven's name, was she to gaze upon him again without blushing and trembling with desire?

Numerous females had certainly done their share of blushing and trembling since his arrival—Arabella, in her sweet, silly way, the mincing Serena Sedley, even the affected Mrs. Monkton.

"I must not appear to love him too well," Fanny resolved, as they reached Henley's entrance.

"What, Fan, ghost still got you?" Kit teased as he

opened the carriage door. "Here we are at the old domicilium. No monks wandering about here, eh, Pater?"

"No, thank God," returned Mr. Feversham. "Dunno what's gotten into Clive. Next, he'll be a strolling player in the provinces."

"Don't trouble yourself about old Clive," said Kit, helping his father out of the carriage. "I've devised a plan for our entertainment." Overriding the loud protests about the lateness of the hour, Kit announced that they would read ghost stories to one another in the library. His recommendation of glasses of wine to warm the ladies, and brandy for the gentlemen, met with Mrs. Feversham's reluctant approval.

They made themselves comfortable in the library, where coals blazed merrily in the fireplace.

"Haven't we had enough of ghosts, Kit?" Neville asked, his gaze lingering on Fanny. "Your sisters appear greatly fatigued."

"Truly, I am all right," she answered firmly. "After all, it is All Hallow's Eve."

"I knew I could count on you, Fan," Kit replied enthusiastically. "As it is nearly midnight we shall start with *The Monk*!"

"And then, the witching hour will be upon us," said Neville in a dramatic voice.

"Oh dear!" Arabella squealed, obviously enjoying the fright.

Kit, his arm outstretched to retrieve the leather-bound book, turned suddenly. "I have it, Fanny! Why don't you read to us from your own novel?"

"What!" Fanny looked up, frozen with horror. "You mean, tonight?"

Neville rested one arm against the mantel and regarded her with barely suppressed humor.

"It is a Gothic novel, is it not?" Kit continued. "Arabella has been your only audience, and we would all be glad to hear it."

"Oh, Kit," Fanny pleaded, "it's just a shabby thing.

I couldn't read it before . . ." Her sweeping gesture stopped at Neville. " . . . everyone."

"Nonsense, Fan," Kit said dismissively. "I have never known you so modest. It doesn't suit you. Come, Bella, be our critic and tell us how it succeeds."

"Well," Arabella replied, chewing her lips nervously, and looking apprehensively in Fanny's direction, "it's very . . . thrilling."

"Then it's settled. Fanny, you will read to us a bit, then we shall all take turns from other books. But we must hurry, as midnight approaches."

Fanny turned miserably toward the library door. Doomed to disaster, she thought. It wasn't bad enough that she had already surrendered to his kiss, but to read her depiction of Lord Rothermere aloud would reveal the full extent of her schoolgirl infatuation. Hearing certain passages, Neville would surely recognize some of his own *bon mots*. If only she hadn't rewritten most of it since Neville's arrival to capture a more lifelike portrait of him.

"Bella, you'd better accompany your sister. She looks quite done in," Mrs. Feversham suggested.

Once they were out of earshot, Arabella whispered, "Fan, what are you going to do? You must not read *The Wicked Lord*. Lord Neville will know everything we have made up about him. You could pretend you'd lost the manuscript," she offered helpfully as they reached the sitting room.

"No, that would only make him suspicious," Fanny said. Seeing no alternative, she unlocked the desk drawer. "How am I going to get out of this, Bella?" she asked mournfully, as she removed the portfolio.

Before her sister could answer, Kit's voice summoned them in imperious tones to return. Fanny reluctantly followed her sister down the stairs, her arms wrapped tightly about the portfolio.

"Capital!" Kit said as his sisters entered the room. Rubbing his hands together expectantly, he peered into the shadows where Fanny had sunk into a cavernous chair.

"Why, Fan, you're practically invisible over there. Like one of Clive's ghosts. Come closer to the fire." Kit patted a chair opposite Neville. "What is the novel called?" he asked brightly as his sister slowly re-seated herself, opening the portfolio barely an inch.

"*The Old Master*," she replied without hesitation, while Arabella stared at her, open-mouthed.

"A promising title," Kit said uncertainly. "Perhaps you would like a sip of wine before you begin?" As he handed her a glass of the dark liquid, he added, "Are you going to begin at the beginning, or read a particularly horrifying part?"

"I'll read you the most recent scene," Fanny said, taking a sip.

"Perhaps you would like to give us a brief description of the story thus far," said Neville in encouraging tones.

"Of course," Fanny replied, fortified by the wine. "You see, the heroine, Miss Melinda Earnshaw, is the governess at Castle Locarno, which is the home of Lord Rothermere . . ." She glanced at Arabella, who had squeezed her eyes shut and appeared to be praying.

"Lord Rothermere is the hero?" asked Neville.

"Yes. He is an older gentleman some call 'the Old Master.' Thus, the title of my novel."

"Indeed," said Neville, frowning slightly.

Fanny produced a sheaf of papers, rattled them noisily and began reading.

That night, unable to sleep and disturbed by fitful visions, Melinda wrapped her cape about her. Carrying a single candle in its saucer, she opened the door to her bedchamber with some trepidation. The silence of the hallway beckoned to her and she issued forth, dismissing as best she could all thoughts of demons and ghosts.

Without realizing where her steps were taking her, she found herself upon the castle's battlements. She shivered in the chill midnight air but was too entranced by the moon to retreat indoors. From her position high atop the craggy walls, she contemplated the planets in their regal procession across the velvety night sky—

"Ah, most poetic," interrupted her father, swirling his brandy in a contented fashion.

"You said she's on the battlements?" queried her mother.

"Yes, Mama," Fanny replied, and accepted another glass of wine from Kit. She stole a look at Arabella, who was staring at her stonily, her features immobilized by fear. Fanny slowly winked and resumed reading.

Entranced by the view, she leaned forward, one hand resting lightly on the rough stone. It was then that Lord Rothermere appeared at the doorway. Leaning heavily upon his cane, he dragged his gamey leg with great effort, his breathing coming in stentorian gasps.

"Lord Rothermere!" Melinda uttered, startled by his presence.

"Be not afraid, my dear," he wheezed, sliding up beside her and covering her hand with his scaly one. He lifted his shaggy brows and Melinda could see his rheumy eyes glittering in the mesmerizing moonlight.

"She must be mesmerized, not to scream!" laughed Kit. "Surely this man is not the hero?"

"Why, yes, he is," Fanny said innocently. "I thought to imbue him with great character and dignity."

"I hope a priest is in attendance," offered Mrs. Feversham, "for the poor man sounds as if he hasn't long to live with that consumption."

"Is he the ghost or the demon?" asked Mr. Feversham, greatly confused.

Just then the door to the drawing room opened and Wilkins entered, bearing another bottle of brandy. He tottered unsteadily toward Mr. Feversham. Neville watched him suspiciously while Fanny resumed.

> As Lord Rothermere leaned toward her, Melinda felt his breath, sour and hot, upon her face. She averted her head slightly, overcome by emotion. She was torn between her respect for his superior rank and her affection for him as a man.
>
> With trembling fingers, he reached to untie the ribbon which bound her chestnut curls, but the gesture evidently taxed him greatly, for he gasped and clutched at his heart which beat unevenly in his consumptive chest—

The sound of someone spluttering into their glass, accompanied by various protests throughout the room, interrupted the narrative.

"Enough!" Kit commanded, alternately choking and laughing. "Really, Fan, you are gammoning us now. We plead for mercy."

"No, it's just as I have read to you," said Fanny with stern rectitude.

Neville deliberately crossed the room. As he passed behind Fanny's chair, he squinted at the manuscript pages, trying to decipher the scrawled letters.

"The old fellow doesn't topple off the battlements, does he?" asked Mr. Feversham with some concern.

"No, Papa," Fanny answered, snapping shut the portfolio as she felt Neville's stare. "He marries Melinda at the end."

"Then he must have discovered an elixir," muttered her father, shaking his head.

"Bella, dear, is this the same story Fanny has read to you?" asked Mrs. Feversham, turning to her youngest daughter.

"It bears a certain resemblance," said Arabella, gazing admiringly at her sister. Fanny seated herself on the floor next to Arabella, calmly folding her hands over the portfolio.

"My congratulations, Fanny, on the ingenious scene you have just favored us with," Neville said dryly. "But your hero did surprise me."

"As heroes are meant to do, my lord," she replied.

He smiled enigmatically and resumed his seat opposite her.

"Now we shall try something slightly more terrifying," Kit announced. He took up *The Monk* and began summarizing the complex plot, to everyone's confusion.

Neville settled back in his chair and regarded the scene before him. The Fevershams could have been a tableau by Greuze, depicting happy family life. Mrs. Feversham looked on with grudging approval as her son declaimed in broad dramatic gestures. Mr. Feversham, Neville thought, could either be listening closely or lightly sleeping. It was impossible to tell which.

His gaze rested on Fanny and Arabella, their hands intertwined, the firelight playing across their faces. Arabella huddled against Fanny for comfort, while her sister drank in Lewis's Gothic images like a cat at a bowl of milk. Neville noted the glossiness of her curls, which only a short time ago he had brushed from her face. His throat constricted at the memory of those soft lips, now parted in rapt attention. He marveled at her delicate beauty, now taking on the sensual curves of adulthood.

How was he to manage what he felt for her? She had reawakened a passion he had known once, then lost.

Could he trust himself to love another woman completely? Oddly, she had mirrored his predicament in her hero. Not the bit of foolery she had just read, but the hero she had described in the grotto. The hero who dared to love again.

11

Fanny awoke so suddenly, it took her a few moments to realize she was safe in her own bed. It must have been the storm, she reasoned. The thunder crashed outside, and rain rattled the casements in an ominous way.

Then she heard the pounding noise overriding the sound of the thunder. She lifted her head and listened. Yes, someone was definitely banging on the front door. At this hour! It had to be well past two o'clock. Making as little noise as possible, she slipped out of bed and tiptoed through the sitting room, opening the door to the corridor. She heard Wilkins fumbling with the locks, and then a stranger's voice asking for Neville.

She saw Neville open his bedroom door, tying the sash of a Turkish robe. He rapped softly on Kit's door. A whispered consultation ensued and moments later they descended the stairs.

Fanny crept further down the corridor. When she reached the stairs, she crouched behind the balustrade. By the flickering candlelight, she could make out a messenger splattered with rain and mud.

"What is it, man?" asked Kit grimly.

"Begging your pardon, sir," said the messenger in a low voice, "but I was charged by Lady Stanbury to see that his lordship received this tonight. I was not to return until I had delivered it into his hands." So saying, he reached into a leather satchel and withdrew a sealed packet which he handed to Neville.

Fanny peered through the darkness, trying to make out the expression on Neville's face, but he merely tapped the packet against his palm irritably.

"Thank you, my good man," he said. "I'll send my valet down with a sovereign for you."

"Wilkins, see that this fellow gets some whisky, and whatever else he requires," Kit instructed.

After reading the message, Neville paced fitfully up and down the hall, swearing under his breath. "Damn the woman! Of all the impertinence!"

Kit opened the door to the library and lit some candles, keeping a companionable silence until his friend was ready to speak. He poured two glasses of brandy while Neville scanned the note once more.

"The devil take her." He balled up the paper and flung it into the grate, tossing down his liquor just as quickly. He held out his glass, and Kit refilled it.

"She pursues you even in your rustication?"

"More than that. Now she adds threats to her troublemaking," Neville snarled. He paced back and forth and paused at the doorway, staring out into the gloom of the hall. "Just when happiness seemed within my grasp." He turned back to face Kit. "She begs me to return to London, without delay. The damnable thing is, I can't see any way to get out of it."

"What is her reason this time?"

"It seems, my dear Kit, that Lord Stanbury has threatened to divorce her by an Act of Parliament."

"Good Lord, why? They have always had a marriage of convenience. Neither can be much surprised by the other's affairs."

"True. But according to her letter, he will institute proceedings tomorrow unless I am there to deny his allegations. Evidently, she has placed him in a position where he can no longer ignore her conduct.''

"Why must you be part of this?"

"There is mention of a duel," Neville said cynically, staring into his brandy, "although that sounds more like her invention than his. Stanbury is no fool." He laughed despairingly. "We are to have it out at last—all in the name of love. What a sordid business."

"You would be well rid of her," Kit said softly.

"That is why I came to Henley, but I was a fool to think that distance and time would lessen her interest. No, she will not retire from the field gracefully." Neville rubbed his forehead and sighed pensively. "Yet, I cannot lay all the blame at Olivia's feet. She is but one small part of my London existence. I cannot say it has been altogether good for me."

"London is a veritable garden of delights," Kit said warmly. "I cannot imagine life without Tattersall's, the clubs, the theater. All the Corinthians are there. You belong there, Neville."

"Perhaps," Neville said shortly. "But, I didn't see my life in its entirety until I came here. Until I met . . . your family. You've been more than a friend, Kit." He clapped his friend on the shoulder. "I should dress now. It's close to dawn and I can reach London by evening. I'd rather not share this news with the household."

As they came out of the library and crossed the entrance hall, Fanny retreated along the upstairs corridor. She could hear Neville's voice clearly now.

"I shall thank your family properly from town. It is a shabby way to repay their many kindnesses, but I must rely upon you to make my amends. Jenkins can follow with my things."

"Perhaps I should follow you in a day or so," Kit offered. "To act as your second and dispose of your bodily remains after the duel."

"It would be capital of you!" Neville said warmly.

"I don't fancy dying just yet, though. Too embarrassing to be pierced by Stanbury. A portlier swordsman I never saw."

Fanny slipped behind the door to her sitting room as Neville entered his bedroom, instructing Jenkins to prepare for departure. Probably the happiest moment in the valet's life, Fanny thought glumly. She sat in a chair by the window, her heart as heavy as a stone.

She hugged her knees to her chest, and stared out the window into the lessening storm. Lightning still flashed through the roiling clouds but struck at the earth less often.

Feeling hopeless, she considered what course of action, if any, she should take. Should she creep into Neville's room and declare her undying love? While Jenkins helped him on with his boots? She could hear drawers being flung open and Neville instructing his valet.

And what of Neville? Would he not pity her for trying, as so many had tried before, to bind him to her in some way with a word, a gesture, a kiss? No, he wanted to depart quickly, without anyone knowing of his predicament. She had no choice but to remain still and silent and watch him ride away.

Would Stanbury challenge him? Somehow, she thought not. Neville was reckoned both an excellent swordsman and shot. Certainly, a duel would not be in Stanbury's best interest. It seemed more like Lady Stanbury's melodramatic invention—the desperate move of a woman playing her last card.

Sounds of movement in the corridor reached her. She ran to her sitting room door and opened it slightly. She could see Jenkins, loaded down with portmanteaux, emerge from the bedroom followed by his master, dressed in a flowing greatcoat and curly beaver hat.

"Don't try to make the journey in one day," Neville instructed quietly.

A beatific smile spread over Jenkins's features. "To think, sir, I'll soon be in Piccadilly." He scurried down the corridor. Neville watched him leave and paused, pulling on his gloves as nonchalantly as if he were dressing for a ball. He turned in the direction of Fanny's room. Narrowing his eyes against the darkness, he said in a low voice, "Fanny, is that you?"

"Yes. I heard the messenger at the door." She opened the door wider as he approached, unmindful of being lightly clad in her nightgown and wrapper.

"Little vixen," he murmured with a concerned look. He stood very close to her. "You heard, then?"

"Everything," she whispered.

He laughed softly. "I am not surprised. A vixen is a very alert creature." With a gloved hand, he stroked her cheek tenderly, then, with an apparent effort, withdrew it. "I must go. Please do not judge me too harshly, Fanny." Forcing a lighter tone, he added, "I thought we would have more time together, but alas, it is not to be." He took her hand in his and kissed it. "I shall miss you, my dear."

"I, too," she stammered out.

His eyes burned into hers for a moment, then assumed a more distant expression. "I suppose the next time I see you, you shall be waltzing with admiring beaus."

Fanny made no reply. A wall of artificiality had arisen between them, making intimacy impossible.

"Julian, please . . ." She reached out, grasping his sleeve.

He squeezed her hand briefly and gently removed it. "Goodbye for now, my dear." He turned and walked away, taking the stairs quickly. The front door opened and closed.

The groom had led Tammuz to the front of the house and now held the bridle, trying to quiet the restless stallion. Neville mounted and adjusted the reins. His glance took in the pedimented doorway, beginning to warm in the dawning light. He wondered if he would ever set eyes on Henley Hall again. Just to the left of the doorway was Fanny's bedroom window. Poor little creature. He had made a mess of things just now, but it was best not to encourage her any more than he already had.

The stallion shifted beneath him, eager to be off. He leaned down and patted its neck. He should never have kissed her. He was sure of that. But then, he had never been so tempted. She possessed a wild and tender spirit. To subject it to town life would be a shame. Without success he tried to imagine her as a Hyde Park beauty, riding a blood bay with haughty elegance.

No, Fanny was cut from a different cloth entirely. He stared at the window and touched his riding crop to the brim of his hat in farewell. What had she said about heroes? That they were meant to surprise people. He was no hero, of that he was sure. The sooner Fanny knew it, the better.

He shook hands with Kit, and spurred Tammuz into a gallop as dawn began to break.

12

Neville's sudden departure aroused little comment from the Fevershams. They deduced from Kit's breezy account that it had been precipitated by an unforseen misfortune. Yet Henley's fashionable guest was held in such high regard that any speculative gossip was quickly discouraged. In due course, a letter arrived from London containing Neville's apologies, his profuse thanks for the family's hospitality and his continued hopes for their good health. The tone was discreet and no mention was made of his hasty exit.

The sight of the monogrammed paper caused Fanny to catch her breath. She touched the letter tentatively, then quickly withdrew her hand. Despite Neville's fine words, it was clear she had been little more to him than a mild flirtation. Their farewell had been tinged with a remoteness that left her feeling unaccountably betrayed.

Kit's leave-taking a few days later sent Fanny into an even deeper despair. He was her last link to Neville and the golden October days they had shared. Despite his promises to return soon, she keenly felt the absence of his high spirits and comforting presence.

During the next few weeks, life at Henley shifted and settled like a great oak tree after a high wind. Gradually the routines resumed a more sedentary pace. Once, Fanny saw Brutus sniffing at the door to Neville's bedroom, looking for signs of Kit's friend. She patted him on the head, murmuring, "Poor Brutus, you must learn not to miss him so much."

There was so much to miss—his elegant air, his quick discernment, his dry humor, his refinement and masculine grace. He had become more than her friend—he had become her lover for a brief moment. But at the final parting, he had taken it all away.

Her wounded feelings prevented her from seeking news of him. The papers and gossip sheets she and Arabella had once so assiduously consumed only seemed to mock her attachment. The reports of his social appearances and *bon mots* that had once fueled her imagination now acted merely as irritants.

One morning, as she listlessly examined the latest copy of *La Belle Assemblée*, Arabella flew in, a newspaper tucked under her arm.

"There you are, Fan—we have been looking everywhere for you. Much news today. I have stolen *The Morning Chronicle* from Papa. It describes Neville's attendance at the opera."

"Oh?" said Fanny, trying to disguise her irritation. "Very well, I can see you won't be gainsaid. Read it, if you must."

"'If you must.' Really, Fan, aren't you a quiz today," Arabella replied, bewildered. "Here it is:

> *Last night the King's Theatre in Haymarket witnessed more than the beloved Catalani making a successful debut as Cherubino in* Le Nozzi di Figaro. *The audience beheld another equally impressive performance as Lord Neville joined the fashionable gathering in the box of Lord and Lady Stanbury. Her ladyship wore a stunning set of rubies, reported to have been purchased by her husband in Paris. Lord Neville's appearance put to*

*rest all rumors of a rift between the two parties.
Lord and Lady Stanbury, accompanied by Lord
Neville and Lady Gramercy and her niece, left before the final curtain. They were later seen at a
waltzing party given by the Countess Lieven ... "*

"Well?" asked Arabella significantly.

"Well, what?" Fanny replied shortly. "I don't see
anything so astonishing about it."

"But, Fan, think of it. Wasn't Lady Stanbury the reason he came to Henley? Kit mentioned something of it
to me. Lord Neville hoped to let matters cool. And now
it appears he's back in the basket."

"What is your point, Bella?" Fanny snapped.

"My point is, why did he bother to come here at all?"

"Why, indeed?" Fanny answered, feeling more mo-
rose each second. She was losing all patience with her
sister and her sap-skulled questions.

"You are quite impossible today, Fanny. I thought
you would like to know the latest about Lord Neville.
That it might inspire you to write about Lord Rothermere. You have quite abandoned him these last few
weeks, you know."

"Yes, I suppose I have," Fanny replied disconso-
lately.

Sensing her sister's black mood, Arabella folded the
paper primly and made ready to go. She dawdled at the
door. "I suppose it wouldn't have anything to do with
you having lost your head over Lord Neville, would it?"
she asked impertinently.

"You noxious ninnyhammer!" Fanny shouted, hurl-
ing a pillow at her sister. "No, it certainly would not!
If anyone looked like a lovesick spaniel the whole time
it was you!"

The sight of her sister's smirking countenance drove
Fanny back to Lord Rothermere that evening. With renewed zeal, she applied herself to *The Wicked Lord*,
writing well into the night.

Often she was tempted to write Neville directly and tell him that she thought him shallow, vain and hypocritical. Once, she took out a sheet of paper, dipped her pen in the inkstand and couldn't find the words to begin. Beneath her overriding anger and disappointment, her emotions were too mixed. To contact him personally would, indeed, be improper. Each day that passed without word from him was more proof of his indifference.

But even when most enraged by his aloofness, her body betrayed her. With an undeniable yearning, she longed to feel his arms holding her again. At times she cursed the passion they had shared. It seemed to have silenced all other forms of communication.

Yet in the safe, anonymous world of ink and foolscap, she could pour out her feelings for him as she couldn't in real life. As Neville receded into memory with each passing week, Lord Rothermere came more alive. Neville's strengths were magnified in Rothermere, just as his faults were.

Every time the *Chronicle* reported him at a ball with a Mrs. Chalmers-Carlyle, or at a rout with a Miss Danvers, or supping with Catalani and a troupe of opera dancers, Melinda reacted as Fanny could not. Although her heroine still loved Rothermere, she was bewildered by his coldness, hurt by his selfishness, and she spoke her thoughts aloud without hesitation. Rothermere's tragic flaw was his pride, which had prevented him from telling his young wife that he loved her. Fanny came to enjoy describing her hero's suffering as he told Melinda how Count Orsini had insinuated himself between Lord and Lady Rothermere.

Lord Rothermere fixed Melinda with a glittering stare. "As soon as Count Orsini saw how it was between my wife and me he began to work upon her, pointing out my infidelities, convincing her I no longer cared for her. She appealed to me. If only I had listened. Within a month of his arrival he had persuaded her to run away with him.''

''Oh!'' exclaimed Melinda, horrified at the scandal.

''When I discovered his infamy I called him out. We dueled and he marked me for life,'' Rothermere indicated his forearm etched with a long white scar, ''as you see. I wounded him, but not fatally. Not six months later, my wife died from illness brought upon by a broken heart. All of this could have avoided had I not been consumed by such damnable pride.''

Fanny sat back, admiring the phrasing in this last passage. She was determined that by story's end, Rothermere would fight, as never before, to win Melinda's love.

Shouts of laughter rang out over the pond where skaters raced and spun in the black December night. As Fanny skimmed across the glazed surface, her spirits soared as they hadn't since Neville's departure. She pirouetted neatly, sending up icy slivers. She plunged her hands more deeply into her fur muff, warming them against the freezing night air.

Carefully tended fires blazed along the bank. Skaters gathered around them to warm their hands and enjoy steaming cups of hot cocoa. Fanny recognized Bella's screams of protest as Brandon Winthrop propelled her away from the fire and onto the ice. Lines of young bucks, their arms intertwined, flew across the ice at dizzying speeds. At a command they changed direction, sending the last man on the line hurtling into darkness.

A lone skater cannonballed toward her, grinding to a stop just a few feet short of collision.

''Care to join the whip, Fan?'' Brandon asked.

''Of course,'' she replied eagerly.

''Not too many girls on this one, but I knew you'd suit,'' Brandon said as they joined the line.

''Am I to be on the end?'' she asked nervously, as

the skaters began to move out slowly toward the center of the pond.

"'Fraid that's the case." Brandon winked.

As the pace quickened, Fanny found she could barely keep up. They were nearing the edge of the pond when their leader suddenly halted, causing the line to wind around him. She spun faster and faster, bending low over her skates to reduce the wind's impact. A dizzying panorama of blazing bonfires whirled before her. She felt her hand gradually slipping from Brandon's grasp, until she could no longer keep hold.

She flew across the ice like a stone released from a slingshot. In the darkness, with no way of calculating her direction, she prayed to be spared crashing against the rocks at the pond's edge.

A half second before colliding with him, she saw a man in a tall black hat, his arms outstretched to receive her. She hurtled into him, knocking them both to the ground. They thrashed about, trying to find their footing on the ice.

"Ooof. Fine go, Fan, I think you've knocked me daffy." The young man rubbed his temple and looked about for his hat.

"Kit!" Fanny exclaimed, almost too stunned to think. "When did you get here?"

"About a second ago. Formerly, I stood ten feet in that direction."

"You clodpole," she laughed, tousling his hair. She looked up to see Brandon appearing out of the darkness. In his dash to aid the struggling pair, he had picked up Kit's hat.

"Look who's here, Brandon. It's Kit!"

"Nice catch, Kit," said their host affably, returning the hat. "Sorry about the whip, Fan. You did dashed better than any of those coves would have." After helping them to their feet, he invited them to warm themselves by the fire and enjoy some hot cocoa.

"Arggh! Bless me, Fan, if you don't pack a wallop."

Kit placed both hands against his back, as if to straighten it, then settled his hat on his head at a rakish angle. "I could do with something hot. Care to join me?"

Fanny looped her arm inside her brother's, more glad than ever for his company.

"Your correspondence hasn't been its usual voluminous quantity," her brother chided, as they found two unoccupied tree stumps near a roaring fire. "In fact, it's been quite lacking altogether."

"I couldn't find much to write about," Fanny said shyly. "Besides, it is much better having you here. We didn't look for you this soon. Usually you can't be pried out of London until Christmas Eve."

"Truthfully, Fan, I come not just on my own account. Like Mercury, I bring messages from the gods."

"Oh? For me?" she asked quickly. An anxious feeling gripped her heart and she immediately thought of Neville. At that moment, a member of the whip skated up, proffered two steaming cups of cocoa and departed.

"Yes, you minx. Had to don a pair of these to find you." Kit unstrapped his skates and held them up for inspection. "Haven't been on a pair of cursed skates since I was ten." Kit took a sip of cocoa, then withdrew a bulging letter from his coat pocket. "My first item of business is a missive to you, dear sister, from our cousin, Alethia, or Lady Lansden as she is better known by the *ton*."

"Alethia? Why is she writing me?" Fanny asked, trying to hide her disappointment.

"Dunno. But I assume it regards your come-out. Our cousin is a great rattle, and she talks of nothing else but when you and Arabella will be in London."

Fanny gulped down her cocoa and stared at her brother. "You mean she has been calling upon you?"

"'Harassing' is the more exact term, if you must know. She pesters me daily for news of your arrival."

"How does this concern me?" Fanny said, turning the letter over in her hand.

"Our cousin has many weaknesses, as you know, Fan," Kit said airily. "One of her greatest faults is her curiosity. Seems it's been whetted by some rumor she's heard recently. Wouldn't enlighten me, but wants to be your chief confidante in London, etcetera." He tapped the letter. "Probably says it all in here."

"How very strange," said Fanny in a small voice.

"My second bit of business," Kit continued, lightly running his finger along his skate's blade, "is to convey Lord Neville's warmest greetings."

"I am surprised," Fanny said with some asperity, "that he could spare time from his entertainments to think of us."

" 'Entertainments!' " hooted Kit, "I like that—if you can call a man who discharges his social duties like a corpse entertained."

"But what of the opera girls, Miss Danvers, Lady Catskin? What of Lady Stanbury?" Fanny asked accusingly.

"What addled wheezebag has concocted these stories, Fan?"

"The papers, Kit. According to them, Neville has attended every revel since his return."

"Take my word for it, Fan," said Kit earnestly, "those reports are greatly exaggerated. You know some of this business about Lady Stanbury. He barely managed to outwit her little plot. Part of his incessant activity is to keep her at arm's length. His interest clearly lies elsewhere. He pleaded fatigue to Miss Danvers and her chaperon, then drank himself into a stupor at Brooks's. I had to see him home."

He stood quickly, taking his sister's cup. "Read Alethia's letter and I'll see about finding us more of this."

Fanny moved to the light of a fire and opened her cousin's letter with some trepidation. Alethia never contacted anyone unless she wanted something from them. The effusive greeting and trivial tone were all-too familiar. On the fourth page, the writer began warming to her subject.

> *... I now come to the real reason for my writing, dearest cousin. It is common knowledge that Kit's dear friend, and no doubt your dear friend, Lord Neville, spent a delightful time at Henley. Now it is rumored he harbors a tendresse for a young girl there ...*

Fanny stared at the page, barely able to countenance Alethia's outrageous speculation, yet desperate to know more.

> *Those who know him well say he is greatly changed. One of his chief critics is Lady Stanbury, who is monstrously jealous of any rivals. According to my valet's gossip, there were two Feversham girls, one a Beauty and the other a Sprite. I imagine Arabella to be the former and you the latter. What of this news? All of London thinks he has chosen the Beauty. It is only I who know her identity. Please write to me if you know anything of this attachment and I will be Silence itself ...*

Fanny gasped. Under no circumstances could she imagine Alethia being Silence itself—not when such a drama was being played out beneath her nose.

She pressed her cold fingers against her burning temples. It was unthinkable that the *ton* might connect Arabella with Neville. Fanny immediately felt protective of her sister, unable to imagine a worse fate than being the subject of the tittle-tattle of Alethia and her set—those sharp-eyed, sharp-tongued ladies of fashion.

Then another thought struck her. What if Alethia, despite her muddled thinking, had gotten it partly right, that Neville did harbor a *tendresse* for a certain Miss

Feversham? What if it was *she* whom he loved, not Arabella?

Fanny shook her head at her own foolishness. She was becoming as bad as Alethia, and she hadn't even set foot in London yet.

She gratefully accepted the cocoa Kit brought her and wrapped her fingers about the steaming cup. Too much Gothic fiction was the cause of these cork-brained ideas, she decided. She took a sip of the sweet, hot liquid and marveled at how much it warmed the world around her.

13

It was just past two in the morning as Neville, accompanied by his friend, William Withycombe, fifteenth Earl of Dunsanay, entered No. 54 Piccadilly Square. Neither appeared especially foxed, although their erect postures only partially belied their true condition.

"You'll find the brandy in there, Dunsanay," Neville offered. His friend, already well-acquainted with the whereabouts of the brandy, steered majestically into the drawing room, listing slightly to the left and ricocheting off the doorjamb.

Neville paused before the heavily gilded mirror that dominated the narrow hallway. He swept off his evening cape and let it fall halfway onto the nearest chair. With slow precision, he removed his hat and gloves and placed them on the marble-topped table. He looked into the mirror with a sour expression. No amount of drinking and dancing could disguise the dissatisfaction he had felt since leaving Henley.

By anyone's account the evening would have been reckoned a success. Yet he was like a gourmand whose palate yearned for something simple and sustaining. He longed to see a certain little Greek dress, trimmed with blue ribbons.

"I say there, Neville, if you've done admiring your-self, I'd be glad for some company," drawled Dunsanay.

Neville riffled through the stacks of invitations that filled the Chinese porcelain bowl. He was about to join Dunsanay, when one caught his eye.

The paper was white, simple, neither thick nor finely grained. The return address was Henley. He was on the verge of ripping it open when Dunsanay appeared, glass in hand, lounging against the doorway. Neville slipped the letter into his waistcoat, causing his friend to frown.

"Must be from a female admirer to make you look like that. I can't think of a single woman I look forward to hearing from, and yet I'm deluged with letters from them each day."

Neville entered the drawing room, followed by Dunsanay, still discoursing. "There are only a few whose scribblings I can bear to read. And if my correspondent is likely to be particularly boring, I give the letter away to whatever friend has come calling that morning."

"I wonder who you punish more: your admirer or your friend?" Neville swirled the dark liquid against the sides of his glass slowly.

"Most acute of you, Neville." Dunsanay strolled over to the ormolu mirror above the mantel and adjusted the points of his collar, which reached just below his ears. Because of the enormous amount of starch they contained, they restricted his movements considerably. Addressing someone not squarely before him required turning his entire upper body. He did so now.

"One of my supplicants was that silly Lady Lansden. She was making great cow eyes at you tonight, by the way."

"Ah, she can lead a ferocious attack, but Lady Stanbury had formed her defensive guard by then," Neville murmured.

Dunsanay stared pointedly at Neville's waistcoat. "Is the lady someone I might know?"

Neville merely smiled. "It is from a member of Kit's family."

"Ah, yes, the Feversham girls. One quite beautiful. The other rather wild." Dunsanay was again engrossed in the mirror, fluffing out his hair with little flourishes. "Shall I like them when you finally introduce us?"

"Kit's family is exceedingly kind," replied Neville, looking away. Usually he was amused by Dunsanay's brittle wit, but tonight he was anxious to be rid of him.

"Kind. Ummm. Something I certainly am not. But then, I like Kit well enough, although he can be a bit racketing at times. Perhaps I shall like them, too. I shall try."

"Please don't try, Dunsanay. That's when you're at your worst."

"Speaking of my worst, I believe my conversation has reached a new nadir." He took out his watch, examined it and snapped it shut. "Really must go, Neville. You look quite prostrate with boredom."

When his friend made no objection, Dunsanay donned his cape in one graceful movement. Neville watched with grudging admiration. The dandy's élan was unrivaled.

Dunsanay paused and rested the head of his cane against Neville's chest. "Have a care for your friends, old chap. Kindness is not rewarded in our world. It is the ones like Lady Stanbury who succeed."

Neville saw him out, watching him disappear into the fog of Mayfair toward a waiting carriage.

He closed the door and immediately removed the letter from his pocket. It took him a few seconds to realize it was not from Fanny but from Mrs. Feversham, thanking him for his latest letter which offered his assistance when they arrived in London. He blinked, disbelieving. Had the brandy so clouded his brain that he had seized upon the first small shred of hope that came his way?

He entered the drawing room and sat close to the fire, running his fingers through his hair. He returned to Mrs.

Feversham's letter, scanning it for any mention of Fanny. "We greatly look forward to seeing you when the Season begins," she wrote. "I believe that our dear Arabella will take at once, for she has greater use for a husband than Fanny."

Neville's smile of recognition froze on his face. A husband. By gad, he had nearly forgotten the whole purpose of the enterprise. He sank back in his chair, struck by the realization that Fanny might actually be wed. But to what sort of fellow? He would have to be a neck-or-nothing horseman, he would have to have at least five thousand a year . . . possibly, a likeable young member of Brooks's.

Neville jabbed at the fire with the tongs. Why did the thought of Fanny marrying fill him with excessive anxiety? Perhaps *he* should marry her. No, no; she was far too young, too spirited, too vulnerable. He had always presumed that if he married at all, it would be to a worldly, fashionable woman, one without illusions, without much expectation of love.

He stared petulantly at the letter that lay on the table. Perhaps her mother was right. Perhaps, with no great use for a husband, Fanny would not find one. He would prefer that. He would like her to remain just as she was at Henley.

But change was inevitable. One day she would marry, of that he was certain. His only choice, then, was to watch her drift away until she became someone else's wife. Or to make her his own. He laughed silently. To think how he had eagerly awaited each day's correspondence. Like a love-sick puppy! Ridiculous! He had been in love before—in love? There, he had said it. Was he in love with Fanny?

He thought again of their kiss in the grotto, of her ardent response, the exquisite feel of her slim, strong body pressed against his. Poor little sprite, he thought. He had been a heartless brute to leave her as he had.

He pocketed the letter, realizing that Fanny was not a

child to be pitied. She had acquitted herself admirably in reading them that make-believe novel. And to reply as she did to his jest about heroes showed she had brains. He slowly savored his brandy and admitted that, thus far, she had always managed to surprise him.

Scribbling away slavishly, Fanny was concluding the final scene of *The Wicked Lord*. Surrounded by several large candelabra, she worked at the big table in the library. Clad in her nightdress and wrapper, she had stolen downstairs to work near the fire.

She paused to stir the flickering flames and shivered, but not with cold. Her nocturnal labor afforded her deep delight. She poured out her passions while, in the bedchambers above, her family slept—with the exception of Kit. Braving the snowdrifts, he had gone to see Little Joey, a notorious local bulldog, fight a sackfull of rats at a nearby barn.

As the flames leapt up, they illuminated the tears that coursed down her cheeks. Fanny's resolve to bring Rothermere to a new low had caused Melinda to despair of ever winning his love. Melinda's abduction by Count Orsini had finally roused Rothermere from his bitter reveries. He had challenged the scoundrel to a duel.

It took place on an alpine precipice. As they fought, Rothermere narrowly missed tumbling into the abyss. In a final desperate lunge, he ran Orsini through. With Melinda clinging to Rothermere's side, they watched as he plunged to his death among the crags below.

Embracing Melinda, Rothermere asked, "Wilt thou have me, my precious angel? I am scarred, and proud as Lucifer, but I am pledged to you, whether you will have me or no."

Nearly fainting, Melinda replied, "We can be happy now, for you are finally free of the past, my lord."

Then he crushed her mouth to his, murmuring,
"Oh, my heavenly one."

Brushing away the tears that were flowing copiously,
Fanny wrote *Finis* at the bottom of the page. There, it
was done. She sighed deeply. She had given her heroine
what she herself most deeply desired—a happy ending
with the man she adored.

Warmed by the thought of a small glass of brandy
and a snug fire Kit entered the library, only to find his
sister with her head in her arms, an unruly stack of papers bulging from her portfolio.

"What's all this about, Fan?" he asked, taken aback
by her distress. He raised her tear-stained face to the
light. "This will never do, y'know." He wiped her
cheeks with his handkerchief. "Good thing I happened
along just now. A minute more and you would have
drowned."

He exhorted her to blow her nose, which she promptly
did.

"You look properly blue-devilled, my girl. You'd feel
better if you'd seen Little Joey go after those rats.
Grabbed 'em as fast as they came out of the sack. Bang,
bang, bang. Even caught some in mid-air." Kit shook
his head admiringly. "Amazing animal, that bulldog."

"Did you win any bets?" Fanny asked hoarsely.

"Only a couple of fivers," said her brother, pulling
some notes from his pocket. "Bet against a couple of
lads from Bradford who said Joey wasn't up to snuff.
But all the farmers were backing him, so I put my money
with theirs."

He sat on the edge of the table and rested his boot
against the grate. "Hullo, what have we here?" He
lightly tapped the cover of the portfolio. "Isn't this your
story about that gouty fellow? If you're crying over that
rubbishy old man, I have a mind to pitch it in the
flames."

He made as if to hurl the portfolio into the fire and Fanny seized hold of it. "No, no, Kit! It is dearer to me than anything!"

"Then it must contain more of a story than that gammon you read us," he teased. "Fan, you must promise to let me read it when you're done."

"I *am* done . . ." she said softly. "I finished it tonight." Struck by an idea, she rested her hand on his sleeve. "Oh, Kit, could you read it, and give me your opinion? Tell me if the characters engage your interest. I trust your judgment in this matter more than anyone's."

He took the proffered volume and affected surprise at its weight. "I hope it has plenty of swagger and adventure, Fan."

"As well as gothic gloom and passion," she said, laughing a little. She watched anxiously as he took a seat and opened to the first page. He undid his cravat slightly and cleared his throat ominously.

"*The Wicked Lord*," he intoned in a thunderous stage voice. "Who could that be, I wonder?" He smiled at her mischievously. "Ripping title, Fan." After several coughs and much repositioning in his chair, he settled down to read in earnest. Fanny gnawed at her knuckles and stared at him.

Would he recognize Neville as her hero? If so, would he see through her thinly disguised fantasy, perceiving her real feelings for his friend? Or would he accept the story for what it was . . . a tale of adventure written to entertain? She couldn't bear the thought of Kit being bored by it. But then, the only book she had ever seen him read was a copy of *Tom Jones*. He read it once a year and always pronounced it a thumping great tale.

Kit emitted a pleased "Aha!" and fell silent again, peering at the page with great concentration. He took out a large cigar from his pocket and Fanny fetched him a lighted straw. She held the flame to the cigar and he puffed mightily until the cigar was lit, never taking his eyes from the page. After a few minutes he glanced up, regarding her closely.

"Demned fine thing you've done here, Fan. Not bad at all. I like this Rothermere chap well enough, although he's a bit proud. Must have been jolly good company in his younger days." He scraped back his chair and rose, still holding the portfolio. He settled onto the sofa, saying in a distracted manner, "Reminds me of someone, can't think who."

Fanny sighed with relief, thankful that he hadn't recognized Neville in Rothermere. She hastily put away the quill and inkstand. "I'm going to bed now, Kit." She kissed him on the cheek. "It's very late. Wouldn't you rather retire?"

"No, I'd rather savor my cigar . . . and my book." He gave her an arch look. "I don't see any signs of the hobbling hero yet."

Fanny laughed. "He figured in it but a short while."

Kit marked his place with some care. "Now, Fan, I must ask you to lend this to me. I promise I'll read it as fast as I can. And I won't let it fall into anyone else's hands." At her sharp intake of breath, he added, "Like Mater and Pater, you goose."

"Very well, Kit. You may keep it."

"I can see that it's going to be as full of twists and turns as *Tom Jones*." Kit riffled through a few pages and marked a passage with his forefinger. "I quite like this swordfight on the castle stairs. Shows Rothermere full of blood and bluster and aching to skewer that cad, Orsini."

"I'm so happy you like it, Kit!" She beamed at her brother and went upstairs to bed.

He puffed contentedly on his cigar, lost in the world she had created.

* * *

A few days later, Kit, wearing a very mysterious expression, summoned his sister to the library. After she had shut the door, he went to the bookcase that held old maps and rummaged through them. At last he produced the green portfolio.

"I've nearly finished it, Fan," he said gravely.

"And what did you think?" She clutched at her throat, unable to read the meaning behind his expression.

"It's spectacular," he said, laughing at her concern. "Easily as good as Monk Lewis. Maybe better."

"Kit, you are too partial." She was both embarrassed and greatly pleased.

"I must ask you one very great favor."

"Yes, whatever you like."

"I would like to take it to London with me." When he saw her look of alarm, he added quickly. "As you know, I'm required to attend Dunsanay's Twelfth Night ball, and I want to finish it." As his sister touched the portfolio affectionately, he added, "Don't look at me like I'm stealing your child, Fan. I have to know how it ends. You have my word that I'll take the greatest possible care of it. Why, you'll be in London in no time and you can reclaim it."

"I suppose it's all right," she said dubiously. She could not rid herself of the trepidation she felt. Kit had never asked her for anything. But what he wanted now was nearly impossible to give. How could she explain what the book meant to her? It was all that was left of her connection to Neville.

Yet it would seem odd if she refused. Reluctantly, she nodded. "You must promise not to show it to anyone else, Kit. I must make this extremely clear. You may want to share it with other . . . friends."

He gazed at her with a gambler's eye, coolly assessing the odds. "I promise to show it to no other friends," he said at last and smiled. "But you do yourself a disservice, Fan, to limit your audience so."

"Oh, Kit, you *are* silly." She smiled back at him, her eyes shining. "But remember, not another soul."

After she left, he returned the portfolio to its hiding place with a thoughtful look. Then, whistling a cheerful tune, he strode out of the library, glad that his bluff had worked.

14

With a sense of awe, Fanny again inspected the Fevershams' London drawing room. It was one of the most agreeable places she had ever seen. Kit had shown remarkable taste in choosing their quarters for the Season. The walls were covered with silk in azure blue and cream stripes. Sunlight streamed through enormous floor-to-ceiling windows, burnishing the elegant furniture neatly arranged throughout the room.

Fanny gazed out one of the windows into the bustle of Duke Street. Never before had she seen so many fine carriages, all newly painted and drawn by splendidly matched horses. High perch phaetons strove to overtake more stately landaulets, while an occasional vis-à-vis caused everyone's head to turn.

"Gemini," she murmured, as a pair of dappled greys drawing a shiny new curricle came into view.

The streets of St. James alone held enough sights to entertain her for months on end. Though she had barely had time to unpack, she was already beginning to feel at home. With each passing day, her longing for Henley lessened a little more.

"Now, Miss Feversham, no more daydreaming."

Miss Wigmore's brisk entrance curtailed all further reveries. The diminutive woman efficiently rearranged a few chairs while Arabella stood patiently, waiting for their lesson to begin.

"Today we shall practice the proper way to enter a room and seat ourselves." Miss Wigmore's tone made it clear that any resistance was useless.

Mrs. Feversham had acted upon Lord Neville's recommendation of Miss Beatrice Wigmore as the ideal person to give the girls polish. It had taken Fanny little time to realize that Miss Wigmore's small stature was misleading, for she possessed the iron will of Old Nosey and the physical prowess of Tom Belcher.

"Please observe."

The two girls watched as Miss Wigmore left the room, and immediately reentered in a gliding motion. She paused before a chair and swept her skirts aside. Then, with seemingly no effort, she sank gracefully upon its edge, maintaining an erect posture and an alert pose.

"You see, girls, carriage is everything. A lady signals her degree of refinement by the way she holds herself." Miss Wigmore made a deprecating sweep in the direction of her hips. "We must triumph over the lower regions by holding the upper regions permanently aloft." She looked pointedly into the center of the room and pantomimed conversation, her head tilting gracefully from side to side in little birdlike movements.

Fanny stared at her mentor awestruck. Miss Wigmore was possibly the most intimidating female she had ever encountered, correcting faults with the precision of a drill sergeant.

"Try it, girls, one at a time," she commanded.

First Arabella, then Fanny practiced gliding through the door, holding their heads aloft, their eyes glassy with concentration.

"How are we to find a chair if we can't look down?" Fanny asked, her eyes glued on the opposite wall.

"You may glance down but do not incline your

head,'' Miss Wigmore responded. ''That's right, Miss Arabella, slowly lower yourself, but keep your body straight. Do not forget to breathe, Miss Feversham. There, you've found the chair. Steady, ah, perfect!'' She clapped politely at her pupils' labors, then said breezily, ''Tomorrow we shall try fans. On Wednesday, we combine fans and conversation.''

Fanny felt overwhelmed. How would she ever be able to talk if she was concentrating on sitting up straight and managing a fan?

''Do not dally, girls. Stand before this mirror, and we will practice our curtsies.''

Fanny sighed despondently. She had never realized that a lady's life could be so complex. Mama had taught them how to be decorous and polite. But Miss Wigmore examined every detail of movement, dress, and speech.

''Now, girls, you must hold your skirt very delicately. *Comme çi.* Observe how I have placed my feet. Very good, Miss Feversham. When you curtsy, keep your shoulders even.''

The sisters copied Miss Wigmore's sinking motion. Fanny struggled not to lean to one side as she slowly descended, keeping her weight on her back foot. With her head bowed, she had just reached her lowest point when Miss Wigmore's voice rang out.

''Ah, Lord Neville, what a pleasure!'' Her teacher rose gracefully, while Fanny glanced quickly into the mirror and saw Neville in the doorway.

He dropped his quizzing glass nonchalantly. ''Most admirable curtsies, dear girls,'' he observed.

Fanny stood hastily, smoothing her dress and trying to stop the blush that crept into her cheeks. The sight of him after so many months filled her with unspeakable agitation. All this time without a word, then to appear so suddenly . . . He was more the nonpareil than ever, she couldn't help noticing, dressed in a tight-fitting bluish-black coat.

''Lord Neville, how happy we are to see you! Mama

has read us your letters. We have missed you greatly," Arabella burbled.

"I can see I am warmly remembered by at least one Miss Feversham," he drawled, depositing his walking stick. He looked pointedly at Fanny.

"It is true, my lord," she said coolly. "We have all been hoping you would call on us."

"Thank you, Miss Feversham. You will pardon my intrusion, Miss Wigmore," he said politely, "but I could not resist seeing how your pupils are progressing."

"Quite well, my lord," she replied.

"Do you think they are civilized enough to be taken out in public?" he asked. "The last time I saw them, they were a bit wild."

"I assure you, my lord, their manners are above reproach." Miss Wigmore busied herself about the room. "Our lesson today is very nearly done."

"Then perhaps you will permit me to invite you and your charges to accompany me tonight to Drury Lane. Along with their parents and brother, we shall be a small army."

"Oh, the theater! How exciting!" Arabella clapped enthusiastically. "Please say we might go, Miss Wigmore!"

"You have already asked their parents?" she inquired sternly.

"Of course. Mrs. Feversham's reaction was much the same as Miss Arabella's, but she felt you would be the best judge of their progress."

"Hmmm." Miss Wigmore was lost in thought. "They are not very good with fans yet, and they know very little of how to converse."

"The bill tonight is monstrous fine," he said with an abstracted air. "Kean is Richard III."

Fanny's heart leapt at the mention of Kean, for she had read Hazlitt's review of him in *The Morning Chronicle*. She could think of no greater pleasure than seeing Kean act. And yet, having been ignored by Neville for the last few months, she was not ready to surrender so easily.

"You go, Bella," she said quietly. "It is best I remain at home tonight. I am not feeling well."

"Fanny, this is not like you!" Arabella said incredulously.

Neville watched Fanny closely. He knew what the girl was feeling. And he didn't blame her in the least. "Miss Wigmore, I should like a word alone with Miss Feversham, if you could manage," he said. "I will only be a moment."

Miss Wigmore considered his request, then nodded her assent, ushering a bewildered Arabella out the door. "I am usually very opposed to any sort of tête-à-tête, my lord. I shall give you five minutes," she said primly.

He stood across the room from Fanny, making no effort to cross it.

"There was no need to do that," she said firmly.

"Yes, there was, Fanny." He searched for a way to begin. "I realize I took unfair advantage—"

"Please," she interrupted, "you do not have to apologize."

"You mistake my meaning. I am not apologizing, Fanny." He crossed the room and stood close to her. "I have missed you. I didn't know how much until lately." He tried to take her hand and she instantly withdrew it.

"Please do not start again, Julian," she said softly. She bit her lip, determined not to cry.

"Fanny, I shall not hurt you, I promise you that." He took her face in his hands. "I was wrong to leave you as I did at Henley."

She looked up at him, blinking back the tears. His tone was gentle and sincere, his eyes encouraging as they had been that night at Burleigh Abbey. She felt her resentment against him melt away.

His intense expression relaxed a little. "That is better, little vixen. I do not know how I came to care for you so, but your happiness means a great deal to me." He brought her hand to his lips with a grave look.

She felt his lips graze her hand with a familiar softness.

"Now, my dear Miss Feversham, it is my turn."

"I am afraid to ask you for what, my lord," she replied warily.

"It is my turn to show you town hospitality, " he said, a slow smile stealing into his eyes. "We shall start with the theater tonight."

Once settled comfortably in Neville's box that night, Fanny decided that nothing she had seen thus far could equal Drury Lane. The brilliant audience, forever gawking and gossiping, was as much of a diversion as any play. In London, it seemed, bold-faced staring was a mark of good breeding.

After reconciling with Neville that afternoon she had felt reassured, although she would be hard pressed to describe the nature of their relationship. More than friends, less than lovers, they had reached a kind of passionate truce.

It was clear that Neville expected little from her. He had never said he loved her, and Fanny doubted if he ever would. Yet it was clear that he was pleased to see her. How long that pleasure would last was another matter.

She turned slightly in her chair and met his glance. He smiled slowly at her, and bent to answer her father's question. At last she was in London, sharing Neville's world! She was surprised to find how well it suited her. She held up her opera glasses and examined the scene before her.

Dressed for the evening's entertainment, the *haute ton* was like a glorious barnyard—the ladies in drooping plumes and the men with heads erect in their cravats, proud as roosters. The buzz of conversation steadily increased, creating a restless energy all its own—a busy hive of speculation, flirtation and intrigue. Kean must be a very great actor indeed, Fanny thought, to command this audience's attention for an entire evening.

Taking a seat directly across from them was the entrancing Lady Cowper. The celebrated Incomparable shed her cloak, revealing a necklace of stunning rubies and a pair of enormous diamond earrings. Fanning herself ceaselessly, Lady Cowper returned her friends' salutations, diamond bracelets flashing from her wrists.

"They say Palmerston is mad for her," whispered Kit in Fanny's ear, his gaze following hers.

"As well he should be." Fanny's glance lingered on the ravishing Lady Cowper, then moved on. "Look, Kit, isn't that Hazlitt?" she whispered excitedly behind her fan, and indicated the intense young man with the face of an angel who had taken a seat in the orchestra. She recognized him from his likeness in the *Chronicle*.

"Indeed it is. He's devoted to Kean and wouldn't miss a performance. He hates sitting in the boxes because of the tittle-tattle."

"By Gemini, he's handsome." Fanny raised her opera glasses to admire the critic's ethereal profile, until the sound of Miss Wigmore's discreet cough made her lower them.

She had just opened her fan to dispel the oppressive heat when, on a signal, all talking ceased. The curtain rose slowly. Placing her fan on the railing before her, she leaned forward, sitting on the edge of her chair.

A medieval throne occupied the center of the stage. There was the sound of a heavy key turning in a rusty lock, and a door creaked open. A little hunchbacked man, clad in a moth-eaten scarlet robe, limped to the edge of the stage and turned fiercely toward the audience.

"'Now is the winter of our discontent/Made glorious summer by this son of York,'" he began, spitting the words out contemptuously.

Fanny was utterly mesmerized. Although Kean's face was thin and sallow, and his voice grated, the small, wiry man conveyed an electric intensity.

He moved upstage, addressing the empty throne, " 'And all the clouds that lowered upon our house/In the deep bosom of the ocean buried.' "

Neville sat back among the shadows, watching Fanny's reaction to the actor. The play completely absorbed her as she listened intently to the long opening soliloquy. While Arabella fidgeted and Mrs. Feversham puzzled over the exposition, Fanny followed Kean's every movement. Neville was pleased for her sake that Kean was in top form tonight. The actor growled and slunk across the stage, rejoicing in each new act of treachery with an exuberant wickedness.

Neville couldn't bear the way Fanny had first looked at him this afternoon. For an instant he had seen himself through her eyes, and he hadn't liked what he had seen. He had wanted to beg her forgiveness for having hurt her. But how could he be sure he wouldn't disappoint her again?

How radiant she looked tonight, in her ivory gown trimmed with seed pearls. Through her, he was enjoying Drury Lane and its audience anew. He watched as she recoiled in horror during the wooing scene. She was outraged by Richard courting Lady Anne before the corpse of her husband, the man he had just killed. As the two assassins sought the whereabouts of the Duke of Clarence, she inadvertently clutched Kit's arm in agitation. Even Kit, Neville noted with some amusement, had ceased perusing the demi-reps and fixed his attention on the stage.

Neville languidly crossed one leg over the other. Fanny's love of the stage was indeed encouraging. He smiled to think of how much she would enjoy Astley's Royal Amphitheatre, Vauxhall Gardens, and Madame Tussaud's. He couldn't wait to show her all the pleasures London had to offer, each one a bright new toy.

" 'I spy some pity in thy looks,' " spoke the Duke of Clarence, begging one of his assassins for mercy. " 'O, if thine eye be not a flatterer/Come thou on my side and entreat for me.' '' As the duke pled for his life, the second assassin crept up behind him.

"He should keep a sharp lookout for that skulking cove," Kit whispered to Fanny just as Clarence was stabbed in the back.

"Oh!" gasped Fanny, "this is too dreadful by half!" As she drew back, she inadvertently knocked her fan off the railing. It tumbled through the air and bounced off the head of a bald man below with a loud thwack. The unfortunate victim rubbed his head and stared up indignantly at Fanny.

Thoroughly embarrassed by her gaffe, she turned around to see Neville laughing softly and Miss Wigmore hiding her face in her gloves.

"Good work, Fan," Kit whispered. "Probably the last time that poor fellow will take his hat off in a theater."

During the intermission that followed Act II the door to Neville's box was flung open, and a high-pitched female voice called out, "Aunt! Cousins!"

Cousin Alethia entered rapidly, flirting with Neville, flattering Mrs. Feversham, teasing Kit, and causing a stir.

Fanny tried not to stare at her cousin's fine clothes. Her daring decolletage was contained in a high-waisted gown of ecru satin, with slit sleeves that buttoned over her upper arm. She flashed smiles at the women and taunted the men with her fan, asked countless questions and ignored the answers.

"So my country cousins have arrived!" She made a little moue, signalling displeasure. "Why did you not tell me instantly? Naughty uncle!" She rapped Mr. Feversham on the knee with her fan. "I could have taken you to the masquerade last Tuesday."

"You see, my dear—" Mrs. Feversham began resolutely.

"Well, no mind. Oh, don't you girls look pretty!" She slid onto the chair next to Fanny and whispered behind her fan, "Isn't it wonderful news about Arabella? I have marked Neville all night and he is very brave, for he shows no trace of passion."

Fanny glanced at Neville who was staring stonily at her and Alethia.

"Actually, cousin, I don't mean to be unkind, but this is hardly the time—"

"Oh, I quite understand, dear Fanny. We shall have a little tête-à-tête later." Alethia stood, her voice regaining its usual pitch. "And now I must fly, everyone. I am immensely relieved the little birds have migrated safely. I shall give you dinner at Lansden House one night very soon."

"Is Lord Lansden in town?" asked Mr. Feversham, straining to be polite.

"Here? In London? Oh Lord, I hope not!" Alethia squinted at the audience as if Mr. Feversham had referred to an encroaching French army rather than her husband. "No, he is in Naples, I think, or is it Rome?" She dismissed the whole idea with a shrug of her shoulders. "Oh, là, how forgetful I am sometimes!" She kissed Arabella and Fanny with a great show of affection. "What friends we shall be, cousins. Come visit me. We shall ride in the park. Oh, I see Kean is about to resume his labors. They say he is perfectly addled with daffy! Adieu, adieu."

Cousin Alethia departed in the same whirlwind of energy as she had arrived. Fanny watched her take her seat in her box, bamming the men and gossiping furiously with the women. Although she could tell Neville disapproved of Alethia, Fanny could not bring herself to altogether dislike her cousin.

Mrs. Feversham adjusted her plumes as if she had been caught in a gale. "I say, that girl puts me in a spin every time."

"She's a prime goer, she is," remarked Kit.

All discussion died away as the curtain rose on Act III. A flourish of trumpets announced the entry of the

Dukes of Gloucester and Buckingham. Fanny rearranged her gown, ready to enjoy the rest of the play.

Had she not been so fascinated with Kean, she would have felt the intense scrutiny being levelled at her from another box.

From the back of the theatre a delicate, dark-haired woman slowly lowered her opera glasses, but her hawk-like gaze remained fixed on Neville's box. So, those were the Feversham girls, she mused. She presumed Arabella was the pretty one with the soft brown ringlets and doe-like eyes—the one Neville was rumored to be in love with. But her intuition told her otherwise.

She raised the glasses again and studied Fanny more closely. The girl had a certain liveliness about her that would attract Neville. Yes, she would wager that the golden-haired Fanny was her rival, not Arabella. How blind people were! So easily misled by a valet's gossip! She prided herself on knowing Neville's taste better than he did himself. Rarely had she been wrong.

But something had gone terribly awry in their affair. The glasses moved a fraction of an inch and took in his profile, half-lost among the shadows. She ached as she recalled his handsome face beside her in the darkened carriage, those broad shoulders and forceful arms embracing her. She smiled bitterly. To think he had broken with her . . . for this chit! A mere girl who couldn't even manage a fan! How could she hope to manage someone as complex as Neville?

"Are you all right, Olivia?" The dashing young man in military uniform leaned toward her, his blond moustache brushing against her ear.

"I'm quite well, James, thank you."

And indeed she was, for a plan had occurred to Lady Stanbury that gave her grim satisfaction. Alethia's visit had not gone unnoticed. She was beginning to see a way to enter the Fevershams' world—the safe little world which Neville protected so carefully.

She saw a way to enter it and destroy it.

15

Mrs. Feversham nervously buttoned her gloves as she awaited her daughters on the landing. Overtaken by impatience, she opened the door of their bedroom to ascertain their progress.

"Là, we are making as little headway as the Congress of Vienna!" she observed. "Cousin Alethia will have to delay dinner unless we depart soon." She fidgeted about the room, then looked askance at the clock on the mantel. "Where is that boy of mine? Has anyone heard from Kit today? He was to arrange for the carriage." Taking in the sight of her two daughters, she remarked, "I must say, you both look quite perfect."

Fanny stood alongside her sister at the mirror. Amazedly, she had to agree. Both she and Arabella had been molded into veritable paragons of fashion. Gone were Fanny's tousled curls. They had been swept up into a neat topknot that cunningly revealed her slender neck. A crimped fringe of curls now adorned her forehead, accenting the upward sweep of her brows.

"Fan, doesn't this remind you of the night at Henley?" Arabella whispered, when Mrs. Feversham was safely out of earshot. "We were standing before the mirror just as we are now, comparing Lord Neville to Lord

Rothermere.'' Arabella giggled. ''To think how little we knew him then. Remember when we used to call him the Wicked Lord?''

Fanny gasped at a memory Arabella's words evoked. What had happened, she wondered frantically, to her manuscript? She had entrusted it to Kit well over a month ago and he hadn't mentioned it since. She didn't particularly relish the idea of it lying among the racing forms and haberdasher's bills which littered his rooms on King Street.

Just then the a door banged open and Kit's voice called out, ''Halloo. Where is everybody?''

''I'll go, Mama,'' said Fanny, glad for a chance to be alone with her brother. She ran down the stairs to the elegantly appointed sitting room.

Kit paced nervously, arrayed in his best evening attire. ''I say, Fan, don't you look dazzling? That pale color suits you. Same shade as the champagne I drank last night with Dunsanay.''

''You're certainly in high spirits tonight,'' she observed.

''I'm in alt, Fan, in alt!'' He approached her, grinning mischievously.

''You haven't bagged the blunt at the gaming tables, have you?''

''No, Fan. I've been soiling my paws with business.'' Kit rubbed his hands together eagerly. ''Business—and don't look at me like that. I will soon have a wonderful surprise for you.''

''I can't say I've ever thought much of your surprises, Kit.''

''You liked it well enough when I brought Neville to Henley.'' Kit chuckled at the indignant look on his sister's face. ''No more clues. From now on, I shall be a perfect sphinx.'' He immediately assumed an expression of stony imperturbability.

Fanny decided to ignore his nonsense. ''Kit, where is my manuscript?'' she asked urgently. ''Have you finished *The Wicked Lord* yet? You promised to return it."

"I repeat, I am a sphinx," he replied with a basilisk stare.

She sighed with exasperation. "Oh, very well, but don't shuffle it about so often you lose part of it. It's my only copy," she said firmly.

As Kit assisted his family into the carriage, he savored once again the delicious secret he had in store for Fanny. Her manuscript lost! Not likely. Why, soon all of London would be reading it.

Just three days after he had presented it to John Murray, the publisher had bought it, pronouncing it remarkable and paying him a handsome sum. He thought what a nice come-out present the money would make, neatly packaged with the three volumes of *The Wicked Lord*.

Why, only today that sly old dog had questioned him oloooly about its author. But Kit had remained mum. "A young lady," was all he had said, and Murray had to content himself with that.

Cousin Alethia opened her arms, greeting Arabella and Fanny with a show of effusiveness. "Heavens, how angelic you both look! Was I ever that young?" Just beyond the entrance to the drawing room, Fanny overheard the murmur of well-bred voices. The evening was definitely underway.

Petting and cosseting her relatives, Alethia steered them toward the drawing room. "As you can see, our dinner has not yet begun. It will be a buffet. So very much the vogue on the Continent. But first, you must meet some people."

As they passed a row of white Ionic columns, Fanny was seized with paralysis at the thought of gliding, sitting, and fanning herself correctly among so many distinguished guests. Those first few moments in Alethia's drawing room had to be the worst of her life thus far. As if on cue, everyone seemed to turn and stare at the new arrivals. Numerous eyes bored into them from behind quizzing glasses and fans.

To make matters worse, Fanny saw that the rest of her family felt as awkward as she did. Arabella had lost the *tonnish* air she had adopted upon arrival, and now hid behind Mama. Papa fumbled a great deal with his fobs and tried not to look at his shoes. Only Kit was his usual self, winking encouragement at Fanny while taking Arabella protectively by the arm.

Just as Fanny had stammered out a bashful reply to a kindly baronet's compliment, a languid voice drawled in her ear.

"What an interesting little creature. Would it like some punch?"

Although her mouth was parched, she immediately stiffened at the patronizing tone. She turned and found a self-possessed fellow staring at her through a gold-rimmed quizzing glass.

"No, thank you," she said coldly.

"Ah, I detect a note of dissatisfaction," he said, quirking an eyebrow. "Perhaps you would accept a glass of punch from Lord Neville."

"Have you seen him?" Fanny asked eagerly.

"I have," the dandy replied. "And I will take you to him, for I cannot bear to be in a clutch of any kind." As he lightly took her arm, Fanny noted that he was a dandy of the highest distinction. He looked neither to the right nor to the left, for his cravat permitted very little motion of his head. Consequently, most of his remarks were not addressed to Fanny directly, but to the air before him, a mannerism she found oddly reassuring once she became used to it.

"You may sit there," he said, pointing to a chair in an out-of-the-way corner. "I shall find Lord Neville."

She sank down, gratefully fanning herself as she waited. She still had no idea as to her rescuer's identity.

"Ah, there you are, Fanny. I have looked for you

everywhere. Dunsanay told me he had tucked you away in a corner.''

At the sight of Neville Fanny eagerly arose. ''Thank heavens you're here, my lord.''

''I hope it has not been very trying for you, Fanny,'' he said handing her a glass of punch.

''A kind gentleman rescued me and went off to find you.''

''That would be Dunsanay,'' he explained.

''Really, Neville, she does me more credit than any of our set. I cannot recall ever being described as a kind gentleman.'' The dandy reappeared, politely bowing to Fanny.

Neville smiled briefly. ''Miss Feversham, I have the distinct honor of presenting you to William Withycombe, fifteenth Earl of Dunsanay.''

''Lord Dunsanay, I regret that I cannot return your greeting,'' Fanny replied, very abashed. ''Miss Wigmore would draw and quarter me, but I can't remember what to do with my glass when I am being introduced.''

''The answer to that is easy,'' Dunsanay replied, a tiny spark of amusement warming his cold blue eyes. ''Simply drink your punch, my dear.''

Fanny did as she was told and instantly felt better. Gradually, the tension seemed to leave the room. She could see Mama, Arabella and Kit conversing in a sociable group, an animated young man making them all laugh heartily. Papa had formed part of an enraptured audience that attended to Alethia's voluble discourse on her spaniel's antics.

Her cousin only stopped talking when a footman whispered in her ear, causing her to glance toward the entry way. A small, dark-haired woman stood there, accompanied by a man in military uniform.

''Now we are complete!'' Alethia cried, extending her hands toward her new guests.

Dunsanay held up his quizzing glass up and said sarcastically, "Bless me, if it isn't Lady Stanbury with the omnipresent Captain Berkeley."

Fanny caught her breath and watched Lady Stanbury glide gracefully to Alethia's side. Neville quickly dismissed the new arrivals, his displeasure evident in every feature.

"I am sorry to say this, Fanny," he muttered, "but your cousin Alethia is a very great fool."

When Dunsanay offered to escort Fanny to supper, she accepted gratefully. Lady Stanbury's presence had created an invisible barrier between her and Neville. He drifted from one group of friends to another, careful never to be in Lady Stanbury's circle. Although he was far too polished to show his true feelings, Fanny could discern his agitation.

The long sideboard in the dining room groaned beneath platters of exotic foods. Overwhelmed, Fanny gazed at the mounds of oyster pâtés, the ducklings, the plovers' eggs in aspic jelly, the roast saddle of venison.

"I do not know where to begin," she whispered to her companion, who held her plate for her.

"It is best to start with turtle soup and a lobster bisque," he said calmly. "I shall instruct the footman to carve you the thinnest slice of roast duck."

As Dunsanay carefully arranged each item on her plate around the porcelain soup bowl, Fanny discovered she had no appetite. She had lost sight of Neville among the guests that thronged the dining room. Eventually she and Dunsanay joined her family at a small table, where the conversation centered on Kean's performance.

"A pity I could not attend," Dunsanay drawled, "I should have liked to have seen his Richard."

He turned to Mr. Feversham in an attempt to engage him in conversation. "Tell me, sir, what did you make of Kean?"

"Well," Mr. Feversham began solemnly, "I think the fellow's a first-rate actor, considering his infirmity."

"And what infirmity is that?" asked the dandy, lifting a fork to his mouth.

"Why, poor lad's got a hunchback and a monstrous limp. Finding parts he's suited for must be difficult."

As Dunsanay's fork clattered to his plate, Fanny stifled a laugh and quickly changed the subject.

When they had finished their supper Dunsanay offered to escort his dinner companions through Lady Lansden's garden, adding that her collection of narcissi was one of the finest. As he helped Arabella with her shawl, Fanny felt a gimlet stare boring into her. She glanced across the room to meet the eyes of Lady Stanbury.

Fanny had never known an enemy before, but her skin prickled under Lady Stanbury's assessment. The woman would have been exceptionally beautiful but for the malicious smile that marred her features. Fanny was suddenly desperate to escape to the garden, away from that vulpine gaze.

Once outside in the cool night, the party ambled along the parterred pathways. Occasionally, they stopped to admire the pale flowers whose trumpet-shaped cups had started to open. While the rest of her family wandered ahead, Fanny paused over a flower bed bursting with delicate white narcissi.

"How very lovely." She bent over an exceptionally tall bloom. "If only it had a scent."

"I believe that is the Francisca Drake you are admiring," Dunsanay said. "I do not like flowers with scent," he added haughtily. "They cause me to sneeze. But then, so does snuff, and I like snuff well enough. A conundrum, no?"

"Perhaps not," Fanny replied. "You do not strike me as the sort of person who enjoys nature much." She caught herself quickly. "Oh, I hope I have not said anything wrong."

"Lord, no. You have described me *point-device*. I find your candor most refreshing, Miss Feversham."

They continued along the path until they came to a

miniature temple surrounded by a yew hedge.

"Here we have the perfect tribute to Lady Lansden," Dunsanay announced. "A temple of Diana, the huntress. Would you care to be seated within, Miss Feversham? I am sure your family will be along at any moment."

They entered the marble enclosure and the dandy sat beside her, taking out a perfumed handkerchief. "The evening would have been quite charming," he said, lightly applying the cambric to his temples, "were it not for one monumental error." He turned sideways so he could look Fanny in the eye. "It was most awkward of Lady Lansden to invite Lady Stanbury. I am afraid it has caused you some embarrassment and has pained Lord Neville."

Immediately all conviviality left Fanny's face. "Have no fear on my account, my lord. Lady Stanbury and I are not acquainted."

"You are most sensible, Miss Feversham. But feel I ought to warn you about her, especially as it appears that Neville displays a partiality for you."

"I know all about her entanglement with him," Fanny said, blushing furiously. Being the recipient of Dunsanay's confidence was distinctly disquieting. She glanced furtively down the path, hoping that Mama would appear and free her from this interview.

"That affair is over," Dunsanay continued. "But the woman is not to be underestimated. She will try any means to get him back." He paused and took a deep breath. "Highly improper of me to mention any of this, of course. But I felt it my duty, Miss Feversham."

"I take your warning," she said. "Lord Neville has, I think, a very great friend in you."

"I have known him for some time," he said diffidently. "Years ago, he suffered a disappointment. As a result, he became a man of the town." Dunsanay examined his handkerchief. "But whereas I was born for a life of pleasure, it has not agreed with him. When he returned from Wiltshire a few months ago, he had changed. The alteration was slight, but those who know him remarked upon it. It was as if he had found his moorings again.'' He paused and gave Fanny a searching look.

Fanny shivered and hugged herself. As chilled as she was, though, Dunsanay's observations had struck a warm chord within her.

''Be assured, Miss Feversham, my lengthy discourse is at an end,'' he said, standing. ''I see you need your shawl. Shall I fetch it for you, or do you wish to accompany me back to civilization?''

Fanny thought of the house teeming with people. More than anything else, she needed time to contemplate Dunsanay's disclosures. ''I should like to remain here, my lord, if you would be so good as to fetch my shawl.''

''Very well, then. I shall return shortly.''

She sat very still, pondering his words. They did not altogether surprise her, but Dunsanay's candor did. That he was both an astute observer and Neville's friend made his warning doubly important. Most of all, he'd confirmed Neville's interest in her, and that gave her renewed hope. It was obvious that Dunsanay knew him as no one else did—not even Kit.

Gradually, she became aware of voices on the other side of the hedge. Although they spoke in low tones, Fanny immediately recognized one of the speakers as Neville. She presumed the other one to be Lady Stanbury. The woman spoke in high, clear tones—the sort that suited a small, determined woman. Their footsteps gradually slowed until they were standing opposite her, separated only by a few feet of yew.

''So, those were the Feversham girls,'' Lady Stanbury began condescendingly. ''I saw them in your box at the theater, you know.''

''No, I didn't know.'' Neville replied flatly.

''Yes, and I thought then how wrong all the wits and wags are that imagine you in love with . . . Miss Annabella, is it?''

"Arabella," he said.

"Ah yes, Arabella. A pretty creature. But I marked a certain fondness in you this evening for her sister. Fanny, is it not?"

There was a pause in which Fanny held her breath for fear they would detect her presence.

Neville finally answered in a tone of drawling superiority that Fanny recognized from his first days at Henley. "How astute you are, Olivia. I never could fool you for long. You are right. There was a moment last autumn when she quite captivated me. But I fear it has passed."

Fanny stifled a gasp while Lady Stanbury triumphed with a low laugh.

"I knew seeing her against a London backdrop would make all the difference, Julian. Besides, you always fall in love at the beginning of the Season. It must have something to do with the time of year. Remember the Horner girl two years ago?"

"What Horner girl?" Neville asked, sounding bemused.

"Oh, come now, how could you ever forget?" she urged. "*Quelle horreur* when you discovered she wore spectacles and read Greek better than you. A regular bluestocking."

"I must confess you have a clearer recollection of this Miss Horner than I do. A Greek scholar, you say?"

"It's of no consequence," Lady Stanbury observed acidly, "as I recall, she didn't take." She gave a long sigh, then added, "As I'm sure young Miss Feversham won't. I must say, Julian, you have a penchant for the truly awkward ones."

"Perhaps it's because I fear the clever ones would detect my flaws." Neville yawned.

Lady Stanbury gave a low laugh and they strolled away, turning to other topics.

As soon as they were out of earshot Fanny began pacing furiously. Never had she heard such hypocrisy, such cruel amusement at another's expense. For Neville to allow Lady Stanbury to mock her so—it was insupportable!

She squeezed her fists against her eyes. She ought to have known the *haute ton* would reclaim him. She was no more to him than—who was it? Poor Miss Horner. Fanny hoped the bespectacled girl had been spared the indignity of hearing herself discussed on the other side of a hedge.

She pressed her forehead against a cool marble column, recalling Dunsanay's assurance of Neville's interest. Evidently, he had also deceived Dunsanay. Fanny stamped her foot in frustration. She was certain of one thing. She would never allow him to dally with her again. She had been a fool ever to believe his fine words.

All composure gone, she ran down the path, colliding with Dunsanay.

"Oooph!" The frail dandy reeled from the impact. "What a start you gave me, Miss Feversham! At first I mistook you for a cannonball. You must be very anxious for your shawl. Here it is."

Fanny mumbled her thanks and pressed her hands against her hot cheeks. Her agitation was immediately evident to Dunsanay, who raised his quizzing glass.

"I trust you suffered no misfortune just now?" he asked solicitously.

"Nothing of any consequence, my lord," she replied, her blazing eyes meeting his. "You'd be surprised at what you might hear on the other side of a hedge."

"Ah?" Dunsanay said. He nodded slightly, then offered her his arm. "I always recommend a stroll as a restorative."

"If you don't mind, my lord, I shall refuse your kind offer. I should like to go inside at once."

"Of course," he responded. Before, she had been all liveliness and youthful chatter. Now, she was a veritable Erinnyes—full of fire and fury. Who could have put her so much out of countenance, Dunsanay wondered. Only one person came to mind.

16

As if to spite Fanny's desire to keep her distance from society, the ensuing evenings were filled with routs, dinners, balls and small card parties. Each day's post garnered new invitations that Mrs. Feversham ranked in order of importance, a task which provided her endless pleasure.

Fanny reckoned herself a silly chit to ever have fallen in love with Neville. The *ton* was his true milieu. It had reclaimed him and he had vanished completely from her world. She would have to reconcile herself to her Season and whatever consequences it brought.

To her amazement, she was beginning to relish her excursions into London society, although there was always a moment of panic that gripped her as she entered a ballroom. She worried that Neville would be present and, if so, that she would have to converse with him out of politeness. One evening Kit casually mentioned that Neville was away, conducting business on his family's estate. She refused to press her brother for details and he offered none, sensing her discomfort.

With each outing, Fanny lay claim to an increasing number of loyal admirers—bucks who frolicked with her on the dance floor, and young pinks of the *ton* who bantered with her over dinner, pausing only to repeat her latest *bon mots* to the rest of the table.

One morning she was roused by a familiar scratch on her door. She instantly closed her eyes and feigned sleep. But the door swung open nonetheless, followed by a dramatic pause. Fanny squinted through one eye at the imposing sight of her mother holding an invitation aloft.

"A voucher," Mrs. Feversham announced hoarsely.

"A voucher—you mean..." Fanny's eyes grew large.

"Yes, my dear. Almack's!" her mother squeaked. "Wednesday—a fortnight hence." She rushed over to the bed and embraced Fanny, tears flowing copiously. "Oh, how proud I am of my two girls!"

"Mama, I am so surprised," said Fanny, returning her mother's hugs and struggling to read the handwriting. "It is on very plain paper, is it not?"

"But very elegant. What a trophy!" Mrs. Feversham tenderly regarded the piece of paper and the names on it. A second scratch sounded at the door and Miss Wigmore entered, followed by Arabella.

While they gathered over the voucher, marveling at its every detail, Fanny quietly arose and went to the window.

"I shall rest much more quietly once we are past Almack's, my girls," Mrs. Feversham announced. "That shall be our final hurdle ... and then you may do as you please."

Fanny wondered what doing as she pleased meant. Once, it would have been returning to Henley. But now she wasn't so sure—not that any of her admirers had laid claim to her heart.

She stared out at the bustling traffic of Duke Street. Each day in London was different from the one that preceded it. Life here was so full of surprises, one could never predict what might happen. She wondered if she would ever see Neville again and, if so, what she would say to him. With Almack's but two weeks away, that night in the grotto seemed very distant . . . as if it belonged to a different age entirely.

Neville raised an admiring eyebrow at the article mentioning the Feversham sisters in *The Morning Chronicle*. During the fortnight he'd been in Derbyshire, the girls had certainly made progress.

He helped himself to a square of toast and reviewed his latest decision. It had been a momentous one. But once he had reached it, he saw how inevitable it had been all along. This latest evidence of Fanny's social success only confirmed the wisdom of it.

After the charade in Lady Lansden's garden, his course of action had become clear. He loved Fanny; therefore, he would marry her. It was as simple as that. Although he had not yet communicated his offer, he was certain she loved him.

He toyed with his breakfast, then rang for it to be taken away. He had only been in Derbyshire a little while before he had realized the depth of his feelings for her. He couldn't get the girl out of his mind. Everywhere he looked, he imagined her at his side. It was as if he were already sharing his life with her. He thought of the callous way he had treated her at Henley. He had been a conceited lout. Well, he had finally seen his folly. But he would not offer for her just yet.

First, she would enjoy a glorious Season. He recalled his mother, decades later, describing the hearts she had broken during her Season at Bath. A girl like Fanny deserved to be unreservedly admired. She was above spoiling. He looked forward to the day when that would be his sole occupation.

"A caller, my lord," his footman announced, breaking in upon his reverie. "Lord Dunsanay."

"Bit early for you, eh, Dunsanay?" Neville offered his friend coffee. "Don't think I've ever seen you in Piccadilly before noon."

"I'd heard of your return from the northern shires," Dunsanay replied in an ironic tone, "and I could not restrain my curiosity."

"As to what?" Neville asked politely.

"Why, as to your appearance. I fairly expected you to sprout a Viking beard or take up living in a barrow with all of your livestock. It would be a pity with Almack's so near." Dunsanay sighed audibly.

"I hope I have not disappointed you, William," Neville replied. "I believe I am much the same."

Dunsanay's eye caught the newspaper folded upon the table. "Ah, you have been reading of our Miss Fevershams. They have become quite the darlings of the *ton*."

"So I see," Neville replied abstractedly. "Tell me, have you seen much of them?"

"Oh, here and there," Dunsanay replied vaguely. "I usually catch a glimpse of Fanny as she is whisked onto the dance floor by one great clodpole or other. I must say, her spirits have greatly improved since Lady Lansden's party. I almost despaired of her that evening."

"Why, what happened?" asked Neville sharply.

"She left quite suddenly. Claimed megrim, or something equally dubious."

"Fanny was ill, then?"

"Rather. Seems she overheard something in the garden that didn't agree with her."

"The devil you say!" Neville's face grew ashen and he moved closer to Dunsanay. "When was she in the garden?"

"Just after supper," his friend answered. "I offered to show her the narcissi—with the rest of the tribe in tow. They promptly scampered down the path and Fanny and I awaited their return in the temple."

"The temple behind the yew hedge," Neville said in a low voice.

"The same," said Dunsanay, watching him closely. "I left her there to retrieve her shawl. When I came

back, she was in a rare humor. She could not wait to
leave.''

"Yes, I'm sure she couldn't," Neville replied softly.

"This must be the first you know of it," Dunsanay
said, toying with his quizzing glass. "You left the next
day for Derbyshire." He regarded the stunned look on
his friend's face, then added, "I take it you have not
heard from Lady Stanbury?''

"No.''

"Very well." Dunsanay turned toward the door, then
added, "Actually, I was just on my way to Brooks's.
Perhaps you would like to join me there? Never too early
for a large glass of whisky, I always say.''

Neville declined his friend's offer and saw him out.
As soon as the door was shut, Neville leaned against it,
staring hard at the carpet.

Oh, God, what had he done? He was revolted by the
brittle, callow part he had played in the garden. He tried
to remember his exact words, then imagined what their
impact must have been on Fanny.

He had misrepresented his attachment to Fanny to
shield her from Olivia's spite. And, granted, he had assumed the mask with some reluctance. Yet not so very
long ago, it had been his habitual pose. He winced at
the thought that once he might have been the heartless
wretch he had played at in the garden. Thank God, his
love for Fanny had changed all that.

Or had it? There was a very good chance that Fanny
would have nothing more to do with him. He quickly
calculated what his best move might be. If he wrote to
her, she might refuse to see him. Better wait. He paced
furiously, cursing himself, then Lady Stanbury, then
himself again. He flung the newspaper to the ground.

If he didn't act soon, there was a good chance Fanny
would be someone else's bride by the end of the Season.

17

Fanny leaned upon the mantel, not knowing how she would manage Almack's that evening. All afternoon their townhouse had been in an uproar. Mrs. Fevoroham had lamented that her daughters' gowns were completely wrong—the necklines were too low and the waists too high. After a hasty consultation with Miss Wigmore, they were suddenly pronounced suitable.

Fanny gazed at her reflection in the mirror above the mantel. The overall effect, she reluctantly admitted, was indeed fine. The bodice of her white tulle gown was encrusted with crystal beads that caught the light as she moved. A silver fillet ran through her hair and held a diamond aigrette, a generous present from Papa.

She rubbed her hands together, trying to warm them. They had turned clammy at the prospect of Almack's. Tonight marked her formal entrance into the *ton*. She would be coldly assessed, then either welcomed or rejected by society's hostesses. The words Neville had spoken to her as they danced to the "Roughty Toughty" came back to her: that everyone at Almack's was "dull and dissipated." She laughed in spite of herself at the memory. They had shared such absurdly happy moments . . . made all the more painful by his betrayal.

"Why, Fan, I almost didn't see you. You're so still and white." Kit had rushed into the hallway and was pulling off his gloves. "I must say, you look quite the thing."

"Thank you, Kit," she replied, smiling. Then her smile faded as she saw that he was far from ready.

"I shall just tear over to my rooms, throw on some knee breeches and catch you up at King Street," he said breathlessly.

Fanny noticed he was carrying a parcel wrapped in brown paper. Despite his hurry, he fairly glowed with glee.

"Fan, I have something remarkable for you," he began.

"Yes?" She could see that he meant to make a present of the parcel. Yet, Mama was already calling to Arabella on the stairs. Within minutes they would all be off to Almack's—without him.

"I must say this quickly." He glanced over his shoulder surreptitiously. "Imagine my astonishment when I stopped by Hatchard's today and found this on the stands! The same day as your come-out. What luck, don't you think?"

As usual, when overcome with emotion, Kit failed to make much sense. "A book," she said, taking the parcel in her arms. "It must be several volumes, it's so heavy! How kind of you, Kit. But, really, I must ask—"

"No, Fan, you don't understand," he retorted fiercely, ignoring his mother's advancing form. "This is a special book. This is—"

"Kit, my boy!" Mrs. Feversham's stunned cry echoed from the stairway. "Not ready? And we're just leaving! You must be at Almack's to escort your sisters!"

"I shall join you in the reception line, Mater!" Kit turned to Fanny and whispered, "Consider this a present, Fan, for tonight."

"Oh, thank you, Kit. I shall open it as soon as I re-

turn.'' She deposited the parcel on the hallway table as
her father draped a silken shawl about her shoulders. Kit
paused at the doorway, a grin lighting his face.

"Famous, Fan. You shall be famous. Mark my
words." In a flash, he was gone.

"What gammon is that boy talking now?" Mrs. Feversham clucked disapprovingly as the family arranged
themselves in the carriage. "We are on our way to Almack's and the lad isn't even dressed!"

"He was in a great hurry, Mama," said Fanny,
smoothing her dress. "I think he has just conducted
some difficult bit of business."

"Business!" Mrs. Feversham sniffed derisively. "Kit
has about as much head for business as Brutus does. It
seems to me, Fanny, that since our arrival in London,
you have grown more sensible and Kit has grown more
flighty."

Neville scanned the crowd that thronged Almack's.
The hot, stuffy atmosphere nearly choked him, yet he
could not deny that the event still held a certain charm.
The rooms were packed with all manner of guests—
pretty girls in white gowns, young matrons in diapha-
nous silks, elegant men in evening dress and anxious
mamas in long gloves and plumes. The orchestra in its
semi-circular balcony was playing a decorous reel that
set couples bobbing down the center of the long room.

The trio of hostesses—Lady Jersey, Lady Cowper and
Lady Castlereagh—stood just within the wide double
doors that led into the ballroom. On the stairs, guests
waited to be received. To parents with unmarried daughters, Neville mused, Almack's must seem a very temple
of matrimony.

He finally found Kit apologizing profusely to an unknown lady for having trod upon her train.

"Neville, how good to see you," Kit said effusively,
glad to be free of his accuser. "We were hoping you
would turn up."

"And so I have, dear boy," said Neville blandly. "Where is your family?"

"I finally found them," Kit answered. "You'll never guess where. Seems Lady Holland has just snared Fanny. They are talking a blue streak."

"Indeed?" said Neville with some interest. "Perhaps I should wait until Lady Holland is done. She is a famous rattle, you know."

"Oh, quite the opposite," Kit said. "You must see Fan! She's in her element."

"Very well. Show me this sight."

The two of them slowly infiltrated a knot of people congregated about two females seated on gilt chairs. Fanny was speaking rapidly to Lady Holland who nodded at intervals, her jet black hair reflecting the brilliant candlelight.

At the sight of Neville, Fanny stopped mid-sentence. He inclined his head to her, never taking his eyes from her face.

"Ah, there you are, Lord Neville," Lady Holland said in a well-modulated voice. She extended a pale hand which bore a magnificent ruby.

"You are looking exceedingly well tonight, Lady Holland." He bowed low, brushing her fingers with his lips. "Italy must have agreed with you."

"It did. Wouldn't you agree, Miss Feversham, this man has the best manners in St. James?" Then, without waiting for Fanny's reply, Lady Holland continued. "Tell me, Miss Feversham, have you have ever travelled abroad?"

"No, my lady," Fanny answered, "but I should like to."

"I think Italy would appeal to you," Lady Holland murmured. Then, turning to Neville, she remarked, "She is very much the *jeune fille*, is she not, my lord?"

"Very much so, my lady."

"You must see to it that Miss Feversham travels to Italy," Lady Holland nodded firmly. "I should like that."

"Very well, my lady," he replied smoothly. "And now, if you will allow me, I should like to ask Miss Feversham to dance."

"Ah," said Lady Holland lightly, "most attentive. I like that in a man. Very charmed, Miss Feversham." She rose slowly in a smooth movement that Fanny recognized from Miss Wigmore's lessons. "Alas, I must take my leave of you, for I see Lady Jersey is debating politics with Tom Moore. The poor man will need my assistance with that chatterbox."

A gavotte began to play and couples had already taken the floor, Arabella and a dashing guardsman among them.

"Fanny, I must talk to you," Neville began.

"There is no need of that," Fanny said coolly. "As to dancing, my lord, I am afraid all my dances are taken." She scanned the room. "I believe this gavotte belongs to Mr. Honeywell."

"A pox on Mr. Honeywell," Neville said in low tones. "Fanny, I insist that you listen to me."

"I listened to you all I wanted to that night in Alethia's garden," Fanny hissed. "Aren't you afraid to be seen talking to someone you find so dull?"

"Fanny, you must know that was a lie," Neville said, taking her by the wrist. He half-dragged her behind a potted palm. "I didn't mean that."

"I don't think you mean half of what you say," Fanny said, her voice rising. The dowagers seated just in front of the potted palm began to whisper behind their fans.

Neville glanced about nervously. They were already causing a scene, but if he let her go now he might lose her forever. He looked down into her furious face. "I have meant everything I ever said to you," he said urgently.

"Ah, what have we here, Lord Neville? This appears to be a strange place to conduct a conversation. I never realized you were so interested in botany." Lady Jersey's eyes twinkled mischievously as she regarded the couple before her.

"Actually, Lady Jersey," he said straightening his waistcoat. "I was searching for you."

"Normally, Lord Neville, I do not reside behind palm trees," she teased, lightly tapping him on the wrist with her fan.

"I was going to ask your permission for Miss Feversham to dance the waltz," he said.

"The waltz is a very romantic dance." Lady Jersey turned, addressing Fanny directly. "Is it to your liking, Miss Feversham?"

Fanny knew that Lady Jersey was offering her a means of escape. Yet the interruption had given her a chance to regain her composure. Neville was most insistent that she listen to him. The least she could do was extend him this one small courtesy.

"I have never waltzed before, Lady Jersey, but I should be delighted to do so."

"Very prettily said," Lady Jersey replied. "Ah, it has already started. Away then, with my blessings."

As Neville led Fanny onto the dance floor, she realized that she was on hazardous ground. Thinking the waltz too scandalous, Miss Wigmore had strongly prohibited it. As a result, Fanny now ran the risk of making a complete fool of herself before everyone.

"I must warn you," she said stiffly as she placed one gloved hand in his, "I am not very good at this."

"You're a hundred times better than anyone here," said Neville soothingly. "Remain calm. Lean against my arm and keep time to the music."

They began slowly, with him purposefully measuring his steps to hers until she became used to the rhythm.

"I have a lot to answer for, Fanny, but when Lady Stanbury questioned me in Lady Lansden's garden, I deliberately hid my feelings for you," he began. "You must believe that."

Fanny started to speak and he squeezed her hand more tightly.

"Please allow me to finish. I would like to assume a noble pose and claim that I acted as I did to shield you. But that would be a lie. I wished to protect myself as much as you."

Neville turned his impassive gaze from the dance floor and stared into her eyes. Fanny tried to detect a trace of irony behind his expression and could find none. She had steeled herself to treat his words as pretty pieces of flattery. But now, like that night in the grotto, they held an undertone of urgency.

"Are you so afraid of Lady Stanbury, then?" she asked cynically.

"I was never afraid of her, Fanny," he replied, a sad smile hovering about his lips. "I was afraid of you."

"Me?" she asked incredulously.

"You were the only one I had let in." He briefly disengaged his hand and tapped his heart. "No one has been here in a very long time."

Fanny caught her breath. She felt his arm tighten about her and carry her along in time to the lilting rhythm.

"You see, Fanny, I love you," he said seriously. "I was a fool to ever think otherwise."

"Oh, Julian," she replied, "I don't know what to say while we are here . . . like this." She indicated the other dancers crowding the ballroom. Long ago she had dreamed they would be together so. Now it was coming true, but her relief was tinged with a sense of unreality. "You have certainly chosen an odd place for this discussion."

"If you must know, little vixen, it was the only place I could think of where you wouldn't run away." He looked down at her lovingly. "You don't have to say anything now. It is enough that you have heard me out."

Fanny smiled back at him. The chandeliers overhead shone with crystal fire as Neville spun her slowly. She longed to close her eyes and drift in his arms forever. As the music came to an end, he held her a moment longer. "I must ask you, Fanny, was the waltz as fine as the 'Roughty Toughty'?"

"Every bit as fine, my lord," she answered as he led her back to her chair.

"Remember how I predicted your success in London?" He squeezed her hand gently. "Here you are, my dear, dancing at Almack's to everyone's delight. But I assure you," he said, lifting her hand to his lips, "no one is more delighted than I."

Neville's confession of his feelings for her left Fanny dazed. He loved her, she was sure of it. As soon as the evening at Almack's was over, they would make a new beginning. With a light heart, she danced reels, gavottes and promenades with a succession of partners.

After a particularly exhausting reel, she sank onto a gilt chair next to Arabella. Kit waited upon his sisters, offering to fetch them lemonade which they gratefully accepted.

Once he was gone, Arabella addressed her sister in a sulky tone. "Are you finding Almack's agreeable, Fan?"

"Yes, Bella, I must confess I am." She fanned herself rapidly. Seeing her sister's downcast look, she continued cheerfully. "Isn't it amusing to mix with all these tulips who give themselves such airs? Poor Bella, are you so very bored? You cut quite a dash with that guardsman during the gavotte."

"It's not that, Fan," Arabella began uneasily. "I simply don't get on with these people as you do. I'm not quick and witty. The girls here are pretty enough, so there's very little that sets me apart. Oh, I wish we were back at Henley!"

To her astonishment, Fanny saw a large tear roll down her sister's cheek. She immediately produced a handkerchief and put her arm protectively around her.

"Come to the retiring room, Bella. You're fatigued, that's all."

"No I'm not, Fan," she countered indignantly. "I'm put out because you are taking and I am not. I hate being here tonight because you've danced twice as much as I have. And that has never happened before." Arabella raised her tear-stained face and glowered accusingly at her sister.

"What's all this?" Kit said, appearing with glasses of lemonade.

"Bella's upset. She's very tired. Make her drink some of this, then we must leave," Fanny ordered. "I shall find Mama and Papa."

She had not gone far when she found her mother attending to a lively debate between Alethia and Lady Jersey. Fanny tried to attract the attention of her mother who was too engrossed to take much notice.

"Oh, there you are, Fanny, I have been searching for you all evening," said Alethia congenially. "But you were so besieged by admirers, I had to concede defeat. Lady Jersey and I have been discussing the most delicious new book. You simply must read it!"

"Indeed?" said Fanny politely.

"I had gone to Hatchard's to purchase Byron's *Hebrew Melodies*, when I happened across an astonishing novel," Lady Jersey explained. "It just came out today."

Her words had a familiar ring to Fanny. She vaguely recalled something about Hatchard's. Oh yes, it was earlier this evening when Kit arrived with that parcel under his arm.

"It is rather scandalous, really. For the hero perfectly resembles someone we all know quite well. Can anyone guess who it is?"

"Mama, I really think we ought to—" Fanny began, but was immediately hushed.

"Lord Neville," Lady Jersey whispered darkly. "Down to the very scar."

"And what kind of a portrait does the author paint?" asked Alethia gloatingly.

"Authoress, my dear Lady Lansden. I think we may all assume it is written by a lady, or rather a *female*. The portrait is extremely amorous. My emotions were so roused that certain passages, I must confess, nearly scorched my palms."

"No!" Alethia said.

"Oh, poor Lord Neville," murmured Mrs. Feversham. "Fanny, do you not pity our dear friend?"

Fanny opened her mouth, but when no words came out, Lady Jersey rushed to her rescue.

"As anyone can tell, Miss Feversham has been very properly brought up. Why, she is probably shocked by even hearing of such a book. I assure you, my dears, that Miss Feversham's character is quite, quite different from that of the authoress—whoever she may be."

"Then it is written anonymously?" Mrs. Feversham asked.

"Such identities do not remain anonymous long," Alethia said slyly. "We eventually discover all secrets, do we not, Sally dear? I'm sure the authoress will be famous within a fortnight."

"Hardly a fortnight. She will be famous overnight if I am any judge of the *ton*," Lady Jersey countered. "Now, tell me the title again so that I may purchase it tomorrow."

"It is called..." Lady Jersey paused dramatically and Fanny awaited her next words as a prisoner in the dock would await sentencing. "*The Wicked Lord*."

Fanny's sharp intake of breath caused Mrs. Feversham to turn toward her daughter. "Why, Fanny dear, you've gone so white. We must get you home at once."

"Yes, Mama, I fear I am very fatigued," she replied weakly.

As they made their farewells, Fanny felt the world sliding out from beneath her like quicksand. She must be sleepwalking, she thought, unable to wake from this horrible nightmare.

"Whatever will Lord Neville say?" Mama clucked disapprovingly.

Yes, whatever indeed, thought Fanny. He would certainly think twice about offering for a girl who had chosen to portray him in a vulgar novel. The mere thought of the unflattering way she had written about him made her feel numb with shock. As she and her mother joined the others in the hallway, their carriage pulled up.

"I say, Fan, you look all peaky," Kit remarked.

Poor, dear Kit. He had been so proud of his present to her—thinking it a splendid idea to take her book to a publisher, no doubt. How could he possibly have understood its consequences?

"I'm all right, Kit," she smiled wanly. Just as she was about to enter the carriage, Neville sauntered down the steps.

"So, you are departing?" he asked warmly, taking her by the arm and helping her into the carriage. "I believe the Miss Fevershams have scored an unparalleled success with our hostesses tonight. Goodnight, everyone. Goodnight, Fanny, my dear. I shall call upon you tomorrow."

"Oh no, my lord, please don't!" she cried.

"Indeed, I suppose everyone shall want a rest. Well then, day after tomorrow." Neville banged the carriage door shut and signalled the driver.

"Fanny, that was very unkind of you," Mrs. Feversham said, "after what the poor man has to face. He will have need of his friends."

"And what does Lord Neville have to face?" asked Arabella.

"It seems that a scandalous novel just has been published containing a speaking likeness of him. It is called *The Wicked Lord*. And now that I've said that, we shall never mention it again."

"A speaking likeness, you say?" spluttered Kit. "You mean the hero is modeled on Neville?" He turned to Fanny with a questioning look then knit his brows together. "Are you very sure, Mater?"

"I have it from Lady Jersey's own lips," said Mrs. Feversham. "Have you ever heard of anything so unrefined?"

Her question fell on deaf ears. To her surprise, all three of her children remained strangely silent.

"Demned fine title, that," Mr. Feversham said, rousing himself. "Is it about pirates?"

"How should I know, you terrible man?" Mrs. Feversham replied tartly. She gave a mighty yawn, and said to no one in particular, "My, but wasn't it a grand evening!"

"Yes, Mama, it was," Fanny said dismally. She felt a small hand slip into hers and turned to see Arabella smiling bravely at her.

They had no sooner returned home than Fanny, waiting until the rest were safely upstairs, unwrapped the package that lay on the hallway table.

There, before her astonished eyes, was her book. She turned the pages, wonderingly. Yes, here were the very words she had written. On the spine was the title, *The Wicked Lord*. "By a Young Lady," she read.

Famous. Kit had said she would be famous. She hugged the volumes to her heart and closed her eyes. If fame meant having dreams dashed to pieces, Fanny reflected bitterly, then she truly knew the meaning of that word.

18

Lady Stanbury propped up her feet on the settee, admiring their shape. She was dressed in a flowing morning coat of taffeta, ruched with a rose-colored silk that matched her slippers. The sun streamed into her pretty boudoir, warming the chintz pillows and delicately striped wallpaper.

She stretched lazily like a sleek little cat as she accepted a cup of cocoa from the handsome man who waited upon her.

"Tell me about Almack's, James," she said, holding the cup to her lips and gazing at him through thick, dark lashes.

"Oh, the usual, as you can imagine," answered Captain Berkeley. He searched through a bowl of fruit until he found a ripe pear, then bit into it with gusto. "The new crop always looks more promising from a distance. Then, after whirling them around the floor a few times, one finds them not so promising after all."

"Now, James, is that fair? You probably leave the poor children breathless," she teased.

A silence ensued during which he savored his pear and she silently cursed his obtuseness. This lull would never have occurred when a pink of the town was her confidant. A dandy would have come straight to the point without being prompted. "What of Lord Neville?" she asked as lightly as possible. "I suppose he was present?"

"Oh, yes," Berkeley replied, giving her an enigmatic look. "Surrounded by a sea of petticoats. He danced with them all. Most diligent about his social duties, I must say."

"Did his attentions linger over any particular girl?" The question came more quickly than she wished.

Berkeley took his time in answering. "No, can't say that he did."

Lady Stanbury hated having to rely on James Berkeley for a detailed report. If only she had been there, she could have told at a single glance how matters stood.

"Tell me, James, did he waltz at all?" she asked demurely.

"As a matter of fact, he did. With the elder Feversham girl. Name of Fanny, I believe."

Lady Stanbury's breath caught. She gently returned the cup and saucer to a nearby table. So, she was right about Neville and that horrid girl. So much for his garden chat, dismissing her as uninteresting.

"Did he dance with the other sister—Miss Arabella?"

"Once, during a reel. But Neville and the other one seemed to suit. They cut quite a dash during the waltz," he added. "Everyone remarked on it."

"How charming," she answered in icy tones.

Berkeley stood and straightened his regimental jacket. These tête-à-têtes always made him restless. As soon as Lady Stanbury had sent for him he knew what her purpose was. He stood by the window and watched the scene in the street below. Why did women always have to be so bloody indirect? If only they could behave more like men. Ask a man an honest question over a tankard of ale and you'd receive an honest answer.

She simply couldn't leave off Julian Carrothers, that

much was plain. Any mention of Fanny Feversham made her hotter than mustard. Dally and begone was his motto. Unless love brought you a bit of the blunt, why chase after it?

He ran an anxious finger along his moustache. Speaking of the blunt, some of it was going to have to turn up rather quickly, or else his military career was finished. He needed funds to rejoin his regiment. A nice, fat widow would serve him very well just now.

"And how do you find Miss Fanny Feversham, James?" Lady Stanbury's ironic tone reclaimed his attention.

"Who? Miss Feversham? Rather fine eyes, I should say," he murmured, resuming his seat. "Tends to chatter a bit, but Lady Holland appeared quite taken with her." He slapped his hand against his thigh. "By Gad, I knew I was leaving something out, Olivia."

"Well, tell me. I am positively prostrate from this turgid account of Almack's," she replied acidly.

"Seems Murray has just published a novel which has taken the town by storm. Everyone was talking of it at the assembly."

"Then it must be quite refined. The Almack's hostesses are all very discriminating." Lady Stanbury examined her rings carefully, showing her indifference to the opinions of those who had ostracized her.

"No, I believe it is quite the opposite and somewhat lurid. Now, here is the part you will like." Berkeley leaned toward her. "The hero appears to have been modeled upon your friend."

"You mean Julian?" asked Lady Stanbury in disbelief.

"Right down to the duel."

"No!" she gasped.

"Evidently, it is someone who knows him well—extremely well."

"A female, you mean," she said, narrowing her eyes. "Does Neville know anything of this book?"

"I'm sure he does by now," he drawled. "The whole town knows of it. The Star and Garter is taking bets as to the authoress's identity."

"I can assure you, James, it is not I," she said smoothly. "I may not be quite respectable in certain matters, but I have never stooped to publishing an account of my amours. How very shocking!" She gave a delighted smile that showed her sharp little teeth.

Lady Stanbury found conversation with James Berkeley was like mining for gold. It was heavy going at times, but patience was often rewarded by striking a vein of the purest quality.

What a delicious scandal for her to feast upon. She would have to discover who had penned this book. There had to be some clerk at Murray's she could set an agent to worm it out of. She was certain Neville would not take this well. Caught up in her own thoughts, she barely heard Berkeley's next words.

"From what I can gather, the novel is really not so much a confession of amours, Olivia. It is more a schoolgirl's fancy given full rein. Moonlight kisses upon battlements, that sort of thing."

"A schoolgirl's fancy, you say?" Lady Stanbury paced the length of the room, clasping and unclasping her hands. Slowly, an astonishing idea occurred to her. There was but one person she could think of who was barely out of the schoolroom, who had an acknowledged connection with Neville, for whom he felt a certain ardor.

Could I really be this fortunate? she thought. It was as if, having been dealt a series of losing hands, she finally had drawn a trump card.

"James," she said, turning suddenly, "I think it would be in your best interests to cultivate that Feversham girl."

"You mean it would be in *your* best interests for me to cultivate her," he retorted, "for Neville appears quite taken with her."

She gripped the back of his chair and whispered in his ear. "No, James. I believe she is going to be very rich soon. You will need a wealthy wife."

She walked over to the bellpull and rang for a servant. "And as you have so kindly pointed out to me, she is likely to receive a number of offers—although I doubt if Neville's will be one of them. If you like, my dear, I will help you devise a way to capture this little bird. Now, hurry along, for I must dress."

"Do you seriously believe, Olivia, that I will carry off the Feversham girl because of some sapskulled idea you have devised?"

"Not carry off, James. Not yet. Simply make yourself appear as amiable as you can. Now, what is this book's title?"

"*The Wicked Lord*," he replied, smiling derisively.

"Ah, how *jejune, n'est pas*? But, I must confess, it has a certain appeal. Something Julian will find most vulgar. Adieu, then."

After her visitor had left, Lady Stanbury poured herself the remainder of the cocoa, slowly relishing its sweetness. A malicious smile lit her face and she murmured, "Dear Fanny Feversham, what would I do without you? Without any help from me, you have managed to lose Neville all by yourself."

Fanny paused as she stepped out of the carriage. She viewed the imposing red brick structure before her with some trepidation, and was finally propelled onto the pavement by a light poke from Alethia's parasol. Although they had ventured into the unfashionable region that lay south of the Thames, the Dulwich Gallery proved to be an attractive neo-classical building that could just as easily fit into the West End.

Fanny had spent the last two days recovering from the shock of seeing her manuscript in print and dreading the inevitable consequences. Her anguished thoughts kept returning to what Neville had said to her during the waltz—about how he had opened his heart to her. He would soon regret those tender words.

Although he had come to call numerous times, she had refused to see him, as well as all her other admirers. That part of her life would be finished forever, she reckoned, once people discovered who was the actual authoress of *The Wicked Lord*. Better to end it now.

Alethia had finally persuaded her she needed a respite from the hothouse atmosphere of St. James. Without further ado, she had bundled Fanny, Arabella and Miss Wigmore into her carriage and driven down Duke Street at an alarming pace.

The vast crowd within made it barely possible for them to squeeze through the entrance. The excited public stood gaping and chattering before the immense collection of prints, paintings and sketches that hung in tiers upon the walls. Fanny had never seen art arranged in such a manner. The paintings stretched into the shadowy reaches of the ceiling, their subjects no longer discernible.

"It is like a Turkish bazaar," said Alethia admiringly, gazing first at the paintings, then at the crowd.

The large, dramatic landscapes all seemed to share a common theme—disaster. In one, a ship foundered upon a gigantic iceberg. All hands plunged to their deaths in an icy sea. In another, the lurid flames of Vesuvius lit the night sky, as the volcano's eruption bathed thousands of fleeing Pompeiians in a stream of liquid fire.

"I find these scenes most unsettling," observed Arabella in a querulous voice.

"But death, even violent death, can be rather beautiful," said Fanny. In response to her sister's questioning look she added lightly, "Perhaps they simply match my mood."

"Don't even joke about such matters, Fan," said Arabella sternly. "Things will turn around. I'm sure Lord Neville will not be offended . . ."

"It's more than that, Bella," Fanny muttered fiercely. "Of course he will be offended. How could he not? But I am offended as well. It is my sensibilities, my very heart, that are so shamelessly exposed to ridicule."

"Kit did not mean to be cruel."

"Kit meant only kindness," Fanny laughed bitterly. "That is the irony of it all. The sooner we leave London, the better. My greatest happiness would be to never again set eyes on any member of the *ton*."

The sisters had been too engrossed in their conversation to notice the tall young man who was determinedly making his way toward them against the crowd. He managed to step forward, nervously adjusting his high cravat.

"Forgive my intrusion, Miss Feversham and Miss Arabella, but I saw you across the room and wished to pay my respects," he said politely.

"Mr. Burleigh!" cried Arabella with genuine delight. Even Fanny welcomed their old friend without her customary rancor.

"It has been ages, has it not?" Clive murmured, nodding to Alethia and Miss Wigmore, who joined the trio.

Arabella introduced Clive to Lady Lansden and their chaperone. Acknowledging the introduction with a slight bow, Clive remarked, "I have heard good reports of both the Miss Fevershams and their Season." Turning to Arabella, he added, "You are, no doubt, flooded with offers, or am I being impertinent?"

"One never discusses offers of marriage until the banns have been posted," Miss Wigmore said severely.

"I shall be glad to tell you, Mr. Burleigh, that my cousins have made London quite merry," said Alethia gaily.

"Nothing like stodgy old Wiltshire, eh?" Clive queried.

"Not in the least," Arabella answered with great feeling.

"And you, Miss Feversham?"

"Each day here brings new surprises," she said evenly, "some more welcome than others. But what brings you here, Mr. Burleigh?"

"A number of things," Clive began. "First, I wanted to see the exhibit. I have heard Mr. Varley's landscapes to be quite fine. Then I thought perhaps to take in Drury Lane."

"Why don't you come round to Duke Street?" Fanny suggested. "Mama would be very pleased to see you."

Clive murmured his thanks with uncharacteristic warmth and made no attempt to leave. His desire to prolong the conversation, Fanny deduced, obviously had something to do with the devoted looks he bestowed upon Arabella.

"And to think, Fanny, until today I reckoned the only entertainments south of the Thames were bear baiting and cock fights . . ." Alethia linked her arm through Fanny's, as if to stroll past the paintings once more. "Adieu, Mr. Burleigh." Under her breath she added to Fanny, "I must speak to you this instant—alone."

Alethia led the way through crowd, prodding those who stood before her with the tip of her parasol. Once outside, they headed for the Lansdens' carriage.

As soon as the door was shut, Alethia began in an excited voice. "Now, Fanny, I am sure you have already guessed what this is about."

"I have no idea," Fanny said dryly. "More horrid scandals pass through Lansden House than letters through the post."

"*Touché*, dear cousin. This concerns you and your book. I think I can help you."

"My book?" asked Fanny blankly.

"Do not play the innocent with me, cousin. *The Wicked Lord*. Soon, everyone in England shall know it is yours. You know how quickly such news gets about. A printer's devil overhears a conversation between a bookseller and a banker concerning payment of royalties. Another person bribes the printer's devil who has never seen a guinea before. So," Alethia shrugged, "*comme çi, comme ça*, in one way or another, all secrets are revealed."

"I can guess who bribed the printer," Fanny replied miserably. "It sounds like Lady Stanbury."

"You are correct," Alethia said briskly.

"Good Lord," said Fanny, burying her face in her hands. "Whatever shall I do?"

"That is why I wanted to talk to you," her cousin replied, taking Fanny's hands in her own. "Do you think I had any interest in those ghastly daubs in there? There is a way to turn this situation to your advantage. It could make you famous."

"Infamous is more like it. Oh, whatever will Mama say?" said Fanny desperately.

"Shame and fame are often closely linked. It is only anonymity that is their true opposite."

"Then I wish to flee and become anonymous again."

"You cannot, Fanny. It is too late. Don't you see? You must ride this storm out. And if you do exactly as I say, I believe you shall have established yourself as one of our most interesting female authors."

"I never wrote because I wished to be thought of as an interesting author," Fanny said softly. "I wrote because I was in love." Her voice broke with emotion. "I never meant for that silly book to be published. Think how Lord Neville must feel."

"Perhaps in the beginning people will read it because it is an unflattering portrait of someone known to them." Alethia toyed lightly with her parasol. "But already they are saying how it is full of mysteries and dashing romance, very reminiscent of Maria Edgeworth. Some readers, I hear, are even asking Murray if there is to be a sequel."

"There will never be a sequel to this disaster," Fanny replied firmly.

"Don't you see? You stand on the brink of fame. This

affaire du coeur with Neville. Pah! It is nothing. You will have many more admirers to choose from.''

"Oh, please, Alethia," Fanny squirmed. "Do not mention such a thing."

"Very well," her cousin replied stoutly, "but we have work to do. First of all, we shall deal with your family. I appoint myself as the one to reassure your parents that your reputation has not been harmed. You have gone from being a rather charming young girl from Wiltshire to being the talk of the town."

"Mama shall be concerned only about my marriageability," said Fanny.

"I shall explain that your prospects are more greatly enhanced as an author."

"I disagree with you there," Fanny countered. "Being the talk of the town rarely confers respectability. And Mama is no fool. However, you are welcome to try to convince her."

"And then, I shall host a number of parties for you at Lansden House," Alethia continued. "Most particularly, we shall invite the Holland House set. They are all quite literary. Lady Holland favored you at Almack's, and I am sure she will approve. This will be our great social coup. After that, Lady Stanbury cannot touch you."

As Alethia continued outlining her plan, Fanny had to admire her cousin's grasp of strategy.

"You are not listening to me, Fanny. You are wearing that look."

"I was just thinking, Alethia, what a shame it is you were not born a man. Wellington could have used a field marshall with your capabilities."

As they alighted from the carriage, Fanny felt somewhat relieved that she had an ally like Alethia to help her sort out her situation. The one subject they had not discussed, however, still weighed on her heavily. No doubt, Neville was reading *The Wicked Lord* this very moment. He would eventually hear that she was its author. Would he ever smile upon her again as he that night had at Almack's? The possibility of that ever occurring, she reckoned, was extremely remote.

19

The next afternoon a very downcast Christopher Feversham presented himself at the door of Grantham House. A suave-faced footman showed him into the library where he nervously paced, waiting for his friend to appear. A book lay open on a nearby desk. Kit's curiosity overcame him and he picked it up. With dismay, he saw that it was the third volume of *The Wicked Lord*.

"Wouldn't you say it's an astonishingly accurate portrait?"

Neville paused in the doorway, a wry smile playing about his face. Despite Neville's assumed nonchalance, Kit saw how worn he looked. "It's taken me several long nights, but I am almost finished," he continued lightly. "Snuff, cigar?"

"No. Thanks, all the same, Julian." Kit indicated the book. "To be honest, this is what I came about."

"Thank you. I appreciate your concern," Neville said. "You know, Kit, I can think of nothing more unsettling than seeing yourself through another's eyes— especially when he, or I should say she, does not hold you in particularly high regard."

"Then you still have no idea who wrote it?" Kit asked tentatively.

"None at all. I've been racking my brains. I even thought it might be that bookish Miss Horner, but surely she would have set it in Greece." Neville shook his head. "I can tell you it has put me in the devil of a mood, Kit. Our unknown authoress leaves nothing of my past to the reader's imagination. She has caught everything—even my affair with Camilla and the duel with her husband." Neville continued cynically, "All that wouldn't be so bad if I came out of it heroically. But in Volumes One and Two I am a vain, heartless scoundrel. My favorite pastime, it appears, is to seduce and abandon women. Have you ever heard of anything so outlandish?"

"Only what I am about to tell you," Kit said quietly.

"Well, out with it, man."

"I wanted you to hear this from me rather than from some damned scandal-monger," Kit began. Seeing Neville's agitation, he decided to take another tack. "Julian, let me ask you a question. In what areas would you consider my development the most deficient?"

"I don't understand," came the reply.

"Well, milling, for instance. Would you say I was a connoisseur of the fancy?"

"An admirable one. I can think of no other fellow with such an appreciation of the ring."

"Then how would you rate my dealings in matters of the heart?" asked Kit.

"Where women are concerned, you've always been damnably lucky," Neville said, impatient for Kit to come to the point.

"Not that. I mean seeing into the hearts of others."

"Oh, well. I suppose we all are blindmen there," said Neville slowly.

"Well, Julian, I have done something terrible to Fanny. Without intending to. I have made an awful mess of things because I did not see—"

"Fanny is all right, isn't she?" asked Neville anxiously, grasping Kit's shoulder.

"Yes, Fanny is all right. But I have hurt her most dreadfully. And I'm afraid I have hurt you, too, old chap."

"I'm sure it's nothing that can't be mended," Neville said, closing the door softly.

Kit watched Neville's face closely as he delivered his news. "I must tell you, my friend, it was Fanny who wrote *The Wicked Lord*."

Neville sat down suddenly, as if receiving a blow. "I don't understand," he said slowly.

"She didn't mean for it to be published. That was all my idea." Kit helped himself to the brandy, then offered Neville one. They would both need some fortification for what he had to say. As to Neville's assurance that the damage could be mended, Kit wasn't so sure.

Fanny examined the tips of her lemon-colored kid shoes and thought how well they complemented the sitting room's dull-blue carpet. Papa sat in the corner, puzzling over *The Turf Register* while Arabella restlessly picked up one book after another.

No matter how you looked at it, Fanny decided, marriage was a nasty business. At Henley Hall, she had feared being bartered off to a feckless husband and interfering in-laws. Despite her meeting with Alethia yesterday, she clearly saw that marriage might be out of the question forever. Her private world was more threatened by *The Wicked Lord* than by any husband, no matter how dissolute he might be. From now on, her future belonged to gossips, scandal sheets and society hostesses. And it wasn't over yet. Not by half.

Mama still had to be told. Was being told, Fanny corrected herself. Alethia had arrived half an hour ago, and they were still closeted in the drawing room.

Arabella moved fitfully from mantel to window and back again, until Fanny could stand it no longer.

"Please, Bella. Can't you find somewhere to sit?"

"I'm as nervous as a cat, Fan," her sister pleaded.

They both stopped and listened. A sound, rather like a moan, had issued from the drawing room. Then all was silence.

At that moment, Kit entered the sitting room at a slow pace. He had just returned from his morning stroll and was looking uncharacteristically dejected.

"Why so down at the mouth, Kit?" Mr. Feversham queried. "This husband hunting business got you down, too?"

"A grave disaster has occurred, Mr. F.," came a sepulchral voice at the doorway. "There shall be no husbands for my daughters."

"Eh, whatever do you mean by that, Mrs. F.?"

"I will tell you, sir, but do not care to shout our business down Duke Street," Mrs. Feversham replied with great dignity. "I must ask all of you join Alethia and me in the drawing room."

After the Fevershams had settled themselves, Alethia explained, as simply as possible, that Fanny had written *The Wicked Lord* and the notoriety that was certain to follow.

"It's all my fault," Kit blurted out. "Really, Pater. I had no idea it was about Neville. All I cared about was the fact that Rothermere makes an end of this rum chap Orsini with the best swordplay you ever imagined. And then Orsini tumbles into an alpine gorge. It's got some exceptional riding and shooting in it, too."

"Do I understand," said Mr. Feversham slowly, "that our Fanny wrote a novel that has been published?"

"Yes, Papa. Only my name does not appear on it. It merely says it is by a young lady."

"And you based the hero on Lord Neville?"

"Well, not exactly, Papa," said Fanny. She glanced quickly at Arabella. "I started the book before Lord Neville ever came to stay with us. Bella and I read all about him in the *Chronicle* and then I made up things—to suit Bella and me, really. And then . . . when he stayed at Henley, I just kept adding to the story."

Fanny sat next to her mother and took her hand. "You see, Mama, I didn't try to portray Lord Neville since we've gotten to know him as a friend," she explained. "I used his background as the model for my hero, Lord Rothermere. As to the duel, it was an unhappy coincidence."

"So far, I see nothing shattering about this confession," said Mr. Feversham judiciously. "It is a tale any schoolgirl could have concocted. Neville is a handsome enough fellow."

"But *I* wrote it, Papa. There are a great many scenes of . . ." She left off, not knowing how to continue.

"Romance?" interjected Mr. Feversham.

"Yes, if you will," Fanny replied limply.

"I still fail to see how this book prevents either you or Bella from finding suitable husbands," he said irritably. "Novel-writing females are under every basket these days. Fanny Burney, Mrs. Gore, Mrs. Cuthbertson. You girls know them better than I. You drag their books home from the lending library by the cartload."

"Yes, Papa, but those authoresses are mostly married," said Arabella softly.

"You are not suggesting, I hope, that Fanny should leave off writing simply because she is not married," he snorted derisively. "Fanny Burney, I hear, was most content to stay at home with her old pater . . . until Queen Charlotte made her a lady-in-waiting, by Jove! I don't recall all of London being in a hubble-bubble over her finding a husband."

"Perhaps I can better explain it to you, dear uncle," said Alethia. "Consider this a puzzle, where each piece, if taken singly, does not mean much. But when all the pieces are added together, they take on a greater significance.

"Fanny wrote, as you said, a schoolgirl's tale. There is no harm in that. Then Lord Neville came to stay at Henley. There is no harm in that. Then Kit read the book and thought it suitable for publication. There is no harm in that. He took it without Fanny's permission because he knew she would never consent to its being published.''

Alethia paused after this last sentence. ''The rest you know. Murray published the book just as Fanny's Season began.''

''So far, I have heard nothing damaging to a reputation,'' said Mr. Feversham stoutly. ''There are unfortunate coincidences, I'll admit. And Kit has shown some rather rackety judgment. But who does not, from time to time?''

''It is just that . . . in London, people talk,'' Alethia began weakly.

''For the first time, madam,'' said Mr. Feversham, half-rising from his chair, ''you have spoken more truthfully than you know. In London people talk and they do not think. They talk because they lead silly, useless lives with little to occupy them!''

''George,'' Mrs. Feversham intervened, ''Alethia only wants to help.''

''I do not see that we require help,'' Mr. Feversham retorted. ''If the *ton* would look to its own business,'' he said, giving Alethia a meaningful look, ''we would all be better off.''

''Cigar, Pater?'' said Kit, stepping neatly between his father and Alethia. ''If anyone in this room is to be chided, it is I for being too sapskulled to see the consequences for Fanny.'' Kit's admission helped ease some of the tension that had been generated. ''As I see it, our only concern is whether *The Wicked Lord* might prevent these pudding-hearted London coves from offering for the girls.''

''Quite so, Kit,'' said Alethia hastily.

''And what is wrong with a novel-writing wife?'' boomed Mr. Feversham. ''Can't see how it is going to hurt when a chap's played too deep one night and comes home with pockets to let.''

"Indeed, uncle," said Alethia. "You have hit upon the solution to all our ills."

Fanny grudgingly conceded that when it came to getting her way, her cousin employed flattery with superb results. Alethia proceeded to explain how they could bring the Holland House set to their side, leaving out the part about outwitting Lady Stanbury. "If Fanny acknowledges her authorship, what scandal can touch her?" she concluded.

"Alethia is right," Mr. Feversham finally concurred. "This deuced business must come out in the open, and I suppose Lansden House is as good a place as any to do it."

He rose to his feet, signalling the interview was over. "But mark my words," he said, glaring at everyone assembled before him, "I'd rather see Fanny married to a red-faced farmer from Bradford than any mincing lord in too-tight trousers. The *ton*, in my opinion, is full of gammon. And the sooner this business in London is concluded, the better."

No sooner had Alethia left than a visitor for Mr. Feversham was announced. With an effort George Feversham put the matter of Fanny's novel out of his mind and went to the sitting room to greet his caller. "When I first heard Mr. Burleigh was waiting to see me, I thought immediately of your dear old father. Presumed he had come to London for another one of those hunting horns he uses." Mr. Feversham chuckled.

"Father did not accompany me to London this time, I am sorry to say." Clive adjusted his posture so that he sat even more upright on the edge of the chair.

"Well, bring him with you next time. Always glad for his company," said Mr. Feversham jovially. What the deuce, he wondered, had brought young Burleigh to his doorstep? Must be something about selling land. Those improvements to the abbey had to have cost a packet.

"Mr. Feversham, you must forgive my awkwardness in these matters," Clive said, wetting his lips, "but I have never made an offer before."

"Nothing to it, my good man," said Mr. Feversham expansively. "Happens every day. Just name a price and I'll tell you if it suits."

"Eh?" said Clive. "I'm not making this offer all over town, you realize."

"Of course not. Wanted to offer to a neighbor first," said Mr. Feversham in a conciliatory tone. He had forgotten how easily Clive took offense. "Don't want some stranger spying on the abbey, do we?"

"No," said Clive slowly. "Although 'spying on the abbey' is hardly how I should have put it."

"Well, then," said Mr. Feversham, stealing a glance at his watch. "Put it however you like, but I warn you, my dear fellow, I like my potatoes plain and my beef well done. I like things said straight out, and the less mincing and chopping of words, the better."

Clive coughed slightly, then stood up and crossed the room, standing with his back to the fireplace. "Mr. Feversham, I should like to marry your daughter." It was the simplest statement Clive Burleigh had ever made. He had planned an elaborate speech, complete with references to Pindar and Thomson, but Mr. Feversham's last remark about the well done beef had dashed his carefully chosen rhetoric.

"What do you say?" Now it was Mr. Feversham's turn to be discountenanced. "That's rather a bare bones approach. A man likes to be prepared for these things. But, never mind."

He stood up and looked out the window. He had known that eventually he would have to give up his glorious daughter Fanny. Yet he had always considered Clive Burleigh a strange sort of fellow, especially after all those popish costumes at the abbey. But, to put another face on it, Fanny would be close to her old home.

He could even see her on Sundays, when she would invite them over for mutton.

It didn't signify that Fanny found the sight of young Burleigh unbearable. Wives seemed to outgrow these initial reactions. If Fanny married Burleigh, things could go on much as they always had at Henley.

"Very well, Mr. Burleigh, I consent," said Mr. Feversham simply.

"Oh, thank you, thank you, sir," said Clive, genuinely moved. "I have loved her from that first moment I saw her after my return from Italy. She is a delicate creature, of great beauty. I shall provide for her handsomely. A reasonable sum, I thought, would be—"

"Never mind that now, Mr. Burleigh," said Mr. Feversham, patting him on the back and opening the door to the sitting room. "We'll discuss the details after dinner next week. I know you'll make my girl a fine husband."

He handed Clive his walking stick and stood by the front door. After Alethia's shattering news, he had despaired of ever finding his elder daughter a suitable husband. Perhaps he had been too hasty in jumping at Clive's offer, for the girl would resist the match. Of that he was sure. But the deed was done, no turning back now.

"Give me a few days, won't you, Mr. Burleigh?" He good-naturedly shook the young man's hand. "I should like to break this to Fanny by degrees. She's always been strong-willed about such things, you know." He held the door open as Clive stepped over the threshold.

"Fanny?" Clive said incredulously, turning around. "I'm afraid there's been a misunderstanding. I meant to—"

"Of course, of course," said Mr. Feversham. "You meant to tell her yourself. Young love is like that, I suppose. You shall have your chance next week. Then you may have a private interview. Until then, Mr. Burleigh, good day."

*   *   *

Dumbfounded, Clive stared at the door that had just slammed shut. A dreadful disaster had just occurred. He could see that Mr. Feversham had not intentionally misunderstood his offer. Clive had never even uttered Arabella's name. George Feversham had simply assumed from the beginning that Clive meant to offer for Fanny.

He recalled his adorable Arabella and her compliant nature—how sweetly she had clung to his arm at the Dulwich Gallery, how devotedly she had attended upon his every word! Fanny had lingered in the distance. No longer impolite, certainly. But definitely unsuited to be his muse, his divine companion.

Like a man suddenly weakened by illness, he grasped the wrought-iron railing. He would have to go back and make his position clear. But not now. Tomorrow, or the day after. When his heart had ceased knocking against his ribs and the spots no longer danced before his eyes. He drew a trembling hand across his clammy brow. The mere thought of Fanny Feversham becoming Mrs. Clive Burleigh almost undid him.

20

Conversation around the dinner table the next night in Duke Street was extremely labored. Fanny barely touched her food and all efforts to draw her out were met with a cold resistance. Her thoughts kept returning to the encounter in Hyde Park that afternoon. Its implications still upset her.

"Fanny, Miss Wigmore tells me that a very amiable officer spoke to you during your carriage ride," Mrs. Feversham began. "Who was he?"

"Captain James Berkeley, Mama," she answered.

"His name sounds familiar," Mrs. Feversham mused.

"We met him at Almack's," Arabella interjected.

"Miss Wigmore said that he spoke to you in a very serious manner." Her mother watched Fanny closely.

"It was nothing, Mama." Fanny put down her napkin. Her appetite had left her completely. "He told me of a mutual friend—who is ill."

"How do you and this Captain Berkeley come to share a mutual friend?"

"A gentleman we both knew from Lansden House." Fanny cast about for a credible answer. She didn't dare say what Berkeley's actual business had been—to warn her of Neville's reaction to *The Wicked Lord*. She had

187

known Kit would spare her. Berkeley had seemed concerned for her future. Neville's outrage, he said, was only fueling the rumors that something more than friendship existed between them.

"He must have been a close friend," Mrs. Feversham observed, "to cause you to look so miserable."

Before Fanny could reply, Mr. Feversham intervened. "Doesn't matter now how close a friend he was. The girl's already taken."

"Taken . . . what do you mean, Mr. F.?" asked Mrs. Feversham sharply.

"I've made a match for Fanny. I was hoping Kit could be here with us, but now's as good a time as any to announce it." All eyes turned on him, the same unasked question on everyone's lips.

"Mr. F., you can't be serious. Why am I to be the last person to hear of my daughter's betrothal? Pray tell me who my son-in-law is to be?"

Mr. Feversham glanced at everyone around the table, then said, smiling expansively, "Clive Burleigh."

"Clive!" exclaimed Fanny. "You must be bamming me, Papa."

"No, not bamming you. Fellow came round here yesterday and offered for you. Nervous as a tick, he was. I couldn't very well refuse him."

"Are you sure he offered for me," asked Fanny, "and not Bella?"

"Ummm, yes, of course," said Mr. Feversham, fiddling with his napkin. "Certainly."

"I really think you should have asked me first, Papa, if I wanted Mr. Burleigh as a husband," Fanny said, standing. "For I don't, and I never will. You have made a dreadful mistake in agreeing to this match." She threw her napkin on the table. "And now, I beg your leave. I am feeling most unwell."

She ran upstairs, ignoring her mother's pleas to return. Flinging herself on the bed, she could no longer hold back the choking sobs that engulfed her.

Poor, silly Papa, wanting to do what was right and

bungling it so. It was obvious that Clive had come to offer for Arabella and not for her. She would rather die than live with Clive at Burleigh Abbey.

And dear Julian. How betrayed he must feel. She had repaid his love with a juvenile prank. If only she could find a way to talk to him and sort things out. But Berkeley had said he was beyond talking to . . . he was deeply hurt and angry.

Fanny despondently reviewed her choices. She obviously couldn't remain in London much longer. To stay with her family would mean acquiescing to the match with Clive. She withdrew Berkeley's card from where she had hidden it in her sash. He had offered her a way out. Although it seemed suspect, she considered taking it.

Just as she felt the most hopeless, a pair of soft arms closed round her. She felt for Arabella's hand and her tears started afresh.

"Oh, Bella, what am I going to do?" she sobbed.

"There, there, Fan. We'll find a way."

"I certainly am not going to marry Clive," she said, drying her eyes. "Poor Papa, what was he thinking of? Whoever would want to marry Clive Burleigh?"

"I would," said Bella softly. "Yes, I would, Fan. You think him foolish and vain, but I think him kind. I have learned a great many things about myself during our Season. I know now that Wiltshire is home to me. I do not fit here in London, as you do."

"You mean, as I once did."

"As you still do," Bella said encouragingly. "You belong to the wide world with a husband as dashing as . . . Lord Rothermere." She smiled at Fanny encouragingly. "I belong at Burleigh Abbey, serving the tenants their Christmas mead."

"In medieval attire?" Fanny asked, the idea causing both sisters to laugh through their tears.

"I must admit, Fan, Clive is eccentric, but I think he adopts those poses out of loneliness."

"Well then, dearest, we must give the poor man what he came for yesterday."

"What is that, Fan?"

"He meant to offer for you, but Papa got things mixed up. We shall have to give him back the Miss Feversham he truly loves."

"And what shall we do with the other Miss Feversham?"

"We shall send her out into the wide world," said Fanny, sliding Captain Berkeley's card back into her sash. "Where, as you said, Bella, she belongs."

The clock had just struck midnight when Fanny saw the carriage round the corner of Duke Street. She shivered in the cool night air, and pulled her cloak more closely about her as she emerged from the shadows. She had packed as few belongings as possible. She realized that the step she was about to take was irrevocable. Once out of London, she was unlikely to see Neville again. She had accepted Berkeley's offer of a carriage to take her to Henley Hall. Now it was her turn to rusticate, she thought grimly.

The carriage pulled up to the Fevershams' door, the horses' hooves sounding unbearably loud against the cobbles. Once more, Fanny checked her reticule for the Mortimer revolver. Inwardly, she thanked Kit for showing her how to shoot. Undertaking this journey as an unescorted female, she prayed she would not have cause to use it.

"Miss Feversham?" came the driver's muffled voice. When Fanny assented, he jumped to the pavement and swung her portmanteau into the back of the carriage. As he opened the door to the carriage, Fanny drew back at the sight of the familiar device.

"But this is Lord Stanbury's coat of arms," she said indignantly.

"So it is, Miss Feversham," came a familiar voice, "but that should not stop you." Captain Berkeley leaned

out and seized her by the arm, dragging her into the
carriage.

The driver hastily shut the door and whipped the
horses into a breakneck pace down Duke Street.

"Stop this carriage at once, Captain Berkeley!" she
commanded. When her companion merely stared at her
impudently, she pounded on the roof of the carriage,
signalling the driver to stop.

"There is no need to trouble yourself so," Captain
Berkeley replied lazily. "The driver is in Lady Stanbury's employ. He doesn't intend to halt until we have
reached our destination."

"Which I assume is no longer Henley," said Fanny
coldly. The realization had dawned on her that she was
being abducted.

"Correct," came the reply.

"May I ask where we are bound?"

"Can't you guess?" Berkeley leaned forward and
leered at her. Fanny could smell rum on his breath. "We
are bound for Gretna Green."

"You are mad if you think you can force me to marry
you," she said with more conviction than she felt.
"Gretna Green is a three-day journey. As soon as my
brother learns of this, he will come after you."

Berkeley's eyes narrowed. Beneath his guise of bon-
homie, Fanny sensed a violent nature. Unlike Kit who
was rendered silly and a little confused by too much
daffy, Berkeley became brutish.

"I wouldn't count on that, Miss Feversham. Lady
Stanbury has taken pains to see that we have the fastest
horses possible. We shall make the journey in two days.
Besides," he added, "this alliance might benefit you
more than you think."

"Don't be absurd," she spat out.

He stared at her with cold blue eyes, then burst out
in a derisive laugh. "What a show of propriety, Miss
Feversham! Forgive me, but I find it all so humorous."

Fanny glared at him. Her hand closed around the revolver in her reticule. She calculated the distance between them and how quickly he might react in his present condition. She would have to time it perfectly. The revolver was her last defense.

"You see, Miss Feversham, I know all about you and Lord Neville from Lady Stanbury."

"I am sure you have received a most factual account," she replied acidly.

"Don't think for a moment I believe her green-eyed nonsense," Berkeley hissed. "But I know what I can plainly see—that you and Neville were once very much in love."

A lump came into Fanny's throat at his words. Pay him no heed, she told herself, he is merely trying to divert you.

"You and I both know," he continued, "that Neville is a proud man. He does not take insults lightly. *The Wicked Lord* created a rift between you that can never be mended."

Fanny turned her head away and Berkeley continued. "I can tell that you do not relish your future as it now stands. You wrote the book because you loved him, yes?"

"Yes," she murmured, gazing out the window at the unfamiliar streets.

"And now the book has killed that love."

"I really don't see how my literary efforts are any of your affair, Captain Berkeley," she replied stiffly.

"Oh, but there you are wrong, Miss Feversham," he contradicted. "You and I are outcasts. We are both looking for ways out of our dilemmas."

"You are a fool if you think there is anything connecting us other than this sordid stratagem," she replied grimly.

"Well then, look again, my sweet angel. For you and I have a future together."

"That is a ludicrous idea."

"Do you honestly think," he leaned very close this

time and Fanny felt his breath upon her face, "that once Neville has read your account of his most private affairs of the heart that he will ever speak to you again?"

"Damn you!" Fanny cried, pushing him away. "You have no right to address me in such a manner."

"Hah!" Berkeley sat back, grinning at her insolently. "You can forget Lord Neville, my child. Poof! He has never existed. Now, what do you have left?" He indicated the passing scene. "You can't go back to Wiltshire and be plain Miss Fanny Feversham again. And you can't become Lady Neville. So, it looks as if it's to be the London literary life for you, my beauty. With your slightly tarnished reputation, you could be an object of lasting interest to the Holland House set."

"No, no," Fanny cried, tearing her handkerchief. "I won't have it!"

"What will you have, then?"

"I . . . I don't know." She stared morosely out the window, seeing how useless it was to return to Henley.

"I'll tell you what you will have," Berkeley said, catching her by the wrist. "You'll have me." With his other hand he grasped her by the waist and pulled her to him.

Fanny averted her face. "Let me go, you blackguard!" Berkeley increased the pressure on her wrist until she cried out in pain.

He released her and she slapped his face as hard as she could. He reeled back, but the blow seemed to bring him to his senses.

"I didn't intend to hurt you," he said thickly. "Look here, I have a bit of money, not much, but it is enough to get us out of the country. I'll join my regiment and you shall go with me to the Netherlands. Being an officer's wife is not such a bad existence. Perhaps you'll even come to enjoy it."

"What do you want with me as a wife?" asked Fanny coldly.

"I like you," he said carefully. "And you're in a bit

of a pinch. This could offer you a change of scene."

"I should say!" she laughed bitterly. "I've always longed to see battlegrounds strewn with corpses."

"Regimental life isn't all blood and gore," he said. "Soon as Boney is run out of Paris, I'd take you to the Opera." He twisted his lips into a smile.

"How much of this idiotic plan is your idea and how much is Lady Stanbury's?" she demanded.

"Does that matter now?" he asked mockingly.

"I know why you need me," she said suddenly. "It's the money, isn't it? You think I'll be a rich woman." When she saw the expression freeze on his face, she burst out laughing. "You are too easy to see through, Captain."

After an unaccustomed silence, she stole a glance at him. He sagged against the corner, his eyes beginning to droop. So, his Dutch courage was wearing off at last. She had devised a plan to escape at the first coaching inn. Once she was rid of him, she would decide what to do next.

She stared at the rows of houses thinning out into clusters. Soon they would be villages. Then open road. The weight of the pistol in her lap reassured her that she would never again have to endure another of Berkeley's boorish embraces.

21

After several unsuccessful rounds of faro, Neville had decided on an early return to Grantham House. He invited Dunsanay to join him in sampling several fine bottles of claret.

Handing his guest a glass, he began, "Now tell me of this mysterious lady with whom you dined at such an unfashionably early hour."

"A mere actress," said Dunsanay, blowing a torrent of cigar smoke across the room with an air of satisfaction. "Just a giddy little thing, easily overcome by champagne." He ruminated in pleasurable silence on his dinner companion, then fixed Neville with a cool look. "And what of you, my dear fellow? How goes it with Miss Feversham?"

"Please," said Neville, grimacing at the mention of her name, "I do not wish to speak of her."

"As bad as that, eh?"

"Shall we just say it is over," Neville said firmly.

"Did you ever learn who wrote that poxy novel?" Dunsanay asked.

Neville watched him closely, saying, "So you know, then."

"Lord, yes. Whole town knows she wrote it. Question is, what are you going to do about it?"

"Let the scandal die a quiet death," Neville replied.

"Hmmm." Dunsanay poured himself another glass and examined the ruby-colored liquid in the light. "And what of Miss Feversham? Will she die a quiet death also?"

Neville shrugged. "I'm sure she will find a husband somewhere."

"That's not exactly what I meant," Dunsanay said acidly. "You are most provoking tonight, Julian. I am being forced to give you advice about love. You know how much I hate that."

Neville quirked an eyebrow. "You think me in love?"

"I know so," Dunsanay responded in an exasperated tone. "What I don't understand is why you should balk at being portrayed in a silly novel. I thought you came off rather well in Volume Three."

"Rothermere was finally quite the hero, wasn't he?" Neville said cynically. "But what of the other two volumes? They were stuffed full of sermons on the fellow's overweening pride and his insufferable vanity."

"What you mean to say is that, because of your vanity, you are turning your back on a beautiful young creature who loves you," Dunsanay observed dryly. "If that is the case, I would say she had caught your likeness quite well."

"Damn you, William. She has already set tongues wagging from Dover to Glasgow. Now must I listen to my own friends abuse me?"

"It must be very lowering to the poor girl to be ignored by the man she loves when she needs him the most."

"What would you have me do, then? I cannot simply call upon her as if I had never read the thing."

"Of course you can," Dunsanay replied. "That

would stop the tittle-tattle at once, wouldn't it? If you acted as though nothing has happened.''

"But a great deal has happened between Fanny and me,'' Neville responded. He remembered the way he had held her during the waltz at Almack's, how she had gazed into his eyes so trustingly. Perhaps that moment was the closest he would ever come to perfect happiness. ''She expects me to be that hero of hers, but I'll be damned if I know how to begin.''

''Action, man, that is the answer. You must take action. No more talk.''

Neville thrust his hands into the pockets of his waistcoat. ''And what kind of action do you recommend?''

''You must carry her off. Sweep her off her feet. Allow her no further argument.'' Dunsanay smiled brightly.

''I cannot believe I am hearing this from you,'' Neville remonstrated. ''It is madness, utter folly. She would hate me forever.''

''She would worship you, Julian. You would have relieved her of all decision and shown your unswerving desire to have her at all costs.'' Dunsanay crossed to the mirror where he adjusted his cravat. ''Of course, I can see why you hesitate. It reminds one, does it not, of a similar occasion in the past?''

Neville stared at him uncomprehendingly.

''The last time I remember you taking such a risk was when you ran away with Camilla.''

A cold fear gripped Neville's heart. Yes, it was very much the same as last time. Damn Dunsanay and his insufferable superiority for pointing it out. Was this why he hesitated to go to Fanny? The old fear of claiming the one he loved, only to lose her again?

''Devil take you, Dunsanay. This is nothing like it was with Camilla.''

''You are right,'' said his friend coolly. ''Pardon my impertinence. You were younger then. More given to indulging your headstrong nature. Perhaps such escapades are unworthy of you now.''

Dunsanay was well aware that he was goading his friend. He knew exactly how much pain this last remark would cause. But he reckoned that Neville could little afford to lose this second chance at happiness.

A knock on the door prevented any further discussion. Neville's manservant announced that a Mr. Burleigh had come to call. Neville stared incredulously from Dunsanay to his watch, which showed nearly one o'clock. ''Burleigh, at this hour? Show him in, Simpson, and bring me another bottle of claret.''

Clive rushed in, looking very disheveled. His face was red and shiny, whether from exertion or drink, Neville could not tell.

''My lord, forgive this uncommonly rude intrusion,'' Clive apologized hastily to Neville, then nodded to Dunsanay. ''But I have received the most dreadful shock.'' He clutched a newspaper in his hands.

''What is it, Burleigh? Here, have a glass of claret. Put your hat down.''

With trembling fingers Clive accepted the proffered glass and quaffed its contents in a single gulp. He began to sort through the crumpled pages with great concentration.

''I think, Neville, Mr. Burleigh would prefer something stronger—perhaps brandy,'' Dunsanay suggested.

Neville was just pouring him a glass when his guest blurted out, ''Imagine my horror when I found myself dining at Colonel and Mrs. Hewett's house tonight—''

''Yes, I can well imagine the horror of finding yourself at Mrs. Hewett's table,'' Dunsanay agreed.

''—when they congratulated me on my impending marriage!'' Clive stared at Neville apoplectically.

''How delightful. I had no idea you were to be wed, Burleigh,'' Neville said politely.

''Neither did I! Not to the wrong woman! That fool,

George Feversham had it published in *The Times*!''
Clive thrust the paper toward Neville accusingly. ''It
seems I am to marry Miss Fanny Feversham!''

''You don't say?'' Dunsanay had actually allowed his
brow to crease before realizing he was in imminent peril
of creating a wrinkle.

''This is not welcome news,'' Neville said grimly,
staring at the paper.

''How well I know it,'' said Clive, sinking into a
chair. ''Certainly most unwelcome to me.''

Neville thoughtfully toyed with his snuffbox. ''Tell
me, why did Mr. Feversham think that you had offered
for Fanny?''

''I went to Duke Street earlier this week to offer for
Miss Arabella,'' Clive explained weakly. ''I suppose I
did not make my intentions clear. Just as I was leaving,
Mr. Feversham said he would convey my offer to Fanny.
I knew then he had mistook my meaning.''

''And what did you do?'' asked Neville sharply.

''I . . . I told him I would be back. I could tell matters
were in a hopeless tangle, but to be quite truthful, I
didn't much relish sorting them out just then.''

''Of course.'' Neville paced, his hands behind his
back. ''Poor Fanny,'' he muttered, ''tossed about like a
bonnet on the breeze.''

''My position isn't exactly to be envied, either,''
Clive moaned. ''I went to ask for one sister and was
given another—one who doesn't find me all that agreeable.'' He sipped his brandy miserably.

''I am beginning to think we have never taken George
Feversham's full measure,'' said Dunsanay, staring at
the plaster cornices along the walls.

''What do you mean by that?'' asked Clive.

''Well, perhaps Mr. Feversham is not the bungler he
seems. Consider. He has a daughter who is rapidly
achieving a certain . . . reputation. He wishes to see her
securely wed. Fellow pops up on his doorstep asking for
her younger sister, and *voilà*, the father substitutes the

other girl just as the chap is leaving. I say, the old fox shows sagacity, Burleigh.''

"I will not have Fanny, just as I am sure she will not have me, and that's that,'' Clive said with great determination.

"I say, the brandy is nearly gone,'' Dunsanay observed. "Shall we have more? I suppose we shall be discussing what to do with the intrepid Miss Feversham for some time.''

Just then a carriage clattered to a stop outside Grantham Place, followed by a loud banging at the front door.

"Neville! Thank God you're here!'' Kit dashed into the room and took his friend by the shoulders. "It's Fanny,'' he blurted out. "She's gone away with Berkeley! No telling where he's taking her.''

"Out with it, man! And quickly!'' Neville said impatiently.

"Berkeley . . . took her away in Stanbury's coach . . . Miss Wigmore . . . was suspicious . . . Fanny sent Berkeley a note . . .'' Kit gasped.

"I perceive Lady Stanbury's mark on this,'' said Dunsanay.

"Never mind her now.'' Neville spoke sharply. "I will see that she is finished forever if this is true.'' He glanced at his watch. "When did they leave?''

"It was late when we returned—must have been shortly after midnight. We had all gone to the theatre. Fanny had pleaded illness at the last minute, and Miss Wigmore was worried. As soon as we set foot in the house, Fanny's maid confessed to delivering a note to Berkeley's lodgings. She was in a state, I can tell you, crying and begging our forgiveness.'' Kit's voice was very low. "Then Miss Wigmore found the letter Fanny left for us, saying Berkeley was sending a coach to take her to Henley.''

"They're on their way to Henley, then?'' asked Neville.

"I doubt it," said Kit. "The maid said it looked as if Fanny was forced into the carriage. That means Berkeley had other plans."

"Where could he be taking her?" Neville asked distractedly.

"Where couples usually go," Dunsanay offered. "Gretna Green."

"I have always detested Berkeley," Neville said coolly, ringing for Simpson. "I am looking forward to thrashing him once and for all." The thought of Fanny alone in a carriage with the scoundrel enraged him.

"Neville, what are you doing?" asked Clive nervously.

"I am going after her, of course," his host replied. "And so are you."

"What!" Clive stared incredulously at him, only to be met with a look of appalling ferocity.

"Here is our plan." Neville retrieved a map from his desk and hastily outlined a route. The others drew close. "I shall need every man in this room." He looked from Kit, who nodded eagerly, to Clive, who assented with less fervor. "And you, Dunsanay, can I depend on you?"

"You know I have always preferred you as a man of action, Neville, to a decoration in society's buttonhole. I shall do anything I can to get your Miss Feversham back for you. That is," he inclined his head in Clive's direction, "if her betrothed has no objections."

Clive looked sick.

"Very well, then." Neville indicated a line that snaked upward. "This is the Great North Road. They are probably just out of London at this point. They might be somewhere near Hampstead Heath, planning to join the Great North Road at Edmonton."

"Unless they mean to change horses at the Angel," Kit interjected.

"Hmmmm. They wouldn't risk stopping so soon," Neville responded. "Berkeley will want to leave London far behind." He glanced at his watch. "They have nearly an hour's start on us. I say our best plan is to head north on Goswell Street, then ride for Finchley Common. From there, we can double back toward Highgate. You say they took Lady Stanbury's carriage?"

Kit nodded.

"It's lightly built and her horses are fast," Neville said, "but we'll be faster. I'll be on Tammuz. Kit, you can handle the ribbons better than anyone else here. I want you to take my carriage and follow us. I'll not have Fanny brought back on horseback for all of London to gawk at."

"Oh, come, Julian. Let Dunsanay handle the ribbons. He's a dab hand. I'd give anything to see Berkeley's face," Kit gloated. "No doubt he'll fear we're highwaymen."

"By Jove, Kit, that's not a bad idea," Neville said thoughtfully. "I'd like to give Berkeley a taste of steel before the evening is out. Let him think he's fighting a bloodthirsty marauder." When Simpson poked his head round the door, Neville instructed, "Send Jenkins quickly, and bring two rapiers."

He threw down the map and strode over to a mahogany cabinet which he unlocked, removing a box of matched pistols. "This is to be kept quiet, do you understand, gentlemen? Our only risk is in giving Fanny undue fright."

"She'll keep a cool head," Kit responded.

"Very well. Now then, Clive, can you ride?"

"Yes," said Clive carefully. "But I'm not a neck-or-nothing."

"Very well. Can you shoot?" Neville sighted down the barrel.

"Shoot?" Clive stuttered.

"Take this," Neville threw him the pistol. "And keep it somewhere on your person. You probably won't have to use it, just look like you might. I want you to keep watch on the driver, while Kit and I—"

"Neville," Clive strove for a light tone, "do you seriously propose that I should ride a horse and brandish this thing in some ruffian's face?"

Neville leaned on the table and looked Clive squarely in the face. "Within fifteen minutes we are going to ride out of here like hell's own fiends. If Lady Stanbury's driver gives you any trouble, you are going to shoot him. Do you understand, Mr. Burleigh?"

At that moment Jenkins appeared at the door, rubbing the sleep from his eyes. "You sent for me, sir?" His expression subtly changed as he saw Clive gingerly slide the pistol into the waist of his trousers.

"Ah, Jenkins, there you are." Neville strode over to him. "Do you remember that ball the Duchess of Rutland gave some time ago? I went dressed as a highwayman."

"I vaguely recall it, sir."

"I should like you to bring me the clothes I wore," said Neville affably. "And enough greatcoats and hats for my friends here. We're going on an excursion."

"So I see, my lord," Jenkins responded. "Will you also have the mask, sir?"

"Yes, especially the mask," his master returned cheerfully. He drew closer to Jenkins and said in a low voice. "And another thing. If I ever hear any breath of this as belowstairs gossip I will gladly strangle you, do you understand?"

"Yes, my lord," his valet responded, his suave expression unchanging.

Neville hastily scrawled a note. "Have a footman take this to Mr. and Mrs. Feversham in Duke Street. I would not have them unduly worried about their daughter's whereabouts. Tell them she'll be back by daybreak."

He sealed the paper and handed it to Jenkins. "Well,

get a move on, man. And don't look so surprised. You'd better get used to serving Miss Feversham. She's going to be your mistress before the month is out.''

As the carriage hurtled through the night, Fanny burrowed deeper against the blue velvet squabs. She wanted to put as much distance between Berkeley and herself as possible.

When he had wakened, he had been tense and withdrawn, constantly checking to see if they were being followed. Gradually, his vigilance lessened and he slipped into a surly familiarity, taking long pulls from his bottle of rum.

''Won't do you any good to hide in that corner, Miss Feversham,'' he laughed mockingly. ''We might as well be on friendlier terms. Eventually, we will be sharing a bed.''

He started to move toward her, but a bump in the road caused him to lurch back against his side of the carriage.

''Bloody stupid driver!'' He pounded on the roof with his sword. ''How's a man to seduce a woman when he's being shaken like dice in a cup?''

''I'd hardly call this a seduction, Captain Berkeley,'' Fanny said coldly.

''You can call it anything you like, but the fact of the matter is, I have you all to myself, and we have a long, long journey before us.'' Catching Fanny off-balance, he pulled her toward him. His hands fumbled with a button at the back of her dress.

''Stop that, you bloody rogue!'' She tried to push him away, then realized she was no match for his superior strength. With one hand cupping her jaw, he forced her face toward his, kissing her with a greedy lust.

''Gretna Green may be too long a wait,'' he rasped. ''I shall order the driver to stop now.''

''No, James!'' Fanny cried out panic-stricken. ''If we

stop now, we are sure to be overtaken."

"By whom?" he laughed derisively, untying her cloak. "Do you really think we are pursued by your rescuers? They are probably still snug in their beds. Which is where I would like to be with you now."

He let go of her and started unbuttoning his waistcoat, his eyes glittering with a cold blue fire. Fanny frantically slid across the seat, and reached inside her reticule. She steadily aimed her pistol at him.

"I'd leave your clothes on for the moment, if I were you, Captain," she said as coolly as possible. "If you dare to lay a hand on me again, I shall gladly blow your head off."

"With that ridiculous thing?" Berkeley hooted.

"I assure you I know how to use it," Fanny said evenly. "It is primed and ready to fire."

"Just as I am, my sweet," Berkeley leered meaningfully. She sat with one leg drawn up under her, her clothes in disarray. A stocking had slipped down to reveal a slender calf. He could see the pulse beating rapidly in her white throat.

"You are a pretty little thing, aren't you?" he said hoarsely, leaning toward her. "Put that pistol away, Fanny." His voice had taken on a menacing tone. "It wouldn't be wise to resist me."

Fanny felt her whole body go cold, but she forced her index finger to tighten around the trigger. "So be it, Captain, but I cannot answer for what will happen." She wrapped both hands around the stock and leveled the barrel with more bravado than she felt. Berkeley grinned at her as if she were an infant.

At that moment a muffled cry came from the driver's box, and the carriage swerved erratically.

"The devil take that man," Berkeley cried. He leaned out the window and shouted at the driver.

"Highwaymen, Cap'n! We're being pursued!" the driver shouted back.

Berkeley quickly glanced at the road behind them. "Damnation!" All amatory intentions were gone. "Give me that pistol, Fanny."

"No." She resisted his outstretched hand. "What do you want it for?"

"There are three highwaymen crossing the heath back there. They're gaining on us. Devil take it," he bellowed, "this is no time to play missish with me. If they overtake us, I'll need a pistol to protect us."

Fanny quickly weighed her options of fending off three highwaymen as opposed to a rum-soaked captain. She decided in favor of Berkeley.

"They won't overtake us if I can prevent it," she cried. She leaned out the carriage window. As Berkeley had said, three riders were approaching at great speed. She could hear the driver's whip lashing Stanbury's horses into a frenzy. But with the weight of the carriage, their chances of outrunning their pursuers seemed hopeless.

The moon was still up. By its light Fanny could make out the lead rider, who had already outdistanced his companions. He was on a superb black stallion and was masked, his greatcoat flapping behind him like the jagged wings of a bat.

She tried to steady her arm against the sill of the carriage, which rocked violently. She carefully aimed at his shadowy form and squeezed the trigger, sending a ball and a blaze of powder in his direction.

"Did you hit him?" shouted Berkeley.

"Can't tell," Fanny shouted back. Whether or not her shot had found its mark, it had not lessened the rider's speed. Fanny began to panic as she frantically searched through the reticule for more ammunition. Loading the pistol was a delicate and complicated process. Her hands trembled so violently she could barely hold the stock.

A second rider had outrun the first, and was drawing even with the carriage. He brandished a pistol at Berkeley and headed toward the team of horses. The third rider, Fanny saw with some surprise, was awkwardly clinging to his horse's neck.

Slowly, the carriage came to a halt. Fanny kept the revolver pointed at their pursuers, hoping they wouldn't discover it was empty.

"You'd be wise to put that pistol away, miss," shouted the highwayman who now aimed his own revolver at the driver. His hat was so lowslung it hid most of his face, but his voice was gruff and demanding as he forced the driver to dismount.

The masked rider rode up, jumped off his horse and threw open the carriage door on Berkeley's side.

"Get out, you cur," he said hoarsely.

"We have little money if your intention is to rob us," Berkeley said. The highwayman, obviously enraged, reached in and dragged him from the carriage, throwing him upon the ground.

"Are you all right, miss?" he asked with some concern. Fanny could see his eyes flash from behind the mask, as he took in her state of dishabille.

"Yes . . . yes, I am all right," she stammered.

"Very well, then. Give me your pistol. I ask that you stand next to that fellow over there." The highwayman indicated his companion who, now upright in the saddle, was pointing a drooping pistol in Berkeley's direction.

"What do you want of me?" Berkeley snarled at his captor, who placed a booted foot on his arm.

"I would have you fight, you spineless mongrel," came the answer.

"I am not armed, as you can see."

"I can soon remedy that." The masked highwayman jerked his head at his companion who still held the driver at bay. The companion quickly produced two rapiers and tossed them to the highwayman, who threw one at Barkley's feet. "There is your weapon. It is more than you deserve."

Berkeley sprang to his feet, warming to the fight. His opponent shed his greatcoat and rolled up the sleeves of his shirt, revealing a sinuous white scar that gleamed in the moonlight.

"Julian!" Fanny gasped, clapping her hand across her mouth. She recognized the horseman who guarded her as Clive. He nodded imperceptibly and lowered his pistol. She then glanced at the other horseman. She could make out Kit's impish grin beneath the low-brimmed hat. He slowly brought one finger to his lips.

"Very well, *en garde.*" Berkeley crossed swords with Neville. "Before one of us dies, might I have the pleasure of meeting my opponent?" he asked cynically.

"No, you may not," came the cold reply. The blades shivered against one another, sending up sparks into the pale moonlight.

The two men edged around each other guardedly, looking for an opening and lunging in tentative feints and parries. Fanny could clearly see that Berkeley had a slight advantage over Neville. His height gave him a longer reach. But whereas the captain fought out of cruel pleasure, Neville was remorseless.

"Since you have made no attempt to rob me, may I ask why we fight?" Although Berkeley's tone was teasing, his eyes glittered dangerously, watching for any lapse in the other's defense.

"We fight for this young lady's honor," Neville responded grimly. "And so that you might never sully another defenseless innocent."

Berkeley made a quick thrust which Neville warded off, averting the rapier's point by knocking it out of his opponent's hands. "Pick it up," he commanded.

"I assure you, the young lady is not as defenseless as you might think," the captain resumed, now moving the blade in small circles before Neville's chest.

"You are a bloody bastard, Berkeley. May you rot in hell." Neville lunged at the mocking blue eyes, while the other's blade sliced against his ribs. Blood quickly stained Neville's left side, spreading across his torn shirt.

"Julian!" Fanny cried. Kit jumped off his horse and

ran to her side. He took his sister in his arms, while keeping close watch on the duel.

"So, it's Julian Carrothers, is it?" Barkley said, a note of fear creeping into his voice.

In a swift motion Neville discarded the mask and threw it to the ground. "You might as well know, Berkeley, I mean to see you dead." His blade hung suspended in midair, ready at any moment for the final onslaught.

"I swear to you, Neville," his opponent spoke hastily, "I never used her ill. She kept me at pistol point."

"Not a very agreeable way for a young lady to have to share a carriage. Wouldn't you agree?" Neville lunged again, this time catching Berkeley off-balance. He slashed the other's face, slicing it from temple to jaw. Berkeley cried out, dropping his blade and covering his face with his hands.

Neville threw down his sword as another carriage rattled into view. "I'll forego killing you this time, Berkeley, but let me not catch you out again." He took the captain roughly by the arm and threw him into Lady Stanbury's carriage. "Let your scar be a reminder to treat ladies more gently."

To the driver he said, "You may go. See that this man finds a surgeon, then return the carriage to Lady Stanbury."

The driver, thankful to have escaped with his life, stung the horses with the whip and wheeled away just as the second carriage, bearing Neville's coat of arms, drew even. Fanny ran to Neville, wrapping her cloak about his side, attempting to stanch the blood that flowed freely.

"Julian, are you all right?" she asked numbly.

"Of course," he answered, gingerly feeling the wound. "It doesn't appear to be very serious." His eyes searched hers. "He didn't hurt you, did he?"

"No, but I'm so glad . . . so thankful." Fanny fought the urge to burst into tears and have Neville hold her forever. But remorse at her foolishness gradually overcame her. Neville would not be standing here bleeding were it not for her decision to run away. "You should not have risked your life on my account." She stared at the ground, not seeing the look of tenderness that stole over his face.

"I should have risked it long ago, little vixen," he said gently, taking her by the chin and forcing her to look at him. "Fanny." He said her name softly. "We have endured much together, you and I."

Dunsanay jumped off the driver's box and came toward them. He gazed with horror at Neville's wound, the blood dark in the moonlight.

"It appears I have missed the brutal massacre," he said, "and that my life as a highwayman is to be short-lived. Was the other man left standing?" He fastidiously offered Neville a scented white handkerchief for his blood-stained hands.

"We packed him off to a surgeon," Neville answered shortly.

"Then it was Captain Berkeley I caught a glimpse of, tearing his shirt into bandages and swearing like a duchess in labor."

Neville held open the door of his carriage and gestured for Fanny to enter.

"If I may presume upon you further, Dunsanay, I would ask that you drive Miss Feversham and me to Duke Street as quickly as possible." He glanced at Fanny's pale face. "I should like to arrive before daybreak. Miss Feversham has had a very long night."

"I should consider it an honor," said Dunsanay, leaping onto the driver's box and adjusting his greatcoat. "I am becoming used to driving a four-in-hand at great speeds. Does wonders for the complexion."

Neville, one foot on the carriage steps, addressed his three companions. "I am indebted to you forever, my friends. After you have refreshed yourselves, I shall expect to see you at Grantham Place for a hero's breakfast.''

Flourishing the whip, Dunsanay whistled through his teeth and wheeled the carriage around smartly.

Kit, still holding the rapiers, searched the ground for any signs of bloodshed. Satisfied that all traces of the skirmish were obliterated, he walked up to Clive who remained mounted, sitting ramrod straight. Patting the horse's neck, Kit gazed approvingly at Clive.

"You did well, Burleigh. Neville is a formidable duelist, is he not? Tell me, how did you like your first taste of a highwayman's life?"

"It was ..." Clive began hoarsely, "most picturesque." Fainting, he fell to the ground with a dull thud.

22

Fanny helped Neville ease his way into the seat opposite her. She was at a loss to decipher the feelings his enigmatic expression concealed, whether he meant to ring a peal over her or treat her with icy decorum. He would have a right to do either, she thought despondently.

"Are you quite sure you are well enough to travel, Julian?" she asked. A bump in the road had made him wince.

"I am well just knowing that you are safe, Fanny," he said solemnly. He pressed his left hand against his side as if to reduce the impact of any sudden movement. Now that the duel was over, shock had drained all color from his face, leaving him pale and haggard.

"I was very foolish," she began, "I should never have consented—"

Neville held up his hand, a plea for silence. "Let us not speak of this now, Fanny. A little later, then we will talk." He leaned his head against the squabs and closed his eyes, as if to ease the pain.

Fanny quietly slid into the place next to him, carefully

placing her hand on his chest. "Julian, I cannot bear to
see you suffering like this."

He put his arm around her, drawing her close as a
brief smile flitted across his face. "There, there, little
one. We must rest now. We shall be home soon."

She lay her head gratefully against his shoulder and
wept tears of relief that, at last, she was out of danger.
Her feeling of security was all the more poignant for its
impermanence. Upon their arrival, Neville would deliver
her to her parents. After that, she could not imagine what
course her life would take. She doubted it would ever
again center around Julian Carrothers.

Neville stirred against her and she raised her head.
"Am I hurting you, Julian?" she asked worriedly. "It
won't be much longer. Look, we are already at Highgate." She laughed bitterly. "Soon you will be rid of
me."

"There is something I have to say to you, Fanny."
Neville pushed himself up against the seat.

She instinctively drew away. It seemed as if she had
been dreading this moment forever.

He looked off into space as if trying to recall a speech
he had memorized. "Fanny," he said sternly, "do you
realize what a confounded farce you have forced me to
play during these last few hours?"

He loosened his shirt from his side, then continued.
"It is truly remarkable. Consider. I have dressed myself
up in a ridiculous masquerade, called a man out, received an injury and delivered an even worse injury."

Fanny bit her lip, trying not to cry. "I know I have
been very selfish, Julian—"

Neville continued as if he had not heard her. "In
short, I have played the fool." He looked levelly at her.
"You have caused me to do things I would never have
dreamed of doing for any other woman, Fanny. I am
truly astonished when I look back on it."

"I am so sorry, Julian. How can I ever . . ." She

looked down, desperate to end the scene. In another moment, she would jump out of the carriage and run all the way back to Duke Street.

A tender smile stole across his face and he lifted her chin with his forefinger.

"Well, I am not sorry, little vixen," he said softly. "Sometimes a man must be willing to play the fool to find out how much of a fool he has been. Dearest Fanny." He caressed her cheek lightly. "I should be lost without you. Pray, don't refuse me what I am about to ask you."

Fanny looked into his eyes, which held the melting expression she had first seen at Henley so long ago.

"Julian, you can't possibly mean this," she said haltingly.

"But I do, my sweet Fanny." He bent over her and kissed her with a fervor that set her heart racing. He drew back, his hand lingering upon her face before falling to his side. "And now, my pretty and picturesque Miss Feversham," he said hoarsely. "I shall ask you the question I should have asked long ago. Will you do me the honor of becoming Lady Neville?"

"Julian," she gasped, "are you very sure?"

"Yes, Fanny, more sure than I have ever been of anything."

"Very well, then," she returned solemnly, "the answer is yes. In fact, Julian, I would find it . . . sublime." She threw her arms about his neck, taking care of his wound, and returned his kiss with an ardor he found most appealing. "You must promise me one thing, Julian," she whispered.

"And what is that, my dear?

"Never to be heroic again," she said softly. "I didn't realize that heroes spilled so much blood."

"Very well. Careful, my angel," he said, wincing a little from her embrace. "You must have pity on your wounded gallant. We shall go slowly now, but once we are wed, I promise you . . ."

The carriage had come to a stop before the familiar house in Duke Street. A discreet tap sounded on the door, followed by Dunsanay peering within. "Have we come to an understanding yet?" he queried, looking from one to the other.

"Indeed, we have, Dunsanay," said Neville, his arm around Fanny. "I should like you to meet the future Lady Neville."

"My dear, may I be the first to felicitate you," said Dunsanay, handing her out.

Mr. and Mrs. Feversham ran down the steps, embracing Fanny and assisting Neville out of the carriage and into their house.

"Thank God it is over," Dunsanay said, crawling into the carriage. "Cupid is most fatigued." Nestling against the squabs, he closed his eyes and fell into a deep slumber.

Mr. Sutcliff looked about him, very pleased with the way the ceremony had gone, and anxious to know the whereabouts of the sherry. Henley positively teemed with guests—some from the most exalted ranks of society.

The raven-haired beauty he presumed to be Lady Holland presided over the far corner of the drawing room. She was talking at a mighty rate with the gentleman publisher from London. Murphy, or was it Murray?

"Here you are, Vicar. The ceremony was extremely moving. Better than anything at St. George's." Mrs. Feversham awarded him the long-awaited sherry, and examined her guests with a beatific smile. "Fanny looked radiant, didn't she?"

"I have never seen a lovelier bride," he said simply. "Ah, here she is now." He lifted his glass to Fanny and she responded by kissing him fondly. Her dress of apricot silk clung to her slim figure, as diamonds flashed from an exquisite necklace.

"At last I have found you, my darling." Neville

caught up to her, gazing at her with the same adoring look he had worn as he repeated his vows. "We shall have to leave soon. It's growing late."

"Yes it is, Julian," she said, gazing up at him tenderly. "But this is the last time I shall see my family for some time."

"Little vixen, you'll be back in a few months for your sister's wedding to Mr. Burleigh." He squeezed her hand. "I've sent for the carriage. It should be here any moment."

"And may I inquire, Lord Neville, where you and Lady Neville will honeymoon?" asked the vicar.

A crowd of wedding guests had gathered around the handsome couple, and all leaned forward to hear Neville's next words.

"I am taking my wife to the Italian Alps," he said in an amused tone. "As I once promised Lady Holland I would."

Before he could extricate his bride from the cluster of well-wishers, Arabella embraced Fanny.

"Goodbye, dearest," she said, alternately laughing and crying. She kissed her sister on the cheek, whispering, "Don't ever regret writing your book. You made *The Wicked Lord* come true."

"You mustn't cry, Bella," Fanny said. "We shall be together soon. By then I'll know more Italian phrases than Clive." Both girls laughed as Kit joined them, a white-haired gentleman in tow.

"Neville, what is your hurry, old man?" Kit called. "Fan, you must meet this fellow. He is John Murray, your publisher."

"Well, I'll be a blind monkey," said Fanny softly. She glanced up at her husband, whose expression remained impassive, then held out her hand.

"My congratulations, Lady Neville," said Murray, bowing. "Lord Neville. This is a very great occasion, and very poor timing on my part, I'm afraid."

"Why so, Mr. Murray?" Fanny asked.

"I must ask you something, Lady Neville, before you take your leave of us. I am sure you know that *The Wicked Lord* is already in its third edition."

"I had no idea," said Fanny thoughtfully. Neville drew her to him protectively.

"I would like to propose, my lady . . . ah . . ." Murray dithered, unable to come to the point. "Lady Neville, you are reckoned famous throughout England. If you would consider writing another book, I would be honored to publish it."

"No more books, please, Fanny," Neville groaned.

"What a grand idea, Mr. Murray!" Fanny cried. She turned to her husband, "After all, my darling, it was fame that brought us together."

"And nearly separated us," Neville said softly. Seeing the expectant look on his wife's face, he smiled ruefully. "Then you must promise me one thing, Fanny."

"What is that, Julian?"

"That there will be no swordplay in the next story." He grinned, then turned away to supervise the footmen who were carrying their bags to the waiting carriage.

"I must tell you, Mr. Murray," Fanny said excitedly, "I already know the title of my next book!"

"And what is that, my lady?"

"I shall call it *The Highwayman*," she said grandly. And with a toss of her head, she entered the carriage where her husband awaited her.

Avon Romances—
the best in exceptional authors
and unforgettable novels!

THE HEART AND THE ROSE   Nancy Richards-Akers
78001-1/ $4.99 US/ $6.99 Can

LAKOTA PRINCESS   Karen Kay
77996-X/ $4.99 US/ $6.99 Can

TAKEN BY STORM   Danelle Harmon
78003-8/ $4.99 US/ $6.99 Can

CONQUER THE NIGHT   Selina MacPherson
77252-3/ $4.99 US/ $6.99 Can

CAPTURED   Victoria Lynne
78044-5/ $4.99 US/ $6.99 Can

AWAKEN, MY LOVE   Robin Schone
78230-8/ $4.99 US/ $6.99 Can

TEMPT ME NOT   Eve Byron
77624-3/ $4.99 US/ $6.99 Can

MAGGIE AND THE GAMBLER   Ann Carberry
77880-7/ $4.99 US/ $6.99 Can

WILDFIRE   Donna Stephens
77579-4/ $4.99 US/ $6.99 Can

SPLENDID   Julia Quinn
78074-7/ $4.99 US/ $6.99 Can

Buy these books at your local bookstore or use this coupon for ordering:

Mail to: Avon Books, Dept BP, Box 767, Rte 2, Dresden, TN 38225   D
Please send me the book(s) I have checked above.
❑ My check or money order—no cash or CODs please—for $_____ is enclosed (please
add $1.50 to cover postage and handling for each book ordered—Canadian residents add 7%
GST).
❑ Charge my VISA/MC Acct#_____ Exp Date_____
Minimum credit card order is two books or $7.50 (please add postage and handling
charge of $1.50 per book—Canadian residents add 7% GST). For faster service, call
1-800-762-0779. Residents of Tennessee, please call 1-800-633-1607. Prices and numbers are
subject to change without notice. Please allow six to eight weeks for delivery.
Name_____
Address_____
City_____State/Zip_____
Telephone No._____   ROM 0595